W9-AEB-280

Appointment in May

Other Walker and Company Mysteries by Neil Albert

APPOINTMENT IN MAY

A Dave Garrett Mystery

NEIL ALBERT

WALKER AND COMPANY
NEW YORK

First published in the United States of America in 1996 by
Walker Publishing Company, Inc.

Published simultaneously in Canada by Thomas Allen & Son Canada,
Limited, Markham, Ontario

Library of Congress Cataloging-in-Publication Data
Albert, Neil.
Appointment in May : a Dave Garrett mystery / Neil Albert
p. cm.
ISBN 0-8027-3279-8 (hardcover)
1. Garrett, Dave (Fictitious character)—Fiction. 2. Private Investigators—
Pennsylvania—Philadelphia—Fiction. 3 Philadelphia (Pa.)—
Fiction. I. Title.
PS3551.L2634A86   1996
813′ .54—dc20   96-1198
CIP

Printed in the United States of America
2 4 6 8 10 9 7 5 3 1

To Les Roberts
Who Does Me Great Honor
Thanks

Acknowledgments

Some books write themselves and some need a dozen revisions before they attain a measure of clarity. This one belongs firmly in the second category. I'm indebted to a number of friends and colleagues whose encouragement, support, and suggestions helped sustain me: Lynne Boyer, Maureen Corwin, Cindy Garman, Richard Goldman, Mary Alice Gorman, Janet Hutchings, Cindy Littleton, Maggie Mason, Otto Penzler, Blanche Schlessinger, David Small, Joel Smith, Roberta Strickler, and Barrie Van Dyke. Thank you, one and all.

A special thanks to my editor, Michael Seidman, for bringing order out of chaos.

And a very special thanks to my devoted secretary, Sandy Renninger, whose typing skill and good cheer in all weathers have made my burden much lighter. Her help and support are very much appreciated.

1

Monday, 11:00 A.M.

IT WAS ALL Lisa's fault.

Anyway, that's what I told her when it was over, when we could relax and share a quiet drink down on South Street. If she hadn't talked me into the brochure, nothing would have happened—or at least, not to me.

Lisa worked for me only when I had more work than I could handle, which wasn't very often. But that hadn't prevented her stream of suggestions on how to lift Garrett Investigations out of its perpetual financial crisis. She'd wanted me to do a brochure. I vetoed it on the basis of cost. She didn't argue with me, but the next morning she showed me her draft of the text, with an estimate from a quick-print shop to set it in type and run a thousand copies for less than two hundred bucks. Even I had to admit it was good stuff. " . . . the personal, one-on-one relationship you'll have with your investigator . . . " Absolutely accurate, since I was the only regular employee. "We pride ourselves on results." Aside from a little concern over exactly who "we" was, I had to agree, especially since, in my last four cases, getting results was synonymous with staying alive. " . . . our undivided attention to your needs." No problem, since I seldom had more than one case at a time, anyway. And so here I was, tramping up and down the Main Line, handing them out to a succession of skeptical office managers, bored receptionists, and indifferent secretaries.

I was in Wayne, a comfortable suburb west of the city just a couple of stops from Paoli, which marked the end of the Main Line. Normally I worked closer to Philadelphia, where my office was located. But my Civic had just gone into a body shop in Wayne, and until my loaner was ready I was on foot. It was a good day to be out of doors. Seventy degrees, a slight breeze, sunny, a few wisps of clouds—as much as I liked to complain about the vagaries of Pennsylvania weather, this was the kind of day that made even me shut up.

Of course, that didn't stop me from complaining about the neighborhood, at least to myself. Wayne wasn't the colonial village it sometimes pretended to be; it got its real start only at the turn of the century, when the advent of commuter rail service turned it into a suburb. When I was a kid it was still a pretty place; the architecture made up in class what it lacked in authenticity. But in the last thirty years an invasion of supermarkets, real estate offices, fast-food joints, and beer distributors had obliterated the town's original character, at least on the main street. A few hardy white stucco-covered stone buildings survived, but most had been disfigured with additions or facades of relentless ugliness. Directly across the street from me was a late-Victorian mansion with gables, matching stone chimneys, and a handsome hipped roof, which had been fitted with a false brick-and-plastic facade and converted into a Chevrolet dealership. As bad as it was, there were uglier buildings in town—like the carriage house next door, for instance, that had been turned into a Burger King. Or the auto-body shop a couple of doors down that had started life as a story-and-a-half cottage. . . .

I walked by the Anthony Wayne Theater and noted that it was playing the same feature as half the theaters in Philadelphia. A hundred movie theaters in the area, showing the same four movies, and they wonder why people stay home. Well, now at least I had two things to complain about.

The building next to the theater caught my eye. A modest one-and-a-half story brick building with blue-gray shutters and brass candles in each window. The foundation was fieldstone, and both the stone and the brick were freshly repointed. A neatly painted sign to one side of the door said "Charles Preston, Counselor-at-Law." Somebody with enough cash to repoint their masonry just might have a little left over. The logic was thin, but I'd turned a dollar on slimmer hopes before.

The door was dark with old varnish, and so massive that it didn't move until I put my weight into it. The tiny brass doorknob, too small to be gripped with more than two fingers, didn't help. I stepped inside, into a narrow hall with brass sconces on either wall and an intricately patterned Oriental runner on the floor. I kicked over a corner, just to be sure. It was real.

At the end of the corridor a dark-haired woman in a severe navy blue suit presided over a desk covered with a telephone console, a computer, and several stacks of papers. Underneath the jacket was a simple white blouse with a plain collar. No jewelry. The stacks of papers were neatly squared off, and each one was aligned with the edge of the desk. No coffee cups, ashtrays, or cartoons. I may be busy, it all said, but I'm in control. Her hair was black, worn in a cut that stopped well short of her shoulders. When I reached the desk I saw I'd been wrong about the jewelry; a tiny gold chain, snug against her throat, peeped out about her collar. Unlike a lot of plain women, she knew how to use makeup, and more important, when to quit. The brass nameplate on her desk said "L Starniski." I wondered what the L stood for.

"May I help you, sir?" Her delivery was businesslike, but she softened it with a hint of a smile at the end.

I smiled right back. "I'd like to see Mr. Preston, please. And no, I don't have an appointment."

She kept her eyes on me while she picked up the phone. "And who shall I say it is?"

"David Garrett."

She looked at me with interest. "Are you the Mr. Garrett from Mr. Richardson's firm?"

"Well, yes, originally, but—"

"Mr. Preston knows him very well." She paused, waiting for Preston to answer. She looked down while she was waiting, and I saw some gray roots. I wondered which side of thirty-five she was on, and then I wondered what difference it made. I was forty-four; and I wasn't looking anyway. Well, not really. "There's a Mr. Garrett to see you. . . . Uh-huh, from Tom's office." She put the phone down. "You can go right back. First door on the right."

"Thanks."

"Are you parked in back? If you are, I need you to leave your keys with me so no one gets parked in."

"I'm on foot, thanks."

On foot in an American suburb, the pedestrian is one step above the homeless. "All right, then," she said a little too brightly. I nodded at her and went down the hall.

I tapped on the jamb. He looked up, smiled briefly, and said, "Just a minute, please." He held up a Dictaphone, and I nodded.

Preston's office was huge, almost three times the size of the offices of the senior lawyers I'd known in Philadelphia. I wondered if rents were that much lower on the Main Line or if he was just the kind of man who needed a throne room as his work space. Everywhere I looked was brass and inlaid panels of dark, polished wood. The desk sat on an Oriental rug that took up most of the floor. I didn't bother checking its authenticity. The walls were covered with diplomas and prints of foxhunts. Stanford undergraduate, Phi Beta Kappa. Then Penn law school, law review, Order of the Coif. Directly behind him on the wall was a blown-up photograph of Preston, in full foxhunting costume, taking a horse over a fence that looked the better part of six feet high.

I sat down and waited while he finished dictating. While he worked I had a chance to get a good look. His face was tanned and lined, with light blue eyes and a thinning head of gray hair. There was nothing wrong with his face, nothing that I could place, but somehow he was less handsome, as a whole, than he should have been. Maybe it was the mouth, which was too thin; or that his chin was too small. Or maybe it was just the way he held his head, pulled in against his chest like he was ducking something. His jacket was an English brown tweed with leather elbow patches and an indistinct pattern that didn't quite come into focus. If he'd bought it at the same place I'd seen one, it didn't even get off the boat for less than a thousand dollars. He wore a button-down off-white dress shirt and a tie of first-quality Italian silk. I had a feeling that under the desk he would be wearing a pair of casual slip-on loafers, custom-made in Italy, that cost $250. Per shoe.

For myself, I was glad it was warm enough to wear a summer-weight suit. My last decent winter suit had given up the ghost, and I was down to three presentable suits—two if you're careful about counting buttons—and all of them were summer weights. What I was going to do in October I didn't know. Pray for an Indian summer, I guessed.

He put down the Dictaphone and stood up, extending his hand. He was tall, almost as tall as me, but thinner. "Charles Preston." He didn't invite me to call him Chuck.

"Dave Garrett." His palm was surprisingly rough. I wondered if he did some of the heavy labor on the country estate I assumed he owned. "Thanks for seeing me."

He sat back down and leaned back in his swivel chair. He took in a deep breath and slowly let it out. "If you're with Tom that's a good enough introduction for me."

"I used to be. Not anymore."

Another breath, shorter this time. "I heard the old firm broke up," he said cautiously. The blue eyes were weighing me. "Which group did you go with?"

"Neither. I haven't been with the firm for a couple of years."

"On your own?"

"Not as a lawyer anymore. I'm a private detective now."

"It must be very interesting—" Then his eyes narrowed. "Wait a minute. Did you used to do litigation? Villanova?"

I just nodded. I knew what was coming.

Another big breath. He was using the time to consider exactly what to say next. "I remember talking to Tom about this. You're the one—you lost your license taking the bar exam for your wife."

"The very same."

"She'd failed it five or six times before and even attempted suicide." He tapped a finger on his blotter and met my eyes again. "Am I right?"

"You seem to know a lot about it."

"I wrote a letter to the disciplinary board for you. Tom called me. I was counsel to the board, you know, years ago. Tom thought it would do some good."

"I didn't know. But thanks for your help anyway."

He waved a finger at me. "Don't misunderstand me. I didn't do it for Tom's sake. They were too harsh on you." His eyes left mine, and he stared into space for a moment. When he spoke again his voice was softer. "I just might have done the same thing myself, if I'd been in your shoes. How long have you been married?"

"I'm not, anymore."

"Oh. I'm sorry to hear that."

I tried a smile. "Well, so am I." I didn't like reflecting on my marriage with strangers. Or, as more than one woman has told me, with myself. "Mr. Preston, I know you're a very busy man and I don't want to make too much of a demand on your time."

He took the hint. "So, then, you have an agency now?"

I handed him a brochure, and he studied it carefully. After a moment he frowned. "Well, we normally use the Shreiner Agency for our work. They have—very substantial resources, you know."

"I sometimes wonder if they give smaller clients the best service."

"Well, so do I." He said it without looking up from the brochure.

"What investigative needs do you have, exactly?" I asked.

It was a moment before he responded, but this time he didn't bother with the breathing preliminaries. "Mmm. More than I used to. I have a general practice, a little of everything. When the construction boom hit I did a lot of real estate. When the Blue Route got off the ground I did condemnations. When the son of a client does something foolish I'm even a criminal lawyer." He smiled a little at the thought. "I'm no specialist in personal injury, and I'd never try a medical malpractice case myself, but with the way things are these days, who can afford to turn away business?" I glanced around the office. If times were tough now, I wished I could have been here in the good old days. "Until recently," he went on, "I had an associate who did most of the legwork." He looked at the paper again. "He's no longer with me. Now, this says here you do domestic surveillance?"

It wasn't quite the anus of the private detective life—I reserved that category for collection work. But if something paid and wasn't illegal, I was game. "I sure do." I tried to sound enthused, but I don't think I succeeded.

"Your rate?"

"Fifty an hour, plus expenses. Normally I need a retainer," I added, "but not when I'm working for an attorney."

He frowned a little and scratched behind his ear. "Well, I have a matter. If you were with Tom you'll do fine, I'm sure." He picked up his phone. "Leah? Can you bring me the Winter file? No, just the domestic subfile. Thank you."

He put his hands together in front of himself on the desk, as if he was going to offer a prayer. But the thumbs kept hitting together, and I realized he was trying to contain some emotion. I couldn't get a sense of what it was, but something about the Winter case was bothering him. I avoided his eyes by making a show of opening up a small notebook and getting out a pen.

"Normally I don't do domestic work," he began. "I stopped ten years ago when they enacted the new divorce code. I took one look at the *seventeen* factors the courts should consider in distributing marital property and said the hell with it."

"But this one's different."

"I'm already doing a major personal-injury case for the husband and a related workers' compensation case. If I don't handle it he'll take everything somewhere else. There's no divorce filed yet, just a separation, but she's told him she wants out."

"What do you want me to do? Find out if there's someone else?"

He smiled again, but from a long way away. "There probably is. Pat just wants to know who and how serious it is."

"From what I know, as far as dividing property is concerned, it doesn't matter if a spouse is playing around or not."

He nodded. "I looked it up myself just yesterday. Surprised me. It would make a difference only if she wanted alimony from him, and she's the one with the job."

I had a thought. "It could make a difference in a custody case."

"No minor children," he said. "There's a son, grown, in Florida."

"Charles, I'm not in the business of turning away work, but this work can be expensive. Even if the wife is seeing someone, I could follow her for weeks before I came up with anything. I could burn through three, four thousand dollars trailing her to the supermarket and the video store, or just hanging around while she shampoos her hair."

He looked at me with new interest. "I agree with everything you've said, and I won't make a secret of the fact that I've tried to talk him out of this. But unfortunately—or fortunately for you—it's full speed ahead and damn the torpedoes. If I don't put a man on this, he'll get someone himself."

"You're sure he can handle the freight?"

"We'll advance whatever it takes and collect out of his settlement."

"Must be a hell of a case."

He nodded. "He fell off an unlighted, unguarded loading dock. There's a pending workers' comp case with a couple of years' overdue benefits, and we've already turned down seven hundred thousand on the personal-injury case."

I had a brief recollection of the day I brought in a four-hundred-thousand dollar fee to my old firm. I closed my eyes and it passed. "If that's the way it is, then I can start this evening," I said.

"Excellent." He indicated the pictures on the walls. "Do you hunt, by any chance?"

"No, I don't." Except for roaches in my kitchen, and I didn't think that counted.

He indicated a large picture next to the one of him jumping the horse. In the foreground was a stone fence; beyond was a rolling meadow; and in the background was a small stone house, half hidden in a stand of sycamores next to the banks of a creek. A new horse barn peeked out from behind the house. "I took up riding a few years ago, when I bought that place. Very relaxing. Gets your mind off the office."

"I'm sure it does."

The receptionist came in, bearing a slender file, and stepped up close to the desk. Below her shapeless suit jacket was a black skirt a lot shorter than I expected and black stockings with a diamond pattern. She saw me looking and lowered her face. With the hand that wasn't holding the file, she tugged her skirt a little lower.

Preston took the file without looking at her and leafed through it. "Leah, you've met Mr. Garrett?"

"Yes, sir." She looked at me briefly, nodded, and returned her attention to him. Preston was studying something near the top of the file.

"He's going to be working with us on the Winter case. The domestic file, that is." From his tone it was clear I was taking out the trash and she was to make sure the door was held open for me and that I didn't leave any bags behind. I didn't take it personally—not many lawyers really enjoyed a tough divorce case, and I'd never been one of them myself. He nodded to himself and handed me the file, along with a business card with his home number scribbled across the front.

"Mind if I sit out front and read it here?" I asked. "I might have some questions."

"Be my guest."

I settled myself in the reception area in a leather armchair with a cup of coffee, courtesy of Leah, and started to read.

The first thing was an assignment memorandum addressed to an investigator I knew at the Shreiner Agency. The memo was dated that day. I smiled a little and congratulated myself on my luck. If I did even six hours of surveillance a day and it took a week, I'd be ahead about nine hundred bucks. And if I got Lisa to cover a second shift I could do even better—I billed her time at fifty but only paid her twenty-five. A fifteen-hundred-dollar week, payment guaranteed. . . .

The facts were simple enough. Pat Winter was fifty and had strained his lower back lifting a window air conditioner at home a few months before he went fifteen feet off a loading dock onto a concrete slab. Two herniated disks. His workers' comp claim for the loading-dock incident was being contested because the carrier was trying to prove that his first injury had caused his disability. No one disputed that he was a hurting cowboy—he'd recently been granted total Social Security disability, meaning that he was unfit to work in any significant capacity.

I stopped reading for a moment. I'd handled a number of bad low-back cases for laboring men when I'd been a lawyer, and they were more the same than different. The husband goes from being the breadwinner who can lift 150 pounds to the invalid who can't bend to tie his own shoes. Chronic pain. Impotence, more often than not. And if he wasn't working, lots of time to sit around and brood. Workers' comp only pays two-thirds of his salary, at most, and much less if he had a good-paying job. Even if comp is paying there are financial pressures—and in this case they weren't. Before the injury the wife might have been able to stay home, or just work part-time. Now she's out working as hard as she can, and probably resenting it.

People are seldom as noble in real life as in the movies, and Mrs. Maria Winter was no exception. According to the memo she and Pat had been fighting more frequently in recent months, and a week ago she'd announced she was moving out. She told him she'd taken an apartment of her own, and except for one brief visit to pick up some mail, Pat hadn't seen her since. Maria had refused to give him her address or phone number, and when he tried to follow her after her visit, she'd spotted his car behind her and eluded him. His only means of contact was through her work. Her car was a red Colt, Pennsylvania registration VAG 545.

I thought about the tail. It was going to be a hard one—she'd already given Pat the slip once, and that told me that she was alert and that she had the capability to shake a tail. Now that Pat had blown it, she'd be even more on her guard.

Maria worked as a Realtor at a Century 21 real estate office in King of Prussia, a small suburb west of Philadelphia known mainly for its huge shopping mall. The address for the office was right on Highway 202, the main street through town. When the Winters had been together, they'd lived a few miles east of Norristown, the county seat of Montgomery County, not far from King of Prussia. Her office couldn't be more than a ten-minute car ride from where they'd lived. She wouldn't be used to a long commute. . . . Maybe that would help narrow it down.

I looked at my watch and then at Leah. "Can I borrow a phone? I need to call my assistant."

She put down her pencil and looked at me longer than she needed to. "Of course."

I used the phone at an empty desk right behind Leah's. Lisa answered on the third ring.

"Hi, it's Dave."

"Good to hear from you. What's up?"

"I need a partner for a tail job. Late this afternoon."

"David, I thought you were going to try to take a week off."

"I was doing some promotion when this came up," I said.

"Sounds like the brochures are working."

I wasn't going to give her the satisfaction. "This is a contact through Tom Richardson." It was, at least, a half-truth.

"What do I need to do?"

"That depends. Your mom still have that old beige Plymouth?"

"It's really white, you know. It's just faded."

"Can you borrow it for tonight?"

"No, she's going off with some friends right from work. I have a car, you know."

"Yeah. A brand-new silver Legend. Where we're probably

going it'll blend in about as well as a nun in a whorehouse. If you can't get another car, I'll just want you to ride along with me."

"Wouldn't two cars be better?"

I wasn't going to argue about it. "The target gets off work at five and I'd like to start tonight. Will that work for you?"

"How late will it run?"

"If she just goes home and stays there I figure we can quit at nine. And even if she goes out she'll probably want to get home by ten. Tomorrow's a workday for everybody."

"Mmn, not everybody. John has tomorrow off but he has to work late tonight. Okay if I come dressed for a date?"

"No problem." We made arrangements to meet at my apartment at four-thirty.

I hung up and turned to Leah. "You can tell Mr. Preston I'm all set. I don't need to see him."

"Then I guess you'll be going now."

"This could take weeks. But you never know. If we get some real luck I might have something for you in the morning."

She favored me with another smile. "Then I wish you luck."

2

Monday, 4:30 P.M.

LISA'S LEGEND, FRESHLY washed and topped with a cellular-phone antenna, glided into a space beneath my apartment window. Seeing it in full daylight made me glad we were leaving it behind. She got out and took off her sunglasses, squinting in the late-afternoon sun.

Lisa was tall, and when she wore heels, as she was now, she came to my eye level. She was athletic, with strong, square shoulders that she set off by wearing tank tops and sleeveless dresses whenever the weather permitted. She was almost forty, but only her hair, which was graying at the roots, gave it away. No sag in her breasts, thickening of the waist, or bulging at the hips. If anything, she exercised and dieted a little too hard. Personally, I thought that another five or ten pounds around the hips wouldn't hurt—an opinion I kept strictly to myself.

I locked the apartment and went down the stairs to meet her. She was dressed for a date, all right. Makeup and a little lipstick, and her dark brown hair was tied back in a loose bun. Even earrings, something I'd never seen before.

I looked her up and down. "You must have some date in mind."

"You like it?" She held out the hem of the skirt and turned around for me. She was wearing something bright yellow, cut somewhere between a sundress and a cocktail dress, and it made Leah's skirt look like a nun's habit.

"It's great," I said. "But isn't it a little short?"

"Well, the neck came too low so I took it up in the shoulders. It raised the hem a little."

"Yeah." If she'd raised it another eight inches, I thought to myself, I'd be able to see her navel. "No problem. We'll look like we're on a date ourselves."

She stepped a little closer. "You look tired, Dave."

"I'm getting my rest."

"Not enough."

"I don't think I'm over last month," I admitted.

"Nobody could be, this fast. I'm surprised you're even working."

I didn't want to talk about it. "I have to keep going."

"How's the nose? Have you been sleeping on it? You know it won't heal right if you do."

"I'm careful, Mom."

"All right, I'll shut up."

She got into my rental, a Pontiac Sunbird with ill-fitting doors, and we headed toward King of Prussia. While I drove I let her read the memo for herself. Even on a simple tail job, I wanted her to form her own opinions. Hah—as if there was any danger she'd do anything else.

She was right about my appearance. In April I'd had a tough case. I'd hardly slept for four days, and I was still in sleep deprivation. My right shoulder, which I'd sprained in February, was acting up again. Add a broken nose, a concussion, and a nasty cut on the back of the head . . . I felt every bit of fifty, if not sixty.

It was just before five when we reached King of Prussia. In that area, 202 was a four-lane divided concrete highway, solidly commercial on both sides.

"You know exactly where the real estate office is?" she asked.

"It's on this road right here. From the number I'd say it's up about a mile."

"Why don't we stop at that gas station and check the street numbers?"

"I'm sure it's a ways up."

Of course, two doors past the gas station was a three-story glass-and-concrete cube with a big Century 21 Real Estate sign on the roof. The parking lot was tiny, and I couldn't risk pulling in. I drove by in silence and parked in the first likely place I could find, a travel agency two blocks up the road.

"Got any binoculars?" she asked.

"In the backseat."

I'd parked parallel to the road, just inside the parking lot. We'd be able to watch for her through the rear window, but all she'd see of us was the rear end of an unfamiliar car with a man and a woman sitting in it.

After some fumbling with the case, Lisa got out the binoculars and focused them out the rear window. "I can see the driveway," she said.

"We've got a pretty good spot right here."

"Well, only if she turns this way." I'd asked for that one.

I was lucky. At ten after five, just as traffic was starting to build, Lisa sat up a little straighter. "Car coming out of the lot," she said slowly. "It's red. It's a Colt, fairly new. One person in it . . . a woman. She's got sunglasses on—I guess it's her." She put down the binoculars and faced straight ahead as the Colt approached.

I picked up the car in my outside mirror. I let her go by, then half a dozen more cars, and then I eased out into the northbound traffic. We moved steadily, both of us in the left-hand lane, slowly climbing a hill crowned with a Hilton Hotel on the right. Suddenly she cut into the right-hand lane without signaling and shot into the hotel entrance.

"Look!" Lisa said unnecessarily. "There she goes!" I stayed in the left lane and went right past, climbing the hill. "What do we do now?" she wanted to know.

"We just keep going till we find a good spot," I said. "That was a sucker play. She doesn't know us or the car. She's just trying to see if someone will do something."

"What if she turns back and goes the other way?"

"Then we've lost her and the hell with it for the night. But there's no point in following her ten feet if she spots us."

"The client isn't going to be happy if we lose her," Lisa said.

"He'll be even more unhappy if she makes us. This woman's so suspicious already, if we get spotted now we'll *never* get anywhere."

"Giving up tonight wouldn't be a very good start," she said.

"No one said we had to get results the first night. If she's got a boyfriend, there's always tomorrow." I crested the hill and parked in a cemetery turnaround near the bottom of the far side. Across the street was a small shopping center, busy with late-afternoon shoppers. The movie theater was showing the same movie as in Wayne.

I slouched down in the seat and adjusted my outside rear mirror for a view of traffic cresting the hill. "Get out and take a look at one of the gravestones," I said.

"It'll slow us down."

"People go to cemeteries to look at graves, not to sit in cars."

"When two people go, one of them doesn't sit in the car."

I sighed. "So you're in mourning and I'm the pissed-off husband."

She hesitated, long enough to let me know she thought it was a bad idea, and got out.

Lisa bent over to read the bottom of one of the nearer headstones and her dress rode up . . . far. I stared into the rearview mirror and tried to concentrate on what I was being paid to think about. The traffic was getting heavier, bumper-to-bumper nearly to the top of the hill behind us. Traffic had its good and bad points. Maria was going to be harder to spot in heavy traffic, but we would be able to stay close without arousing her suspicions. God, Lisa had gorgeous legs. . . . I saw the Colt, in the right-hand lane, a tractor-trailer right behind. "Lisa! Here she comes!"

She was in no hurry to get inside. I wasn't sure if she was playing the part of the mourner or just giving me a hard time. Maria missed the red light at the far end of the shopping center, and I had plenty of time to position us in the left lane about six cars back. The tractor-trailer gave us good cover.

Without being asked, Lisa was already taking notes. She checked her watch and then put down her pen. "Why do you think she's so scared of being followed? Afraid of her husband?"

"I hope I'm not working for that kind of guy."

"Me, too."

We crossed over the Schuylkill River on a four-lane concrete bridge and made a gentle turn to the left, passing a string of factories and warehouses. Maria signaled for the first Norristown exit. I followed her up the exit ramp, three cars between us. She headed up the hill on Main Street. An assortment of low-rent businesses went by on both sides—check-cashing operations, secondhand stores, mom-and-pop groceries. Families in shorts and T-shirts sitting on their porches. "This isn't the Norristown I know," I said.

"A lot of it's pretty nice," Lisa said. "This is just the poor part of town."

"It's funny how—" Maria went past a McDonald's, signaled, and made a left. The three cars in between all kept going straight. "This is where we start earning our money," I said.

"Think she spotted us?"

"She wouldn't have signaled. But I'll bet a buck she'll be watching to see if anybody makes the turn. How lucky do you feel?"

"Oh, pretty lucky, I guess."

I speeded up and shot past the turn, running a yellow light. "Then let's hope she goes straight for a couple of blocks." I reached the light at the next block as it was going red but made a left anyway. I was a quarter of the way up the block before the honking died down behind us. "Did you get the name of the street she turned on?"

"Cherry." She was already writing it down.

We made another left, slowed down, and then made an easy right onto Cherry. It was a working-class street, a mixture of white, Hispanic, and black. The street was one-way, with parking on both sides. Kids were riding bicycles the wrong way toward us. The houses were mostly stucco over brick, two-story, with concrete porches. Aside from a few broken-out windows and a couple accumulations of trash, the houses were in pretty good repair. A number of families were out stoop-sitting, but no one paid us any particular attention.

We went another block, crested a slight rise and there she was, half a block ahead. As we watched, the Colt pulled over and parked on the right side of the street. I speeded up and drove right past, Lisa and I both looking straight ahead. "When I pull over," I said, "get back there and try to see where she's going. Don't run, and try not to let her see you." At the corner I made a right and stopped as soon as I was out of sight.

Lisa was out of the car before it had even stopped moving. She was a little overdressed for the neighborhood, but other than that she did a fine job of blending in. Her walk was cool and deliberate and her arms swung casually. I was sure she was sweeping the houses with her eyes, but there was no motion of her head to give her away.

Lisa turned left onto Cherry, in the direction where Maria

had parked. I found a spot where I had a view of traffic passing through the intersection. I gave myself five minutes, then walked down to the corner myself. A person, especially a man, sitting alone in a car for any length of time in a residential neighborhood is bound to draw attention, and that was the last thing I needed.

I walked right past Cherry Street—and as I did, I saw Lisa talking to a large black woman in a turban. Several children were listening from the porch. I got a glimpse of Lisa nodding and gesturing before I stepped out of sight. I walked to the next corner, checked to see no one was watching, and started back toward my car. What was she doing?

I crossed Cherry again. Out of the corner of my eye I saw Lisa, still talking to the same woman. Then the two of them climbed the porch stairs and went inside. For an instant I lost it and came to a stop in the middle of the road. Then I made a conscious decision to put one foot in front of the other and walked back to my car.

I couldn't keep walking the street, and sitting in the car would cause trouble sooner or later, so I fell back on the old dodge of checking under the hood. I'd read every serial number four times and my neck was starting to hurt when I heard heels on the sidewalk. While pretending to check out the radiator hose, I turned my head slightly and saw Lisa.

She bent over the engine with me. "It's not broken, is it?" she whispered.

"No. What happened?"

"Maria and I had a nice talk. She has to go out this evening, but we're supposed to get together to discuss being roommates. I've got her unlisted phone number. Want to get something to eat? Her date isn't till seven and I'm starving."

I was a professional. I was in control. I didn't even hit my head on the underside of the hood. Not too hard, anyway.

3

Monday, 6:00 P.M.

WE WENT THROUGH the drive-through at the McDonald's on Main Street and ate in the parking lot with the car pointed toward Cherry. I nibbled at Lisa's fries and kept my thoughts to myself.

"Want to hear what happened?" she asked.

"That's putting it mildly."

If she noticed my tone of voice, she didn't react. She just gulped down a third of her drink and offered the rest to me. I took a sip. "I watched her go into a house," she said. "I saw it had two electric meters so I figured it was an apartment. Then the woman on the steps asked me if I was coming about the ad for the apartment, so I said yes."

"It could have been a setup."

She took a big bite out of her hamburger and chewed while she thought it over. "Well, yeah. But I had to either take it or walk away. I couldn't think of any other reason to be there. She said Maria'd rented it just a couple of weeks before, but it was a big place, three bedrooms and two baths, and the tenant was thinking of a roommate. She took me upstairs to meet her." She took another bite and wiped the corner of her mouth with a paper napkin.

I sighed. "Lisa, I hope you know how close you came to blowing everything. This is the woman who dodged into the Hilton just half an hour ago, remember? What if she saw you back at the cemetery? Or what if she was just generally suspicious and started grilling you? Did you have a story ready?"

She stopped eating and looked at me, her chin thrust out a little. "I didn't have a story and I didn't need one because I'm so good at this she trusted me from the first moment she laid eyes on me. Now, you want to know what happened or don't you?"

I regretted my little lecture as soon as it was out of my mouth. "I'm not saying you didn't handle it right," I said. "I just mean that you have to be careful."

She returned her attention to her food. "She's there on a year lease. She took the place two weeks ago. It was more than she could afford but she was in a hurry to move. I didn't get a reason why. The guy she's seeing isn't a first date. She said she'd be home by ten, which means to me they have the evening planned out already."

"Any idea who he is?"

She took another gulp of her drink before she answered. "No. And no one stays over, at least not that the landlady's seen. Maria keeps a regular routine, no noise, no visitors, no deliveries."

"How did you find out *that*?"

She swallowed the last bite of her hamburger. "I told the landlady that I hoped her tenant wouldn't expect a roommate to be home all the time to accept deliveries, because I worked, and she said there hadn't been any."

"Good thinking. What about the apartment?"

"I didn't get a really good look, but I can tell you what I saw. Purely feminine. Lots of pale pastels. If a man lives there his stuff is hidden pretty well. Not much furniture. She still hasn't gotten around to hanging pictures."

"Any mention of her husband?"

"She just said she was separated. I told her I knew a good domestic-relations lawyer, but she didn't seem interested."

"Either means she just wants to be alone, or she already has an attorney."

Lisa tossed her paper bag into the dumpster and we went back up Cherry. I cruised past Maria's car to make sure it was still there, then circled back. I parked on Cherry between a van and a pickup truck about half a block behind her and settled down to wait. I watched the street while Lisa took notes on what had happened. Just about the point where I was getting bored, I saw Maria come out of her house and cross the street. "Keep low," I warned Lisa. "We can't let her see you."

"Want to try and get a picture with the telephoto?"

"Nah. Even *I* think that's overkill. We've already got the address, the landlady's name, and the unlisted phone number."

I hunched down till I could barely see over the dash. Maria was looking around carefully. She wasn't on her way for groceries. She was wearing a black dress, longer than Lisa's but with a deep square neckline. High heels. A white necklace of some kind, maybe pearls, that wrapped around her neck and fell down inside her dress. Her eyes swept the cars, including mine, and then kept going up and down the street. Then she got in her car and started off. I waited till she was out of sight before we started after her.

"You're not going to wait till there's a car in between?" Lisa asked.

"I wish I could. But there's nothing around."

I came over a rise and saw her a block and a half ahead. I slowed down till she went over another hill, then speeded up again. I wished I had the luxury of turning onto a parallel street and following her that way, but with only one car for tailing, the risk of losing her was too great.

After a few blocks the neighborhood turned a little rougher, with some weed-choked yards and a couple of abandoned buildings. Lisa locked her door. We almost lost Maria at a red light, and by the time we caught up three cars were in between. Fortunately she was a little slower than the cars ahead of me, and we gradually closed the distance till she was less than a block ahead. As we continued up the hill the neighborhood changed steadily for the better—enclosed porches, bigger houses, bigger lots, more expensive cars in the driveways. Two of the cars turned off into a couple of the nicer houses, leaving only one in between. "Maria's getting a long way from home," I said. "What's out this way?"

Lisa studied the map. "Not a lot. Looks like a couple of shopping centers, a hospital. Maybe she's going to Lansdale."

"I thought you knew the area."

"Just around the courthouse. I was never out this far north."

"I don't like it. Things are thinning out. We get out of town, she's likely to spot us." I started to drop back.

I shouldn't have worried. The northern edge of town was bursting with activity—Pizza Huts, real estate offices, chiropractic clinics, gas stations, pet stores, and all the traffic I could want. A large shopping center appeared on our right, and Maria turned in at the first entrance. I went past and turned in further down. "Got her?" I asked.

Lisa was using the binoculars. "I see her, over the tops of the cars . . . hey, be careful."

"How so?"

"She's not close to the stores. She's stopped at the edge, right where she came in."

I pulled into the nearest space and banged my fist on the wheel. "Shit! She's made us! I shouldn't have tried to follow with only a one-car cover."

Lisa kept her binoculars trained on Maria. "She's out of the car . . . looking around. She's just standing there. Now she's locked up her car. She doesn't look worried. I bet she's just waiting for her date."

"Sure she's not looking at us?"

"Sure."

"Well, I hope you're right." I rummaged around the back seat, found a white paper bag, and put the camera inside. "I'm going to get a closer look."

"Sure it's a good idea?" Lisa asked the question without looking at me.

"We should be fine," I said. "If she hasn't made us already."

"What if the boyfriend comes by and you're away from the car?"

"Then at least I'll get a look and maybe a picture."

From around the binoculars I saw her frown. "Well, if you say so . . ."

I took off my tie and jacket and opened my collar. With the bag, I looked like any of the early-evening shoppers. I walked toward the stores, checked to see that Maria wasn't looking in my direction, then cut across to the aisle where she was parked. Someone walking *across* the parking lot was unusual, but no one would think anything of someone coming from the direction of the stores.

I walked slowly, craning my neck as if looking for my lost car and trying to look annoyed. It's an expression that comes to me easily. As I walked I tore a hole in the bag big enough for the lens.

I came around the back of a Grand Wagoneer. Maria was less than twenty feet away, standing next to her Colt and looking out toward the main road. She was shorter than I expected—not more than five four, if that, in her stocking feet—but her heels made her as tall as Lisa. Her hair was dark blond, and pulled back in a single braid over one shoulder that fell down nearly to her breast. She was playing with the end as she waited. I kept moving, looking around for my imaginary lost car. When we were about ten feet apart I brought the bag up to waist level and snapped off three quick shots. Without aiming I couldn't be certain what I'd shot, but it was worth a try. I lowered the camera and moved closer. Large blue eyes, high cheekbones, and smooth, regular features with a light sprinkling of freckles. She had a fine body, tanned and curved. The only hint of middle age was a gentle broadening at the hips. I liked the softness there; it kept her from being a perfect, remote beauty. She was a flesh-and-blood woman, one you could grab from behind at the kitchen sink before dinner. Or after dinner. Or both . . .

I walked past her without pausing, intending to make a circuit around the next row of cars and work my way back to where I was parked. I continued turning my head from side to side, giving her a quick glance each time I was all the way to the left.

I must have been about ten feet past her when I saw her looking dead at me.

My first thought was to freeze, which was the worst possible response. I flushed and tried to keep my head from sinking down to my chest. I struggled to keep moving but my stride was already broken. It looked suspicious as hell and I knew it. Christ, what was I going to do now?

I planted one foot in front of the other. It didn't look a bit like an appropriate walk, but at least it was putting some distance between us—unless she was coming after me. I was afraid to look back and check. How had she made me? Did she see me raise the camera? Or maybe she caught a glimpse of the lens in the bag. I wondered if she might have seen me driving. No, that was too much of a long shot. But I'd crossed Cherry Street twice on foot. It was half a block from her place, but how did I know she didn't have a window facing my way? She would have seen a strange man walk one way and then come back just a couple of minutes later. Damn, damn, damn.

I reached the end of the line of cars and started to swing around back toward Lisa. I wasn't even bothering to look up. A car door opened almost in front of me and a powerfully built man with short blond hair in a blue sports jacket got out. I waited for him to shut the door so I could pass by, then went on.

I was no more than three feet past him when I heard him say, "Hi, honey. Sorry I'm late." So she'd been looking at him, not me, all along.

I'm not as much a professional as I sometimes think I am. My first thought wasn't what my next move should be—I was just relieved that I hadn't screwed up.

When I was a couple of car lengths away I took a chance and looked back. It wasn't much of a risk. They had their arms around each other, oblivious to the rest of the world. I felt myself smiling for them. They might be a couple of adulterers on their way to a sleazy rendezvous, but for the next few hours they had each other. No bills or work. No distractions at all. I felt glad for them, and a little sorry for myself.

My car glided up and stopped in front of me. Lisa had tied a scarf over her head and was wearing big sunglasses. I got in.

She put it into gear and drove toward the edge of the lot. "I got some pictures of his car through the telephoto," she said. "It's a late-model Audi 4000. If they come out all right we'll have the plate."

"You know, I used to have an Audi," I said.

"Oh?"

"The husband of one of my divorce clients found out where I lived and pissed in the front seat."

"What did you do?"

"When Terry and I got divorced, I let her have it."

"David!"

"She left me in the winter. It didn't smell then."

Maria and the blond got into his Audi and headed for an exit near them but half a dozen aisles away from us. By the time Lisa could get there, a van and a station wagon were between us. The four of us waited for a break in traffic.

"Well, we've got good cover, at least," I said.

"This isn't very good, David. We may lose them."

"It's the nature of tails. We've already done better than I thought we would."

The Audi made a right, but both the van and the station wagon were signaling for lefts. I tracked the Audi through the binoculars as it went east. It stopped for a red light about a block away. I tried to read the plate, but it was too far away and the late-afternoon sun was glaring off the metal. "Hope your pictures come out."

"No guarantees," Lisa said. "I'm not even sure I had a view of the plate."

The van started to make his turn, then lost his nerve and stopped. "Hmm," I said.

"Too bad we didn't have two cars," Lisa said.

"Don't try to tell me yours wouldn't have stood out on Cherry."

"It would have fit in around here just fine."

"Two cars without communication doesn't do much, and the rental doesn't have a phone."

"Your regular car doesn't have a phone, either," she pointed out.

"Which costs money I don't have."

"What if you had a couple of CBs, or a handheld cellular phone?" The van finally made its left and we moved up a few feet. The light changed and the Audi started pulling away.

"At the risk of repeating myself . . . ," I began.

"Well, don't you think the right equipment could make you more productive?"

I didn't answer and just kept my binoculars focused on the Audi. It made the next light and melted into a long line of traffic headed away from the shopping center.

The station wagon made its turn, and Lisa was hard behind him, turning right, but we hit the same red that had held up the Audi. When it turned green we followed the road through three name changes, all the way to the turnpike, and never saw them. Lisa pulled over just before the turnpike exit. There was nothing to say. I'd screwed up.

"I'm sorry," she said.

"For what?"

"I should be helping, not criticizing."

"For what it's worth, you were right about every single thing you said. It's my own damned fault. Now let's just go home."

She pursed her lips. "Mmm, maybe not just yet."

"What are you thinking?"

"Let me see that map. I've got an idea."

4

Monday, 7:00 P.M.

"YOU FIGURE THEY'RE going to a motel, right?" she asked.

"Either that, or the house of a friend."

Lisa looked at the map. "Think they'd go very far?"

"Not if he's married. He can't afford to be away too long."

It was a while before she said anything. "There's a place I know about that isn't far."

"Motel?"

"Uh-huh." She paused. "Shall we give it a try?"

"It's either that or go home," I said.

"We could stake out Maria's place and wait for her to come back."

"Whenever she goes home, we're not going to learn anything we don't already know."

"Unless she takes him there," Lisa pointed out.

"If they were meeting there she never would have left."

Lisa didn't say she agreed, but she didn't offer any more

objections, either. She just put the car into gear and headed back toward Norristown. We rolled through several miles of residential area, most of it lower-middle-class housing dating from the early fifties, before she turned and headed down a steep hill that ended on a busy highway.

We were back in the working-class area of town, not too far from the courthouse, but the neighborhood was Italian this time, not black. Scarlotti's Electric Supply, Perrogene's Produce, Armen Cadillac, Terrente Realty, and the usual gas stations. But what interested me was the building right at the corner where our street ran into the highway—the Goat's Head Tavern and Motel. It was a rambling wooden one-story building with a big electric sign on the roof and a parking lot crowded with pickup trucks and Japanese subcompacts. A couple of young men in T-shirts were standing around the back of one of the pickups, drinking beer and watching the traffic go by. Neither gave us more than a glance as we pulled in, which was fine with me.

I looked around the lot as best I could without getting out of the car. "What makes you think they'd come here?" I asked.

"It's close, and cheap, and they rent by the hour." She brushed the hair away from her face, a habit that told me she was ill at ease.

"You see them?" I asked unnecessarily. My real question was how she knew they rented by the hour, but I knew I wasn't going to ask that one.

"No. Maybe they stopped for a six-pack or something."

I couldn't think of any response. Lisa was looking around, but I could tell her heart wasn't in it. This place was bothering her. It was, I realized, our very first awkward silence. "You want to talk about it?"

She looked at me. "This place . . . I have a lot of trouble dealing with my past."

"Well, God love you, because so does everybody else."

She brushed at her hair and crossed her arms over her chest. "Some more than others."

"Lisa, there's—"

She looked at her watch. "How long shall we give them?"

"Half an hour," I said arbitrarily. I was surprised that she didn't argue. For a while we just shared the silence while we both kept watch. We talked a little, about our other cases and about Kate. It must have been about ten minutes before she put her hand on my sleeve and said, "Here we go."

I looked out toward the highway and saw the red Audi as it pulled into the lot. We both ducked down, but not so far that we didn't see the driver get out and go into the motel office.

"When he comes out," I said, "I'll follow him on foot and you use the car." I stood in the darkness to the side of the bar entrance and waited. It didn't take long. The blond man came out and then the Audi moved off, around the corner of the building. Once it was out of sight I got out and sprinted across the parking lot. I reached the corner in time to peek around and see them go into the end room.

Lisa was right behind me with the car. I leaned into her window. "They took the room here on the end. I don't like it."

"What's the matter?" she asked.

"They have more windows to look out, and it means there's only one adjoining room, not two. Stay out of sight and make sure they don't leave."

"Not much chance of that."

I headed back to the office. The registration area was simply a counter with a tiny desk behind. Presiding over the office was a stocky, bald man in a tank-top T-shirt. A forest of thick black hair protruded from the top of his shirt. I gave him an implausible story about how my wife and I had taken the room next to the room on the end on our honeymoon, and now it was our tenth anniversary, and she was kind of sentimental. . . . I don't think he believed a word of it, but the extra twenty was a great convincer. Five minutes later Lisa and I were tiptoeing inside.

It was one large room, dominated by a king-size bed with a headboard that was chipped and stained. No chairs, tables, or television. The muddy brown carpet was crisscrossed with cigarette burns. No pictures, but the wall opposite the bed was covered with a mirror that ran from two feet above the floor almost to the ceiling. The only other furniture was a cheap veneer bedside table with an ashtray propping up one of the legs. The door to the bathroom was open, revealing a generous stack of fluffy white towels on top of the commode. Around here, getting clean was almost as important as getting dirty.

She set down the equipment case on the bed. "Boy," she whispered. "The place must have gone downhill. I can't remember ever being this desperate."

We opened the equipment bag. While Lisa fiddled with the tape recorder, I put the stethoscope against the wall. They weren't talking, but that didn't matter. I was mainly interested in checking the level of extraneous noise, and the news was good. No roaring air conditioners, rumbling pipes, loud music, or noises from other rooms. The only background noise was from the traffic on the highway outside. I checked my watch and hoped that the traffic noise would lessen as the evening wore on.

I planted a suction-cup microphone against the wall and ran the cord back to Lisa, who plugged it into the tape recorder. She put on a pair of headphones, plugged them into the machine, and sat down on the bed with a notebook. She made a circling motion to tell me we were running, and I turned back to the wall with my stethoscope.

A soft steady thumping came from the wall. After just a few beats it became so loud that I had to put down the stethoscope. I turned to Lisa and drew my finger across my throat. She turned off the tape and made a note of the time.

I sat on the bed, rewound the tape a little, and replayed it.

The audio quality was acceptable, but they weren't saying much that was germane to the investigation. I would have been surprised if they were.

"I'm going to check the car," I whispered. Lisa was busy taking notes, and just nodded at me without looking up. When she concentrated, I noticed, the tip of her tongue protruded from the corner of her mouth.

Once I was outside, in the cool spring evening, I realized how musty and stale the room was. I took the time for a few deep breaths before getting down to the business at hand.

I looked over the Audi as quickly as I could. I wasn't afraid of Maria and her friend, just then, but the motel was a busy place, filled with people self-conscious about their privacy. Someone snooping around a car could attract attention from passersby. I made a note of the plate and the dealer's sticker—Swedeland Motors. A child's seat in the back and some children's books in the backseat. Candy wrappers, crumpled papers, and a dirty pair of panty hose rolled up in the front. It wasn't the kind of car I would have expected to find at a hot sheet operation—or, then again, maybe it was.

My next stop was the motel office. The clerk didn't look surprised—if I was a betting man, I would have laid odds I was expected.

"Hello again," I said.

He just looked. He wasn't going to make it easy for me.

"The couple in the next room, number eight?"

"Uh-huh?"

I flashed my private investigator's identification. "I'd like to know his name and address, please."

"Do tell."

"I could use a little help, friend."

He shrugged and pulled out the registration slip from a pile on his desk. I noticed that in the twenty minutes since they'd registered, three new couples had checked in.

He handed me the slip. *John and Jacqueline Kennedy, 1600 Pennsylvania Avenue, Washington, D.C.*

"Funny," I said. "He looks different in his pictures."

"You know what else?" He looked both ways, leaned closer, and lowered his voice to a whisper. "I don't think that's Jackie."

"Were they ever here before?"

"Sir, we respect the privacy of our clientele. You're going to have to show me some authorization."

I put a twenty on the counter, which vanished so fast I never saw the hand move.

"Make it two," he said. "This ain't my first rodeo."

"When I hear it."

He hesitated, but then I realized he was only getting his breath. "Once or twice every week, starting the week before Thanksgiving last year, but never on holidays or weekends. Never a reservation and a different name every time. Always pays cash and always the same car—and the same girl. He uses two Trojan extrathins and if they do anything kinky they clean up after themselves."

It was easily forty dollars' worth, but I didn't want to contribute to driving up the prices. I frowned. "That's all very nice, but what's his real name?"

"As far as I know, it's John Kennedy."

"Anything else?"

"For another ten you get the story about the really fat couple that rents three every Sunday afternoon."

"I'll pass. Anybody ever ask about them before me?"

"No. Say, is that the guy's wife with you?" he wanted to know.

I put down the second twenty, which vanished as quickly as the first. "How did you know he was married?"

By way of an answer he snorted and let his eyes wander around the office.

I let myself back into the room. Lisa was sitting upright with her legs straight out and crossed at the ankles, her notebook in her lap. The tape recorder was at the foot of the bed, still shut off, with the headphones wrapped around it. The thumping continued through the wall, as loud and as regular as ever.

I sat on the edge of the bed, leaned over to Lisa, and told her what I'd learned. From time to time we heard Maria moaning and shrieking. "Anything new here?" I asked when I was done.

"Just that this is bothering me."

"I know. I don't like this part of the job, either."

She blushed and pulled her hair away from her face. "I— didn't mean it that way."

"Oh. Well, then, this'll be John's lucky night."

"David!"

"Then tell me it's not true."

By way of an answer she stuck out her tongue at me.

We were silent for a while after that, listening to the noises through the wall. Then Lisa asked, "What are we going to do when they finish?"

"Listen for any pillow talk, then go home."

"Aren't we going to follow them?"

It was already after nine. "No. Traffic'll be too light at this hour. Too much chance of being spotted. Anyway, we know where she's going and we have his plate."

The thumping showed no signs of ending. I stretched out on the bed next to Lisa and looked at the ceiling. Lying down made my shoulder feel a little better. "Did you see how she was wearing her hair?" I said. "That big braid on one side?"

"You liked that?"

"Yeah. And I think a lot of men would."

She took hold of a fistful of her hair and considered it. "Maybe I'll give John a surprise."

We lay that way for a couple of minutes, each with our own thoughts, till the thumping suddenly speeded up and then stopped.

Lisa flicked on the recorder and put on her headphones. She looked at her watch. "Not bad for a woman her age."

"Or him, either." I went to the wall and picked up my stethoscope.

For a while I heard nothing, and then a couple minutes of the usual postcoital endearments. I turned to Lisa. "You think they—" but she put up a single finger and pointed to the wall. I put up my stethoscope again.

"What do you mean?" he said.

"I've done my part."

A pause. "Yeah."

"And—now it's your turn."

I heard the squeaking of springs and for a moment I thought they'd gotten up. I heard him whispering, but couldn't catch his words.

"I know, I know," she said softly. "Don't you think it was hard on me?" More movement of the bed. "Tom," she said, "you have to *decide*."

"It's not that easy, you know."

A few exchanges, again too low to hear, and then Maria again. Her voice was sharper now, and louder. "I don't want to hear it!"

"Calm down, honey."

"Don't give me that!"

More noises of movement, then silence. When I heard the voices again they were fainter, as if they'd moved to the center of the room. I hoped the tape was picking it up.

"I can't believe you want to end tonight like this," he said.

" . . . more than just tonight like this, you son of a bitch!"

"Hey, come on now."

"Just don't talk to me."

"Maria . . . " The words trailed off.

"You think I've got nothing to do but sit and wait. . . . "

She moved away from the wall and I lost the rest.

"Don't talk like that." It sounded more like a command than a plea.

"And why the hell not? You think it was easy for me?"

"No, but—"

"I'm *tired* of sneaking around. . . ."

I couldn't hear his response, but hers was loud and clear. "Take me home right now!"

"No problem!"

They must have been dressing while they were arguing, because it wasn't more than ten seconds before we heard their door slam and the clatter of her heels on the walk. We started packing up as quickly as we could. I would have preferred to get out ahead of them and wait in our car in a dark corner of the parking lot, but they had moved too quickly. The car doors slammed and the engine started. It sounded like he was revving it. An instant later his headlights lit up the room through the curtains. He jerked into gear, squealing the tires, and abruptly the headlights were gone.

We rushed out. Lisa shoved the equipment bag into the backseat while I started the engine. We made it to the highway in time to see the taillights of the Audi disappear in the direction of the shopping center. I knew where they were going, and there were no cars in sight to give us any cover. "Following them doesn't make much sense," I said. "All we'll do is blow the tail."

"They're too mad to be looking around," Lisa said, which was probably true. But I wasn't feeling lucky anymore. I felt ragged and tired and ready to make a mistake if I kept going.

We got on the turnpike at Plymouth Meeting and headed back toward Wayne. "What are you thinking?" I asked.

"That the evening didn't end the way Maria wanted."

"Or Tom. She sounded mad."

"She was the one who was surprised," Lisa said.

"Tom's wife must be really something. Maria seems like quite a woman."

Lisa was quiet for a moment. "It's not enough to get a better offer. You have to be ready to give up what you have already."

I mulled that one over the rest of the way home.

5

Tuesday, 7:00 A.M.

I SLEPT BETTER than usual that night, which meant I only woke up once. In the bad old days I could count on the Vietnam dream to wake me every night, sometimes twice, and leave me in a cold sweat, shaking, in a tangle of sheets and bedclothes. Since Kate the dream had stopped, but I was still a restless sleeper. That night I had one of those vivid, disjointed dreams that left me wishing I knew more about psychoanalysis. Terry, my ex-wife, was trying to find the site of a plane crash. We tramped all over the fields where the plane had gone down but couldn't find it. She was dressed for a safari and I was wearing a business suit. Then we were on the run from people who were shooting at us, and suddenly Terry was Lisa, but still dressed the same. I remember stopping to throw dirt clods at the men with guns, but somehow, I didn't get the worst of the exchange. Then I was in a reception area in an office building, by myself, waiting to see someone. I think it was the man who had stolen the wrecked plane. It was a huge, cold room and when I looked up I couldn't see the ceiling. Then I woke up.

When I opened my eyes I was half asleep and still agitated from the dream. At first I wasn't sure where I was.

In the dim light, with the morning shut out behind thick drapes, it looked like the motel room in Lancaster that Kate and I had shared back in February. I stretched out my hand, but all I found was air. We'd had less than a week together; afterwards, just months of long-distance telephone calls; and now, not even that. I tried not to feel sorry for myself. I hadn't known she was married when we first slept together, but I knew it soon enough, and I'd kept seeing her anyway. . . .

My apartment was a second story, in a garden apartment complex that catered to Villanova students, the recently divorced, and the financially distressed in general. It dated from that period in the late fifties and early sixties when the quality of construction started going downhill. The walls conducted sound like the head of a drum—more than once I'd found myself answering a question from the woman in the next apartment. The kitchen cabinets were some unsuccessful ancestor of particle board. They warped, twisted, and split with every change of temperature. Right now the corners were starting to curl up, a preview of what the summer humidity would do.

I showered, dressed, and warmed some of yesterday's coffee in the microwave. I usually brewed a big pot on Monday and rewarmed it by the cup through the rest of the week. Of course, by Thursday each cup needed a spoonful of sugar; and by the time I reached the end of the pot each cup needed two.

While the coffee was cooling I did some toast and read over Lisa's notes. God bless her, she was thorough. Page after page was covered with her small, regular handwriting, detailing the previous day from the time we left my apartment till I dropped her off again. Completing my report wouldn't involve much more than some editing and typing.

By a quarter to eight I was back on Cherry Street, parked half a block up from Maria's apartment. I hadn't seen her car on my first pass, and for a moment I thought I was too late, but then I saw it on a side street about two blocks from where she lived. Served her right for waiting so late to come home, I thought.

At eight-twenty she came out, wearing a white blouse and dark skirt. I followed her out of Norristown and back to King of Prussia on 202. This time she wasn't on guard—no sudden lane shifts, changes of speed, or unnecessary turns. Anyone with a driver's license could have made the tail with no problem. At eight-thirty she turned into the parking lot of the real estate office.

I kept going, south, towards Marcus Hook, a small borough on the Delaware below Philadelphia, just north of the state line. It had an evil reputation dating from the seventies when the Pagans motorcycle gang used it as a headquarters. Those days were long gone but the impression lingered. A lot of lifelong Philadelphians wouldn't venture into the town on a bet, which was too bad for them. It was much like any of the working-class small towns around Philadelphia, and better than most. Its industries, by and large, had stayed open, the neighborhoods were stable, and it even had a pretty little riverfront park where the kids flew kites and the old-timers played bocce ball.

I parked on a side street near the Marcus Hook Borough municipal building, an odd gray stone cube that dated from WPA days and looked like one of those sugar-cube buildings kids make as arts-and-crafts projects. I went into the police station by the side entrance. It was dark and cramped, with cheap wood paneling, few windows, and low ceilings. The receptionist recognized me and gave me a smile. "Lookin' for Joe?"

"Sure am."

"He's in. Go right on back."

Detective Joseph Ianucci Jr. was sitting behind his tiny desk, struggling to read a fax under bad light. He was the youngest of three sons, and both his brothers had gone into the family funeral-home business. From his appearance you'd think he was in it, too—a black suit, narrow, dark tie, pencil mustache, and a narrow-brimmed black hat, which at the moment was tipped back on his head. He glanced up when I came in. "Dave, how you doin'? Hey, look at this here, in the middle of the page, this DOB—think it's '66' or '68'?"

It was a fax of part of an extradition warrant from Essex County, New Jersey. Evidently it had been faxed off a bad photocopy of the bottommost carbon copy of the arrest warrant. "I can't make heads or tails of it," I confessed. "If I had to guess I'd say '60.' " I handed it back.

"Shit. We're holding a guy on a fugitive warrant, wanted for jumping bail on a rape charge, I've got to prove it's the same guy, born in '66, and look at the crap they send me." His eyes narrowed. "Say, Dave, you ever do any bounty work?"

"Hell, no. Too dangerous."

"You can live pretty well, taking in creeps like this."

"Especially since you don't need to save for your old age."

He grunted. We'd had this argument before, and neither one of us had changed our minds. "Anyway, what can I do for you?"

"Need a registration check from PennDOT."

"Well," he said thoughtfully. "I could do that from here."

In Joe's world, people fell into some clearly defined categories. I wasn't one of those that his family had adopted as their own; but he knew me and we trusted each other. He would help me out, as long as it was understood that the obligations were mutual. I handed him a slip of paper with the Audi's plate and another of my dwindling supply of twenties.

"Need to know if the title's encumbered?"

"Not if it slows things down."

He went into the next room and sat down in front of a massive gray Teletype machine that covered the entire top of a large metal desk. In less than three minutes he was back with a barely legible computer printout created by the world's oldest dot-matrix printer outside of a museum. "Here you go, Dave. Registered to Thomas and Virginia Evans, 1442 Walker Road, Broomall."

Marple Township. Northern Delaware County. Not far from my own place. "Nice middle-class suburb," Joe said. His voice dropped a little. "We got some relatives up there." He seemed proud they'd done well, but not so proud of how they'd run out on the old neighborhood. "Need an introduction to the chief? I don't know him but I know the township detective." Joe was offering an unsolicited favor—it was his way of telling me that there was room in the Ianucci family if I was willing to spend more time down in the borough.

"Thanks, Joe, but not just yet. But I appreciate the offer."

"So what you working on?"

I tapped the printout. "Thomas here's been putting it to my client's wife."

"Thomas and Virginia," he said slowly. "Unless she's a mother, or a sister, he's got a wife. Kids, too?"

"I think so."

Ianucci shook his head sadly. "Kids. They didn't ask for this."

"They never do."

"Dave, that woman you were in about last month, Kate McMahan?" Like most detectives, he had a phenomenal memory for names. "Did that work out for you?"

"Nope." I said it in a way that discouraged any more questions.

"Sorry to hear that." He paused. "So, you seeing anybody serious these days?"

"No. How about you?"

He grinned. We talked about Joe's family after that—two kids in high school, one in the eighth grade, and now another on the way—and he then inquired gently if I wanted to come for dinner sometime. We agreed he'd talk to Theresa and call me back. I had a feeling that dinner was going to involve a fixup with a friend of the family—not a family member, of course, since I wasn't Italian or even Catholic—but it still sounded good. The prospect of any kind of connection was cheering. I headed up to Broomall in a better state of mind than I'd known in at least a month.

Broomall looked like half the suburbs of Philadelphia. A resident of Swarthmore, Ambler, Media, or any of a dozen other towns who was dropped into the center of Broomall would have trouble realizing he wasn't in his hometown. After a while all of the houses on quarter-acre lots, strip malls, car dealerships, and fast-food joints start to look alike.

By the time I located Walker Road a warm breeze was picking up, tossing the leaves on the trees. I followed the street through a development that looked like it dated from the late fifties, with old shade on both sides. I reached a cul-de-sac at the end without spotting 1442. Then I spotted a narrow road, no more than fifteen feet wide, between two of the houses. I followed the road over a hill and into a patch of scraggly woods. The road stopped at a mailbox with "1442" in crooked decals. It wasn't much to write home about. A small rancher, probably no more than two bedrooms. No garage, and weeds growing out of the gutters. I parked and centered the place in my viewfinder as I took a few shots. Not that they were essential for my report, but I'd started the roll and I needed to have the other shots developed anyway. The yard sloped steeply away to the rear, as if the house were slowly sliding backwards, barely hanging on by its fingernails. The yard was in bad shape, riddled with bare patches and crabgrass. Several small gullies told me it was losing its battle with erosion. The house looked a little newer than its neighbors, perhaps twenty years old instead of thirty. Probably because no one had been willing to build on the lot until every other one was taken.

I put down the camera and went to the front door. On the

way up the driveway I saw children's toys scattered about in the grass. The metal ones—a tricycle, some small shovels, and a remote-control car—were rusting.

I didn't bother with the front doorbell and just knocked. My guess was that it was probably out of order. I gave it thirty seconds, knocked again, and then another thirty. I was about to give up when I heard movement behind the door. Not footsteps—a single, heavy thump as if something was being dropped on the floor. A shadow moved across the lens of the peephole. I stayed still and tried to look presentable.

"What do you want?" came an edgy female voice through the door.

"Mrs. Evans?"

A pause. "Who are you?"

"I'm an investigator, ma'am. I'd like to talk to you for a minute."

"I want to see your identification!" The woman sounded halfway to calling the police already. I smiled meekly and held up my photo identification to the peephole. I must have stood that way for almost a minute. I'd just about decided she was trying to memorize it when she spoke again. "I want to see your identification close up. I'm going to open the door a little, but I warn you it's on a chain so don't try anything. Pass it through when I open up."

I heard another thumping sound, like the first, a rumbling, scraping noise, and then the sound of several dead bolts being worked. The door opened a hairsbreadth and I slipped my ID inside. The moment she had it the door slammed with a bang and the bolts flew back into place.

This time, at least, she wasn't long. "I'm going to call and see if you're who you say you are."

"Fine. You want the Clerk of Courts, Philadelphia County."

She gave no acknowledgment. I must have stood there for five minutes. I wished I could say that I was able to use the time wisely, but I didn't. I was afraid to run the risk of alarming her by moving off the porch, and from where I stood there was nothing to see.

Finally she came back to the door. "What is your business?" She spoke so slowly, with a pause between each word, that I wondered if she was taping us.

"I'm here about an investigation."

"Investigation?"

"Your husband, Thomas."

"What's this about?"

"It's something I'd rather discuss face-to-face."

Even through the door I heard, "Oh!"

"It's hard to talk out here like this, ma'am."

"This is about Tom?"

"That's right."

"You understand, the place is a mess."

"I don't mind, ma'am."

After a pause the bolts were thrown back, but the door didn't open. Instead, I heard her voice, distantly. "You may come in now."

The door swung open into a narrow hallway. The bright sunlight didn't penetrate beyond the sill, leaving the rest in near darkness. Dimly, I saw her at the end of the hall. To one side were three large cardboard boxes, which I assumed she used to barricade the door.

"Get inside, please. It—bothers me when there's a door open."

I shut the door behind me, plunging us into a darkness so thick that I was afraid to take a step.

"I'm sorry," she said. "Your eyes will adjust in a minute."

"Thanks for letting me in."

"It's been a long time since we've had visitors."

"Are the children at home?"

"How did you know about them?" she asked sharply.

I answered in my gentlest voice. "Just from the toys outside, ma'am. That's all."

"Yes," she said. "They left toys out in the yard, didn't they?" It sounded like an insurmountable problem.

My eyes were adjusting, and now I could begin to get a look at her. She was a broad woman, with short, frizzy hair, in a loose housecoat, backed up against the wall. "Could we sit down for a minute?" I asked.

"Oh," she said. Every request presented new difficulties that had to be carefully considered. "I guess so. Follow me."

She turned to the right and entered a cramped, dim living room, overstuffed with furniture and cheap knickknacks. It smelled of mold, and the air was stale. Every item was precisely arranged; the chairs were parallel to the wall and every lamp and dish was centered on its table. She sat on a sofa that took up one entire wall, and I sat in a wing chair opposite her. The curtains were tightly drawn, but enough light came through for a good look. She was enormously fat, so fat I had no idea how old she was, with chins cascading down where there should have been a neck. Her bloated cheeks nearly submerged her eyes and nose. Her arms were as big as my legs. The housecoat hid her legs as far as her ankles, but her bare feet looked nearly as broad as they were long.

"Now, why are you here? Is Tom all right?"

"Yes, he is." It was time to decide how to play it. If I were Tom, what would be my cover story? He meets Maria only on weeknights, after dinner. He's not at a phone, so he can't say he's at the office. "I met Tom at the club."

"Oh—the racquetball club?"

I'd been hoping for the Lions or Jaycees, but it would do. It never failed to amaze me how little one member of a couple seemed to know about the details of the spouse's life. "Yes, that's right. And I do investigations for insurance companies, too, which is a coincidence, because I got assigned Tom's policy.

He gets a small policy through his work—nothing big, five or ten thousand dollars, I think, but we have to do an investigation anyway. It's just a formality, of course." I leaned closer and dropped my voice. "And I'd appreciate it if you didn't tell him I was here. Technically I'm not supposed to turn in a report on anyone I know personally, even a little. I just thought I'd do him a favor."

"Is this life insurance or medical insurance?"

"Life."

"Oh."

"You sound disappointed."

"It's nice, but our real problem is the medical bills." She paused and moistened her lips. "I—wasn't always like this."

"None of us were, ma'am. Things happen."

"Yes, Mr. Garrett, things . . . happen. I'm glad you understand."

"Nobody knows what card we're going to draw tomorrow."

"That's not true. I know exactly what tomorrow is going to bring."

"It must be hard for you."

"I don't normally go on like this, but you listen well, and I don't get many visitors."

"You must be lonely."

"You have no idea."

"I can tell you're not happy."

She swallowed. "When we were married I weighed one hundred and ten pounds." She said it slowly, to make sure I understood. "I can see by your face you don't believe me." She raised a gigantic forearm and pointed at a table next to me. It was her wedding picture—a pretty girl with flowing black hair wearing a tight sheath wedding gown that left nothing to the imagination. She looked at the camera with a ready-for-anything bridal smile.

"You made a very pretty bride."

"Then we had Josh. It was a horrible pregnancy, and afterwards I found—do you know what agoraphobia is?"

"Fear of heights?"

"That's acrophobia. No, it's fear of going outside, of open places. A lot of people haven't heard of it."

"I'm sorry, but I guess I'm one of them."

She was so set to tell her story, I'm not even sure she heard me. "It starts out that you feel nervous in crowds. Then you can't stand any place that isn't familiar. You can't stand being in Center City. Then you get nervous at King of Prussia. Then it's the neighborhood mall. Then the corner store, and then it's the front lawn. You don't think you can face the world, so you stay home, and then the next day it's that much harder. So you force yourself, but you get so *scared* all you can think of is getting home again, and pretty soon you can't leave at all. Then you don't even like to leave your room." She looked around the room, a little nervously. "I only come in here to clean and then I go back to my bedroom."

"I'm sorry."

"I haven't been out of the house, except for doctors' appointments, in four years. I haven't been able to work. I just eat and eat and now look at me." She looked down at herself. "If I got over it tomorrow I couldn't stand to go out, anyway."

"You said you had medical bills?"

"Psychiatrists and counselors. And medications for my anxiety and my weight."

"You must be very lonely."

"I have the children, but Josh is in school and Clarissa is in day care."

"You and Tom must be very anxious that they'll find a cure soon."

"A cure." She said the word slowly, turning it over with her tongue. I wondered if she was drugged or whether she was just not used to communicating with strangers. Or both.

I decided it was time to get to work. Or maybe she was just making me nervous. "What's his date of birth?"

"November 19, 1958."

"Does he have any personal habits that would affect his longevity?"

"He'll outlive me by years." She said it with bitterness, as if she blamed him for his good health.

"It must be a hard thing to accept."

She looked at me, puzzled, and didn't answer.

"Aren't the doctors helping?" I asked.

It was a stupid thing to say, and her laugh told me so. "Sure, look for yourself. I'm a picture of health."

"How's Tom taking it?"

If she thought it was an odd question for an insurance investigation, she didn't say so. It could have been months since she'd talked to an adult, other than Tom or her doctors, face-to-face. "He—how do you think he takes it? How would I take it if it were him and not me?" The question hung there for a moment. I was sure she asked and answered it every day; I wondered what her own answer was, the private one she only admitted to herself. "But he says he married me for better or worse, sickness and health, and he knows it's not my fault." Her voice became insistent. "He *knows*."

When I started to ask where he worked, I realized my cover story wasn't as good as I'd thought. If I was investigating for his employer I'd already know that. "You've been very helpful, but could I trouble you for one thing more? One of his business cards? I like to clip one to the report."

"Well, those would be in the kitchen." I had the sense that I should understand how much of a problem that was.

"I can get one, if you'll tell me where to look."

I saw her lips working as she wrestled with what to do. Then her mouth set in a straight, determined line. "Come with me."

I followed her into the kitchen. It was just as dark as the

living room, but at least it smelled of cooking odors and soap instead of mold. Next to the phone was a pile of his cards. I squinted at one in the half-dark and put it in my pocket. SWEDESTOWN AUDI-BMW, THOMAS EVANS, SALES REPRESENTATIVE, and an address not far from Norristown.

"He gets out," she said. "Every day."

I thanked her politely and got the hell out of there myself.

6

Tuesday, 1:00 P.M.

I CALLED PRESTON from a WaWa convenience store on West Chester Pike. Over the noise of traffic, the gas pumps, and a popcorn machine placed thoughtfully right beside the phone, I told Preston I was ready with a report. We agreed to meet at two-thirty, enough time for me to have the photographs developed.

I don't know exactly how I decided on my next step. Maybe because the case had gone so smoothly, or maybe I felt I had to do as well as Lisa. I pointed the nose of the rental north and headed for Maria's office.

It was a small operation, pleasant and well lit, with a play area in the front with lots of children's books and toys. Right behind that was a large desk, obviously belonging to the manager; behind that were half a dozen desks for the salespeople. I was in luck; besides the manager, she was the only one on duty.

She stood up from her desk, walked up to meet me, and gave me a brisk handshake. When our eyes met she gave no sign of remembering me from the parking lot. Her hair was down today, and she was wearing makeup. Small diamond earrings and a gold bracelet. No rings.

"I'm Maria Winter. How can I help you?" She had a wonderful voice, smooth and clear, and just a little breathy. I wanted to keep her talking, just to listen some more.

"Michael King," I said. "I'm interested in a place in the Norristown area. Something simple, just for myself. Maybe a little row house, something around a hundred thousand."

I followed her back toward her desk. She moved with an easy, fluid sway that a man couldn't mistake for anything but sex. She was wearing a sheer ivory blouse that glided slightly from side to side as she walked. Underneath there was no slip or even a bra, just some kind of stretchy lace thing with broad shoulder straps and a deep plunge in the back.

We sat at her desk. I assumed she shared the desk with other realtors, and that it was hers for only a few hours a day. Her only token of possession was a framed photograph of a young man in a suit.

"Your son?" I asked.

She nodded. "That's his high school graduation. He's an engineer now."

"You don't look old enough to have a son out of college."

She ignored the compliment. "He's a lot older than that, actually. He's with a big firm in Orlando." She looked at the picture. "It's funny; he's all grown up and I keep putting out his graduation pictures. I guess I can't deal with him being away." She asked me a few questions and then started leafing tentatively through some multilist books. "You'll have to excuse me," she said. "I just started."

"Oh? When?"

"Last week."

I indicated her clothes and jewelry. "You look mighty prosperous for someone who's only been working a week," I said.

"I had another job, before."

"It must have paid well. Is it open?"

"You wouldn't want it."

"Oh, I don't know. Try me."

She opened her mouth to answer, and then shut it. After a pause, she said, "Trust me, you wouldn't."

"What kind of work was it?"

"Real estate, sort of. Uh—property management, I guess you'd call it."

"If it paid well enough I'd be interested. Where did you say you worked?"

She met my eyes and held them. "Look, I'd rather talk about selling you a house, okay?"

She showed me some printouts, and I came up with varying excuses about why each property wasn't right. "Maria," I said. "I don't know this area real well—you from around here?"

"All my life."

"I'm a single guy and I'm looking to meet people." I made a point of noticing her ringless hand. "So where do the singles hang out?"

"I'm a little old for the singles scene." And so are you, she implied.

"I wouldn't say that at all. You're gorgeous."

She nodded, accepting the compliment, but the smile turned wooden. She leaned a little closer. "Mr. King, please don't get upset, but I don't date my clients."

"Are you spoken for?"

"I'm married," she said automatically.

"You're not wearing a ring."

She looked uncomfortable. "My life's complicated enough right now."

"I'd just like to take you out to dinner. No strings." It was an easy offer to make; I knew she'd turn me down.

She didn't disappoint me. "No, I don't think it's a good idea."

"It might make your life simpler."

She smiled at the thought and then looked down at her desk. "That would be a nice change."

I let her think I was misunderstanding her. "All right, then. Can I pick you up at six?"

I saw genuine alarm in her face. "Oh, no. I'm sorry. Dating someone else is the last thing I need. I just meant I'd like things to be simpler."

"That bad, huh?"

"Thank you for asking, but I'd rather not discuss my personal life anymore." The words were mild enough, but the tone left no room for disagreement.

I hadn't learned much, but I'd gone as far as I could. I took a couple of brochures on the joys of life in Montgomery County, plus the office's newest handouts on properties in my price range. I stood to go and asked her for her card. It didn't have a home phone, and I asked her about that.

"If we need to set up a showing after hours you can always reach me through the office."

I fingered the card. "I hope your life gets less complicated, soon."

"It will," she said. "One way or the other."

7

Tuesday, 2:30 P.M.

LEAH LOOKED UP the moment I came in the door, and she seemed glad to see me. "Hi, Mr. Garrett. Here to see Mr. Preston?"

"I believe we have an appointment."

"I'll tell them you're here. Parked in our lot?"

"My car is blocking a white Ford. And the Ford is blocking somebody else. Hope you have all the keys."

She put up her hand, palm open, and I tossed her my car keys. She made the catch without effort and favored me with a smile. "Thanks. If I'm on break when you get through, just ask whoever's here. Have a seat, please."

I found myself a small but comfortable flame-stitch chair near the fireplace and considered. "Them" could only mean Preston and Maria's husband, Pat. I wished Preston had warned me. Preston and I, by ourselves, could talk as one professional to another. Of course, Preston knew that every bit as much as I did. I was certain it wasn't his idea to have the client present.

He'd told me—warned me—that Pat was difficult. Now I knew he was demanding, too.

Leah was dressed like a grown-up schoolgirl today. A brown sweater, buttoned nearly to the neck, and a plaid skirt that ended well below the knee. When I looked at her hands I saw that her nails were short and plain. Just when I started daydreaming about asking her out for a beer, I saw the engagement ring. The diamond was tiny, but there was no mistaking it. I contented myself with wondering what sort of a fiancé she had, and what she was like outside of the office.

As I watched, she checked Preston's daybook against a similar book, occasionally adding appointments or making erasures to make sure the books were identical. Normally that would be a job for Preston's secretary. I wondered if that was somehow part of her duties as a receptionist or whether she was one of those hyperenergetic people who just take on more and more work—making coffee, opening the mail, calling for supplies, making sure the lot gets plowed in the winter—until they virtually run the office by themselves. Unfortunately, their capacity for work is usually matched by their capacity to complain about how busy and unappreciated they are. Advising them to take things a little easier never works—they're not made that way. But if you can keep them happy they're worth their weight in gold. They'll stay late, come in on weekends, deliver documents to clients' houses—whatever it takes.

I thought about my days practicing with Tom Richardson. He had a secretary like that, Margaret. She ran his practice and the rest of the firm so efficiently that we were barely aware that over the years she acquired a husband, three children, and four grandchildren. I'd started out with a take-charge secretary of my own, but after a couple of years she grew bored and went on to law school. The secretaries wanted to be paralegals and the paralegals wanted to be lawyers. And once you'd been a lawyer for a while, the odds were that you wanted to get the hell out, but that's another story.

A small red light blinked on her console. "They're ready for you, Mr. Garrett. The small conference room, first door on your left."

It was a cramped, bare room, dominated by a polished wooden round table that seemed a little too big for the space. Preston rose and shook hands. "Dave, I'd like you to meet our client, Mr. Winter."

Pat Winter stood up, at least as much as he could. In his prime he'd probably been as tall as me, but now he was half a head shorter. The best he could manage was a round-shouldered, bent-over stance that left his chin only a few inches above his chest. "Mr. Winter, glad to meet you."

He gave me a flabby handshake. I smelled beer on his breath and saw that his face was flushed. He still had most of his hair, but it was nearly all gray, and badly combed. Deep crow's-feet marked the corners of his eyes. He was a big man, with a broad chest and shoulders, but like most big men who couldn't exercise, he was turning to fat. His gut protruded from underneath his shirt and hung over his belt. I remembered what Virignia Evans said about not always being the way she was now.

We sat down, and for a moment no one said anything. It would have been easy for me to speak up, since I was the one with the information. But I was a little annoyed with Preston for putting me on the spot with Pat Winter.

Preston cleared his throat. "Dave, first of all I want to tell you how happy we are that you got results so quickly. We're very impressed, even though . . . our worst fears are confirmed. I told Pat what you told me this morning. Perhaps you could give us a summary."

"Sure." But before I could start, Pat interrupted, pointing a stubby finger at me. "Now you're gonna swear to all this in court, right?"

"If I need to, yes."

I looked at Preston. "I didn't know if I'd have a chance to

see you face-to-face, and I figured you'd want something to show
your client, so I've already prepared a written report."

"Written down? Already?" Winter asked.

"It's only a partial report," I said. "It covers just last night.
I haven't had—"

"Here, right now?"

I opened my briefcase and extracted four single-spaced
pages, with the photographs paper-clipped to the top. I handed
it toward Preston, but Winter snatched it away from me. Preston
and I both gaped at him. Preston dropped his eyes before I
did—except for finishing up with the names and details on the
Evanses my job was done, and I didn't care if Winter knew what
I thought of him. But my glare was wasted. Winter wasn't paying
attention to either one of us, or even to the report. He was staring
into the distance, his mouth open a little and breathing hard. One
beefy hand pressed the papers to the table. I knew what he was
thinking; I'd seen it in clients' faces a dozen times. This wasn't a
couple of pieces of paper about a quickie in a motel. This was the
Grail itself. He was dreaming of the power this gave him, how Maria
would come back to him once he confronted her, how the boyfriend
would back off now and leave her alone, how it was going to make
his back strong and his dick hard again and get him his old job
back and make everything the way it had been before.

His eyes cleared and he went to work. He read the report
closely, but with surprising speed. I noticed that his lips moved
as he read. Then he studied each photograph carefully, especially the ones of Maria waiting in the parking lot. They'd come
out better than I had expected, one of them in particular. It was
a profile shot of her looking into the distance, showing her pearls
and a lot of cleavage. She looked, as Lisa said, loaded for bear.
"How long this been going on?" he asked.

I didn't feel like sparing his feelings. "No telling. The desk
clerk said since last November, but they could have been going
someplace else before that."

He looked at me. "This guy's married, maybe?"

"With kids, too."

"How did they meet?" he asked.

"Neither of you have been looking at German cars, have you?"

"I buy American," he said proudly.

"Then I don't know."

"When the two of them had this fight—she sound mad?"

"Real mad." I said. "He was trying to calm her down but she wasn't having any. She have a temper?"

"She tell him they were through, anything like that?"

"She wants him to leave his wife."

Winter's hands drummed on the table. "He gonna, you think?"

"I'm just an investigator, Mr.—"

The finger was pointing again. "You're a smart guy. You've seen my wife, got told all about her. You've seen this guy. So who knows if you don't?"

"Maybe nobody. I'd be guessing."

"So give me a smart guess."

"Okay. Without ever meeting him, I'll guess for you. Your wife is a very attractive woman, she's pressing him hard, they've been seeing each other a long time—I'm going to say that he'll leave his wife."

The muscles in his jaw tightened as he listened. "Huh." He was quiet for a moment, digesting what I'd said. "So," he continued, "who all knows about this?"

"I can tell you who *doesn't* know—his wife. And your wife's landlord. Maria's putting a lot of energy into being discreet."

"Discreet," he repeated slowly, giving the word an ugly, sarcastic sound. "Discreet."

"I have no idea who else knows. Answering that question would take a long time, Mr. Winter. I'd say, quit while you're ahead."

His head snapped up like he'd been given an electric shock. "Quit? I ain't *never* gonna quit, hear that? That son of a bitch cocksucker's never gonna have my wife! He's gonna be sorry he ever fucked with me. I—"

"Take it easy," I said. "I didn't mean quit about your wife. That's up to you. I just meant about following her, that's all."

"Oh," he said, and sat back in his chair. "I'm sorry. I didn't mean to piss you off. These pills I take—I don't know."

"You're under a lot of strain right now."

"Yeah," he nodded softly. "Sometimes, it's like everybody's against me." He glanced over at his attorney. If Preston thought Pat meant to include him, he gave no sign of it.

I turned to Preston. "If you don't have anything else, I'll be on my way."

"Hey," Pat said. "You ain't quittin' on me now, are you?"

"You want me to keep following her? What for?"

He jabbed his thumb at my report. "She'll say it was a one-night stand, or mistaken identity or something. The once ain't enough."

"Come on, Mr. Winter," I said. "You don't believe that."

He looked uncomfortable. "I watch a lot of TV. When the cops do drug busts, they always buy from the guy two or three times first, not just the once."

"This isn't criminal law. You've got all the proof anyone would ever need." I realized it was Preston's part to decide how much evidence he needed, but it was too late.

"I got my reasons."

"I need to know what they are."

"No, you don't."

"Then get somebody else."

"I just wonder if we know it all."

"You think there's someone else? Besides this guy?"

"I don't know. I just figure maybe there's more to know."

"Like what, exactly?"

"Like, I don't know. Like what she's doing, how come she just changed jobs like that, makin' less money? She trying to stick me for alimony or something?"

"She didn't talk to you about the old job?"

"Not after the first few weeks, not a peep."

"You know she was quitting the old job?"

"Nope."

I started to say something, but then Preston sighed heavily and touched my arm. "Dave, let me see you in the hall a minute, please." We left Winter studying the photographs of his wife again. Beauty and the Beast.

Up close Preston smelled slightly of Old Spice. "Pat's under a lot of pressure," Preston said. "His personal-injury case isn't going to trial anytime soon, his workers' comp case still hasn't been decided, and this business with Maria . . . I don't know."

"Did he sound surprised when you told him about the affair?"

Preston put a single finger to the side of his face and considered. "No. He was angry—angrier than he was in there, and hurt and jealous. But no, it wasn't a surprise."

"How long were they married?"

"Thirty-two years this August."

"You have a hell of a memory," I said. "He seeing a psychiatrist?"

"A psychologist, for chronic pain management. Biofeedback."

"Any counseling? I wonder if he's a suicide risk. Right now, he's got to be wondering what he has to live for."

"He's been worse," said Preston. "You should have seen him the day he was told they weren't going to hold his job for him any longer."

"Still, he still had his wife then. This could be the last straw."

Preston pursed his lips. "I'll see if his counselor can see him right away."

"I guess I'm still on the case."

"Would there be a problem, staying with it a couple more days?"

"Not if there's a reason."

He sighed again. "Pat is a very . . . suspicious man. We don't have the best relationship, as you can see for yourself. He may think it's all been too easy."

"He thinks you and I are in cahoots?"

"If he thought that, he wouldn't want you to continue, would he? No, I think it's simpler than that. I told him it might take a couple of weeks, and he was already resigned to spending it. You've whetted his appetite while he still has money set aside."

"Well, I guess it can't hurt."

He allowed himself a very small smile. "Thinking of having Mrs. Winter show you some houses?"

"If I wasted any time, it was interviewing her. No, I was just thinking about a new suit."

"I reviewed your bill to date and it's very reasonable. If you can wait a minute I'll have Leah draw you a check right now."

"I'd appreciate that."

We shook hands. "Dave, I'm impressed. You're doing a hell of a job. Keep it up."

I waited in the reception area and thought about how Maria and Tom had been kissing, how she'd looked when she first saw him. I thought about Tom and Virginia. And I thought about Pat. A few minutes later, when I walked out to my car with the check, it didn't feel like a hell of a job at all.

It was a long way from Wayne to my office in west Philadelphia—even if the drive took only thirty minutes. My neighborhood had been called "decaying" by idealistic reformers around the time I was born. The area wasn't dead—people lived there and business survived. But poverty and crime and hopelessness left its mark on everything. There were churches, but nothing very grand—just storefront operations that were tightly pad-locked when not in use. Garages and service stations, too—but ringed with high chain-link fences topped with triple coils of military concertina wire. Restaurants, but none were open all day. Places specialized in breakfast, lunch, or dinner, and were tightly shut the rest of the time. No one would work outside of the restaurant's busy time because of the risk of a holdup. The only legitimate businesses that thrived were the bars, which bustled till closing and frequently beyond. They were busiest of all on days when DPW or Social Security checks hit the streets, but I didn't begrudge anyone their relaxation. If I didn't have my work and my education I'd probably be at the bar rail with them.

The politicians and the planners were right when they said it was decaying. But there was renewal, too, if you knew where to look. Right in the middle of a block of abandoned row houses a family would be trying to make a go of it. Freshly painted trim, usually bright green or purple, a fenced yard, and window boxes. And usually a brave little hand-lettered "No Drugs" sign on the gate. The signs didn't seem to accomplish anything, except for making personal statements. Drugs were sold as openly as ice cream, and in much the same way—the seller would drive slowly down the street till someone hailed him, then pull over to the curb or just stop in the middle of the road while business was done. Traffic waited patiently for the deal to finish. The other drivers might be poor and uneducated, but they weren't crazy.

I was sitting at my office desk writing out checks when the intercom buzzed. I'd learned to hate that noise. The receptionist worked for the landlord, and one of her jobs was to remind the tenants when our rent was overdue.

I picked up the phone. "Yes?"

"Somebody here for you," she said, and hung up. I put on my suit jacket and headed downstairs. There was no point in trying to tell her that she should let me know who it was. Her attitude was that if I wanted to know that I ought to come down and see for myself. Like I said, she worked for the landlord, not me.

It was Lisa, wearing the same dress from last night. The dress looked a little worse for wear, and for that matter so did Lisa. Her makeup was gone and she looked like she could use a good night's sleep. She was wearing her hair like Maria's, pulled into one braid as thick as my wrist, hanging forward over one shoulder. Each half of her face looked so different, one bare and the other nearly hidden by her dark hair. And that big hunk of hair, flowing down her breast, almost daring a man to unbraid it and let it down . . . When she saw me she grinned and waved the tip at me.

I motioned for her to follow me back upstairs, and she took a seat across my desk. "So how did he like your hair?" I asked.

She tugged at her skirt till it went at least a quarter of the way down her thigh and gave me a slow smile. "Just fine, thank you."

I was going to tell her that John was a lucky guy and then decided it was none of my business. "Looks nice," was all I said.

She flushed and started fiddling with the braid. "Uh—John and I wound up going Dutch. If you could pay me for last night, I could use it."

I got out the agency checkbook and started to write. I'd already written a number of checks to clear up overdue bills, and this last one put me back almost exactly where I'd been three hours before.

"How can a woman who affords a Legend need seventy-five dollars so badly?"

She opened her mouth, hesitated, and then shut it again. "Well, if the job's over, why not get paid for it?"

I wondered what she'd been about to say. "None of my other assistants asked for their money this fast."

"I figure I'm worth the trouble."

I shut up. I wasn't getting anywhere, and besides, she was right.

"David," she said after a moment, "you're right. There is something I wanted to see you about."

"Go ahead."

"You're going to have to get a loan. You'll never survive this way." She didn't gesture at my grimy office—she didn't need to.

"We've had this conversation twice already." It sounded harsher than I'd intended, so I went on, trying to soften it. "If I got a loan I'd just have to pay it back."

"If you had a loan you could afford better equipment, advertising, and an office that would impress the kind of clients you want to attract."

"My credit sucks."

"But you agree that a loan is a good idea?"

"The concept is okay."

She looked out the window. "The money you got me for my case, back in January? It's just sitting there. I could become an investor."

"I've got no collateral. Why would you want to risk your money?"

"Because I know you're good. I know, sooner or later, people will recognize you and things will take off. So why not sooner?"

"I don't think I like the idea of being beholden to one of my employees like that."

"I'd be a partner."

"A partner," I repeated. It had a nice ring. Until you got to the part about sharing decisions. "You given any thought to the terms?"

She leaned closer and put her elbows on the desk. "I'll put in fifty thousand and take back a note payable over five years at ten percent. I get a fifty percent ownership as security; when the note's repaid the business reverts to you. I sign a noncompetition agreement covering Philadelphia and the surrounding counties for two years after I leave. You promise to recommend me for my own license when the five years are up." It tumbled out in a rush, so fast I wondered how many times she'd rehearsed it.

"It's very generous," I allowed.

"You don't sound too enthused."

"I'm just tired."

"Then let me help with the tail. I'm free tonight."

It would have been easy to say yes, to have some company on the Winter case. But Lisa was pushing too hard. "I'll be fine," I said.

"What if I just ride along? We could talk about the deal—"

"Lisa, thanks very much, but I need to think about it, okay? Alone."

She blinked, and her mouth went into a tight line. "Okay."

"I'm not turning it down. I just need to think about it."

She picked up her purse and drummed her fingers on it. "If you're not going to need me, maybe I'll give John a call."

"No problem. Besides, nothing's going to happen tonight, anyway."

Well, nobody's right all the time.

8

Tuesday, 5:30 P.M.

I WANTED TO make it to Maria's real estate office by five, but I decided to stop in Wayne to drop off my supplemental report to Preston first. I'd never been in a traffic jam between Wayne and King of Prussia before, but this was my lucky day. The traffic kept me pinned on Lancaster Avenue till the five o'clock rush was in full swing. I patiently inched my way the four miles to King of Prussia and found that her red Colt was still in the lot. I drove on by and found a spot in the parking lot of the Valley Forge Hilton where she'd turned in the night before. Sure enough, about fifteen minutes later I saw her cut into the hotel's driveway without signaling. She stopped for a minute, then drove slowly through the lot and turned back onto 202. I waited till she'd made her turn and followed her home.

I found a spot on Cherry a half block from her apartment that gave me a view of both her front door and the spot where she'd parked her car. I made a few notes and settled in, trying to get comfortable in the cramped front seat. I took my time, studying the houses, the trees, and patterns of traffic, periodically looking at her front door. When I'd reached the point of complete boredom, I stretched and checked my watch again.

Eleven minutes had passed.

Someone—I think it was Red Barber, the sportscaster—

said that watching yacht races was about as exciting as watching grass grow. Compared to a stakeout, I'd take grass anytime; if conditions are right, you can have the thrill of seeing a lawn shoot up a good quarter of an inch a day—and that's not counting the weeds. Lawn watching is an amusement park of excitement compared to watching a closed front door and a parked car. I sat there regretting a lot of things, like not taking some Motrin for my shoulder and not bringing Lisa along. I hoped she wouldn't be too upset to know that my most immediate regret was not bringing along a milk bottle. . . .

After half an hour I moved a block down, a little past her house. It wasn't as good a spot, but I didn't want to attract attention sitting in the same spot any longer. Another half hour, and I took the risk of a quick trip through the McDonald's drive-through. I might as well have driven all the way into Center City for the early seating at Le Bec Fin; the Colt stayed at the curb like it was planted there. The evening wore on that way, with a high point at eight-thirty when she switched on a front room light.

I'd originally planned to stay till nine, on the theory that if she was going to leave at all, it would happen by then. But when the time came I decided to give it another thirty minutes. I based my decision on intuition born of years of experience, plus the fact that I'd reached the real estate office at five-thirty, and I wanted to rack up an even four hours.

It was worth the trouble—in a way. I was just about to call it a night when her light went out. A couple of minutes later she came out the front door, dressed in tennis shoes, jeans, and a sweatshirt. She crossed the street with nothing more than a glance for oncoming traffic and started her car.

I followed her as she headed north. We passed by the shopping center this time and left the borough. The country gradually became more open, but traffic stayed heavy. I was able to keep almost continuous eye contact from just three cars back.

We reached the intersection of 202 with Germantown Pike, and she surprised me by signaling for a left. I cut through a shopping center and avoided the intersection, then waited for her to pass me as she headed west. Her car was easy to spot from the front. She was one of those drivers who love to use fog lights. I thought it was just one more way for car manufacturers to separate drivers from their money, but some people thought they did some good, and Maria was one of them. Anything that made her car more conspicuous was fine with me.

Germantown Pike was two lanes, straight but rolling, so that the cars ahead of me floated in and out of view as I drove west. Traffic was lighter, mostly eastbound cars heading for Norristown or Philadelphia. As I drove west the area became steadily more suburban, with touches of rural. Genteel rural, that is— horse farms behind dry-jointed stone walls, with the farmhouses set so far back they were invisible in the dark. Interspersed with the farms were strip malls and roadside businesses, especially near the major intersections.

We entered a dip where both sides of the road were forested. Evansburg State Park, said the sign. We crossed over a bridge spanning a creek, which another sign told me was Skippack Creek, and then gradually climbed till the trees stopped and we were back in farmland again.

A sign for Collegeville came up, but we never got there. Maria signaled and turned off. As I drove by, I caught a glimpse of a stand of trees, and beyond them, a crowded parking lot. Further back was a white stucco building surrounded by flood-lights. I kept going till I was out of sight, then made a U-turn and parked in a closed gas station across the street.

Using my binoculars, I picked out her car, at the very end of the lot, and then Maria herself, heading towards the building. She was a good fifty yards away, maybe seventy-five, but she looked like she was in a hurry. She went up the front steps and disappeared inside.

I scanned the building. Through the leaves I saw a sign: COLLEGEVILLE CROSSING TAVERN—FOOD AND SPIRITS. I checked my watch—ten after ten. I wondered if she was late for a ten o'clock appointment. The hour of the night and her clothes didn't make it likely she was on a date.

On the theory that she wouldn't be leaving for at least a few minutes, I went around the back of the gas station to answer the call of nature. I got back to the car, rubbed my eyes, and thought about my next move. If I hadn't gone to her office that morning, I could have gone inside, tried to get a table nearby, kept an eye on her. But I'd let myself be seen, and for nothing. . . . The interview had been a dumb idea. Why did I think she would open up the details of her personal life to a new sales prospect? I'd handled it badly. I should have had a better story. But what? I couldn't have posed as a headhunter without knowing about her last job, and that was what interested me the most. Life insurance? She would have brushed me off. How about a credit investigator? She'd just signed a lease. Yeah, I decided, it would have worked. Even if she'd already been interviewed by a real credit investigator, I could have said it was a follow-up. I could have asked about her income sources, expenses, and she would have been glad to cooperate. The more I thought about it, the more aggravated I became.

I picked up the binoculars again. Two couples came out of the bar, but no Maria. I surveyed the building. As far as I could tell, customers were only using the one door. I kept my eyes on it, waiting. People drifted in and out, mostly couples, but a few groups that looked like families, or double dates. Hardly any singles.

I had the binoculars down, resting my eyes, when I saw a small light come on in the parking lot. That in itself wasn't worth noticing—the interior lights of cars came on every time someone arrived or left. But this light was from the area near where Maria had parked. I picked up the binoculars again, but the light was gone. Through the trees I saw a figure near her car. Maria? I couldn't tell, no more than I could see what the person was doing. Then the figure was gone, lost behind the screen of trees. I watched for a couple of minutes, but the car didn't move. So why would someone open the door and then not drive off? Maybe she went out to get something. Okay, so why not go back inside with it? If she had, I would have seen her. Was she sitting in her car, in the dark? Or was someone else?

Taking a penlight, I slid out of my car and crossed the street. The lot was dark, but the ground was flat and it didn't take me long to reach her car. I looked around, but I was alone. I checked the hood latch, trunk, and doors, but everything was secure. I turned my light inside, checking the front and rear, but there was nothing in the passenger compartment bigger than a paper clip. The glove box was closed. I walked around the car. The tires were inflated and there were no foreign objects under them. I even checked the exhaust; not only was it clear, it was still damned hot. I made a final circle of the area and then went back to my car.

Did Maria come out and take something from the car? Or did somebody else take something? If they did, they were careful about it. More likely, I decided, somebody else took something from some other car. From across the street, I couldn't be sure the light came from her car in the first place.

I was still puzzling about it, a little after eleven, when she came out, alone. She wasn't hurrying this time. I watched her cross the lot and open her door. The light that came on was no different from any of the other interior car lights in the lot. I had no way of knowing if the light I'd seen earlier had been from her car in the first place.

I had started my engine when the tavern door opened again and a single figure emerged into the light. Through the binoculars I saw it was Tom Evans.

Maria's car was nosing up to the edge of the road, its headlights on, but I'd made up my mind to follow Evans. It was hardly a good use of my client's money to determine where Maria was going, but Evans just might lead to something. It was a long shot, but it was the better of the two.

Maria pulled out onto Germantown Pike, heading east back toward Norristown. Another car was right behind, with Evans bringing up the rear in his Audi. I waited for another eastbound car to give me some cover, but no one appeared. As they disappeared over a hill, I went after them.

It was the shortest tail job of my life. Less than three hundred yards away, on the reverse slope of the hill, Evans pulled into a WaWa convenience store. Two sets of taillights were ascending the next hill ahead of us. I parked as far away from Evans as I could.

My job couldn't have been any easier. Evans was at the pay phone on the outside wall of the building, his back to me. I hefted some quarters in my hand and pretended to be waiting. I caught the tail end of his excuse to his wife, something about delivering a car to Camden with Sam. When he got to the part about promising to be home in half an hour, I drifted back to my car.

He headed east again, but a short distance down the road it forked, and he went to the right, so suddenly that I overshot. For a second I wondered if he was checking for a tail, but then I saw that he'd signaled for his turn. I pulled over to the shoulder and checked the map; he was taking Ridge Pike, which looked like it would get him back to 202 a little faster than Germantown Pike. I let him go. He was going home, and Maria had gone in the direction of her home. Time for me to go home, too.

I pulled back out onto Germantown Pike and settled in for the ride back to my apartment. I wasn't feeling too sleepy; maybe I'd type up my report tonight while it was still fresh in my mind. That way I wouldn't have to take notes and then transcribe them. Let's see; five-thirty to eleven-thirty would be five hours. Guessing, I probably had a solid ten-hour day, maybe as much as twelve—and more important, I had something to show for it. The fact that I didn't know what it meant didn't matter; at least I'd seen Maria do something.

When I crested the next hill I saw a flicker of light, like heat lightning, but more yellow than white. I looked closer and it was gone. I looked around the sky, waiting for another flash. I liked summer storms, the stronger the better; how they cleared the air and rinsed everything clean. When Terry and I were first married, we used to go out in the backyard in the worst storms and make love. We'd come in afterwards, wet and covered with mud, leaving our clothes in a soggy trail on the way to the shower. That had all been a long time ago, before she flunked the bar the first time. . . .

I came out of a dip and the light was there again, distant, but flickering steadily, like a tiny candle. What could be burning? It was awfully close to the road, and too late for it to be a farmer's brush pile. Campers in the state park near the creek? Maybe, but it seemed too big, more like a bonfire than a campfire.

I went down into another dip and lost sight of the fire. I took my foot off the gas and coasted up the next rise. Somehow, the fire up ahead seemed like trouble, and I wanted to see what I was getting myself into.

I crested the hill. Ahead of me was a long straight stretch and then the bridge over the creek. And right in the middle of the bridge was a car, blazing furiously.

I hit the gas again and slammed to a halt just short of the bridge. I could see the sparkle of glass and chrome on the roadway, and streaks of fresh red paint where the car had slammed into the abutment. I left my headlights on the high beams and raced to the car, which was facing toward me. Yellow-orange flames engulfed it from nose to tail, sending off thick clouds of black, oily smoke. Through the roar I could hear popping and groaning noises as components exploded or melted.

I doubted that anyone could be alive inside, but I had to try anyway. I ran back to my car and frantically searched the trunk. I snatched a small fire extinguisher from a bracket, pulled the pin, and ran to the driver's door. I stood as close as I could and shot foam in through the open window. The fire paid no attention. I could feel the heat baking the skin on my face and hands. The wind mostly took the smoke away from me, but every so often I collected a lungful of searing black gunk that took my breath away. I could feel the skin on my hands starting to tingle. I covered them with foam, to insulate them from the heat, and they felt better.

A muffled explosion came from the rear of the car, and I started to think about the gas tank. If the tank was full, the gasoline would probably just burn off. But if the tank was mostly fumes it was going to explode. I pressed in closer till I was almost touching the car, feeling the heat through my clothing as I played the pathetic little stream of foam into the flames. Finally, just when the extinguisher began to sputter and quit, the flames began to die down in the front seat. Shading my eyes against the heat, I leaned closer.

The driver's seat was empty.

I dropped the extinguisher and backed away as the fire regained the ground it had lost. The night air was eighty degrees, but it felt like ice against my face and hands. For the first time I had a chance to give the car a careful look. Even though the smoke and flames hid the roof and upper body, the general outline was all too familiar. I realized it was a Colt. Maria's Colt.

The work wasn't finished. If Maria wasn't in the car, she was somewhere close by, probably ejected by the impact with the bridge.

I didn't bother to try to yell. My throat was parched, and if Maria wasn't interested in the inferno on the bridge, I doubted she'd be motivated by hearing me shout. I just walked back to my car, watching the roadway. A short set of skidmarks leading up to the abutment, and the debris at the point of impact. No one on the roadway or the bridge but me.

If Maria wasn't in the car and wasn't on the bridge, she was either in the creek or on the bank. I got my penlight from the car and started searching the brush along the bank. It was slow work. The light only gave off a narrow beam, and the fire had destroyed my night vision.

I found what I was looking for by sound, not sight. When I got away from the roar of the flames I heard a low, irregular noise, somewhere ahead and below me. Not like any noise I'd heard before, at least not since the war; soft, between a whine and a moan. Not even distinctly human. An animal could have made it, if it was in enough pain.

I pressed through the blackberry bushes and the weeds until I came to a clearing near the edge of the water. Maria was there, faceup, her arms and legs twisted at every angle. Blood covered her sweatshirt and jeans. Her face was covered, too, and her hair was matted. As I watched, her chest rose and then fell and she made the moaning sound again. Her mouth was open wide, and a trickle of blood ran out.

I got on my knees next to her and gently raised her head in both my hands. Her eyes were open, but unfocused. I don't think she had any idea I was there. I checked her airway, and it was clear. I pulled up her sweatshirt and felt her ribs. They seemed all right; at least none of them were protruding, and there were no sucking chest wounds. No blood under the sweatshirt. So where was it coming from? And why the trouble breathing?

Above me, I heard a siren and then saw red flashing lights. When I heard a car door slam I yelled as best I could, "Call an ambulance! There's somebody hurt bad down here."

I heard the car door again and the muffled sound of the radio. Then from above me, a woman's shout. "Where are you?"

"Down here, near the stream. Watch out; it's steep."

She crashed through the bushes so fast I thought she was going to go right past us and into the water. As she got closer I saw the beam of her flashlight through the brambles. "Over this way," I yelled. The light moved toward me, and I made out a bulky figure topped with the regulation state police broad-brimmed campaign hat. When she knelt beside Maria I saw she was young, no more than twenty-five, and black. Handcuffs, baton, holster, radio, and spare ammo clips hung from her belt. The body armor under her uniform made her look more like a paratrooper than a cop.

She looked at me. "Can you do mouth-to-mouth while I do her heart?"

I tilted Maria's head back, checked again to make sure her airway was clear, and started breathing into her mouth. Her chest rose, and she seemed to relax a little. The cop pulled up Maria's sweatshirt, then brought her fist down, hard, between the cups of Maria's bra. She leaned on Maria's chest, pressing down with both hands as hard as she could, then releasing. Then she repeated, every few seconds.

The fact that we were trying gave me hope. Maybe it wasn't as bad as it looked. An ambulance was on the way, and hospitals were close at hand. Maria had lost blood, but not enough to be fatal. Twenty minutes and she could be in intensive care. If she could just hang on a little longer . . .

Maria didn't have twenty minutes. Her mouth moved, like a fish gasping for air, and I pulled back. A choking sound came from the back of her throat, and her mouth opened wide. The cop stopped working on her chest; we both knew what it meant. Her arms and legs twitched weakly, and her head fell back. Her eyes rolled back into her head and she was gone.

The trooper checked Maria's carotid arteries, then pulled back the eyelids and shined her light into her eyes. I winced at the bright light, but Maria was beyond caring.

I smoothed her sweatshirt down and felt for the back of her head. I felt the top of her neck, the top of her skull, and the soft cushion of her hair. Nothing else. I pressed gently and felt hard edges where the skull had fragmented. My fingers came away coated with brain.

"The back of her head's gone, Trooper." I held up my hand for her to see. Our eyes met and she shook her head. I closed Maria's eyes and laid her head down gently.

We started up the bank, with the trooper in front. Before I reached the top, I turned for a last look. Maria seemed smaller now, as if she were already beginning to sink back into the earth.

It was a long climb. When my head reached the top of the bank I found myself dazzled by a set of headlights, on high beam, directly in my eyes. Above the lights, I made out a state police cherry light. I raised my hand to shield my eyes.

The trooper lifted her portable radio and repeated her call for an ambulance and an advanced life-support unit, describing it as an auto-accident victim with head injuries.

"You've got to be kidding," I said.

She held up a hand covered with spinal fluid and bits of brain. "I haven't hit the Cracker Jacks box with the M.D. degree yet. Pronouncing is somebody else's job."

Her voice was steady, but her flashlight was still on, and I saw that the beam was wavering. "My name's Dave Garrett."

"Roz Carter."

"The woman down there, her name is Maria Winter."

"How do you know that?"

"I know her, a little. Thanks for trying."

"Hey, that's why we get the big bucks, so we can get brains all over our hands in the middle of the night."

A team of fire-fighters was spraying foam on Maria's car. She took me to the far side of her patrol car and asked for some identification. I handed over my driver's license and she started taking notes on a gray metal clipboard.

"The information here current?"

"Yes, it is."

"Is this your car?"

"It's a rental."

"If you live around here, why are you renting?" she asked.

"Mine's in the shop. You mind telling me why you want to know?"

"You see it happen?"

"No. I was a little behind. The car was already burning, stopped, when I got here."

"Wait right here."

She went to the other side of the cruiser and spoke quietly into the microphone. While I waited I had my first chance to really study the scene. The fire, the headlights, and the fire and police emergency lighting made the area bright as day.

Before and after the bridge the road was at ground level, and the shoulders were wide and flat. But the bridge was several feet above grade, and the road rose to meet it. The shoulders narrowed and sloped down, away from the road, at an angle I estimated at twenty to thirty degrees, and then terminated at the abutments. I took a close look at the shoulders. If a driver got onto the shoulder near the bridge, he would be funneled right into an abutment. It would take some real presence of mind and a fair amount of physical strength to wrestle the car back onto the road. If Maria's belt wasn't fastened, she probably went out the windshield when she hit, or a second later while the car was spinning around. At least it was over quick. I wondered if she'd felt anything after the impact. I hoped not.

I glanced into the interior of the cruiser. Trooper Carter's clipboard was on the front seat. Most of the writing was too small to read, but at the very top, in large letters was "2321—veh (fire) Skipp Cr—per Mike Arronomick" and a phone number. I repeated it to myself till I had the number memorized.

The trooper put down her microphone and went over to my car, studying every inch of the body with her flashlight. When she was finished she went around again, even slower. Finally she came back to me. "What were you doing out here?"

I decided to play it straight. I don't know why; maybe because she was a woman, or because of what she said about the

Cracker Jacks box. "I'm a private detective. I'm working a case."

"Tail job? This woman here?"

"That's right."

"Who do you work for?"

"The lawyer for her husband."

She didn't ask the name, which was fine with me. "What about your hands?"

"I tried to get the fire out. I gave up after I saw there was no one inside."

"You want me to get you somebody about your hands? They're going to smart."

I shook my head. "They'll be fine."

"So give."

I told her what I knew of Maria's movements that evening, including everything I'd seen and done at the tavern. I left Evans out; no point in having the police on Virginia's doorstep for no reason.

"Any reason to think this wasn't an accident?"

"I sure as hell hope it was."

"Could her husband have followed her? Or you?"

"I don't think so. I sat in the parking lot for a hour. I don't think he was anywhere around."

"So why are you worried?"

That was a very good question. "I'm just not a big believer in coincidence. You mind telling me why you're so interested in my car?"

"Yeah. I just cleared you in a homicide investigation. For the moment, anyway."

"Oh?"

"There was a complaint to Lower Providence Township Police about a suspicious person in the parking lot at the Collegeville Crossing Tavern, around ten-forty."

"That could have been me."

"Your car is clean. You didn't run her off the road."

"I could have had help."

She shook her head. "Then you wouldn't have got yourself half fried playing firefighter. And you wouldn't have been down there."

"Thanks, Trooper."

She handed me one of her cards, and I returned the favor. "Don't get mushy on me," she said. "You're still a suspect, just a damn remote one. Besides, it looks like an accident, anyway."

"Her car going to be looked at?"

"If they follow standard procedure, they'll be taking a look later this morning, at the state police garage."

"Okay if I come see?" I asked.

"Not up to me; I'm just a traffic cop. Go to the garage and ask for yourself. Behind the Limerick barracks."

We talked a little more after that; I don't remember about what. I couldn't just go home. I'd touched death that night, and its stink was still on me. Trooper Carter had it easier; she was busy being in charge of an accident scene. Her time would come later. A tow truck arrived, and she started giving orders about clearing the road. I took one more look around and started back toward my car.

In a couple of hours Carter would be getting near the end of her shift. She'd go to her barracks and sit down to make out her report, filling in the dozens of tiny boxes on the Department of Transportation form with every detail of the accident—except the important ones, that is, the ones that bring nightmares. Someone would write "Fatal" in big block letters across the front, and it would be assigned an incident number. It would be cited in traffic studies and duly recorded in all the proper places. Maria Winter had stopped being a person who liked dressing up for dates and got angry and knew how to show her boyfriend a good time—she was well on her way to simply becoming the operator of unit number one in a State Police Incident Report. . . .

It was a long drive home; and crowded, too, with Maria in the front seat with me. I tried to remember if her eyes had shown fear, or pain. As best I could recall, they were dull. At the end, she didn't suffer. If she'd been wearing a seat belt she'd be in the hospital instead of the morgue. If she'd had an air bag she might have walked away. And if she'd stayed home to shampoo her hair? She might have slipped and hit her head. . . .

I had a brief image of her, smiling in her little black dress and waving at Tom. Then I shook my head and it was gone.

9

Wednesday, 2:00 A.M.

WHEN I DRAGGED myself into my apartment the answering machine was blinking with a frantic message from Preston. Could I please investigate an auto accident on the bridge over Skippack Creek? Very important. If there was a premium for emergency work, that was no problem. Call me whenever you get in. . . .

I looked at myself in the mirror, bloody, sooty, unshaven, my hair going in every direction. My suit jacket was ripped down one side; I must have snagged it on something and never noticed. Could I investigate Maria Winter? What a question.

He answered on the first ring. "Yes?"

"It's Dave Garrett." He didn't thank me for calling and I didn't apologize for the hour.

"You got my message."

"I just got in the door," I said. "I was there. I almost saw it."

"What happened?"

"What do you know already?"

"Pat called me, got through my answering service saying it was an emergency. Must have been around one. He said there'd been an accident and he told me where. That was all he knew, except that Maria was dead. What about the other car?"

"One-car accident, at least it looks that way."

"Drinking?"

"Possible, but I doubt it. But it might be a good civil case anyway."

I gave him the basic facts of how the car hit the bridge, nothing more. "It's got the makings of a road-defect case," I said. "There's no suggestion there was any other vehicle. It looks like she just drifted off the road a little and then got caught in the sloping shoulder near the bridge." I described the bridge in detail. "You ought to see this for yourself—it's the Venus flytrap of bridge approaches. I'm no engineer, but it looks like there's something to it."

"Any indication it was the car? Steering? Brakes?"

"No, but you're going to have to know for sure, one way or the other."

"You see this as a conflict of interest? Taking her wrongful death case when I've been adverse to her in a domestic case?"

"No. You never entered your appearance in any case against her. And for all we know there isn't a filed divorce. And with her dead, he's the surviving spouse. Unless there's a will, he's the administrator of the estate—he has every right to call the shots."

"Keep on it for me, please."

"First thing in the morning." I told him about the state police garage and we hung up.

I showered and went to bed. It was a troubled sleep, punctuated with dreams of fire and blood. At six-thirty I said the hell with it and got up.

Michael Arronomick, the eyewitness, wasn't home when I called at eight, but his wife gave me his work address at a garage in Conshohocken. I didn't know the exact address but I knew the town well. It was an old railroad and river town, about ten miles west of Philadelphia on the banks of the Schuylkill. The town had started out at the base of the steep north bank of the river, then gradually built uphill and north till it covered a square mile of bluff overlooking the river. It was an old town of red-brick houses and gray stone churches, invisibly divided into fiercely independent ethnic enclaves of Poles, Italians, Slavs, Croats, and who knew what else. Apart from a smattering of restaurants and bars catering to the small yuppie population, the town hadn't changed much—churches where your son could meet a nice girl; family restaurants for after church on Sundays; corner bars with fifty-cent beers and maybe a room in the back for a little gambling, if your name ended in the right vowel.

The garage was in the northwest corner of town, in a rusted and dilapidated Quonset hut that was almost hidden behind a gaggle of trucks and backhoes in various stages of disrepair and disassembly. A rusty sign, "Entrecken's Garage—Towing All Hours," hung a little out of level. The parking lot was a crazy quilt of dirt, brick, and asphalt. I parked between a couple of truck tractors with open hoods and no engines and went inside.

I found myself in a small, dirty office, decorated with the usual pinup calendars from the auto-parts suppliers. I was as much an admirer of female flesh as anyone, but I'd never been able to appreciate the erotic appeal of a tall willowy redhead in a filmy negligee holding an impact wrench.

"Yeah? Whatdayawant?" The interior of the garage was dark except for a few work lights, and I couldn't tell where the voice was coming from.

"My name's Garrett," I yelled back. "I'm looking for Mike Arronomick."

"Yeah, that's me. Gimme a minute."

I heard the clanking of tools on the concrete floor and then a large shape came into view in the dimness. He was about my age, but that was about all we had in common. Short, no more than five six, and looked like he'd given up the battle of the bulge without much of a struggle. It wasn't more than seventy degrees, but his face was red and he was perspiring freely. He was wearing a toupee that was noticeably more curly than his own hair. It was also crooked, which gave him a Cubist appearance. An unlit cigar protruded from one corner of his mouth.

He wiped his hands on a rag that was filthier than anything else in the garage, but he didn't offer to shake. That was fine with me; my hands were starting to tingle already. "What's up, bud?"

"I'd like to talk to you about the accident."

"Who'd you say you were?"

"Dave Garrett. I'm a private detective."

I might as well have told him I was an alien sent to kidnap him for ritual sacrifice on my home world. He froze dead on the spot and his complexion went from red to white. He swallowed hard and then looked away. "I don't know nothing. Beat it."

"I really am a private detective. Want to see my ID?"

He shook his head and backed up a step. "I know about yous guys."

"What do you mean?"

"I know what you're here for, so just beat it!"

"You *are* Mike Arronomick, aren't you?"

He folded his arms across his chest as if he'd been challenged. "And so what?"

"And you were on Germantown Pike, between Collegeville and Norristown, last night about eleven?"

"The hell I was. I don't have to answer your questions. Now get out before I call the cops."

"Speaking of cops, you already answered some questions, remember?"

"I don't know what you're talking about." He wasn't much of a liar.

"I'm investigating the accident you called in last night. I'm working for the family of the dead woman. And I couldn't care less where you were supposed to be last night."

"How did you find me here?"

"Your wife."

As he considered his reply, his cigar angled upwards. "You workin' for my boss?"

"No."

"Maybe you're playing some angle."

"No angles. I'm not going to tell your boss and I'm not looking for money. I'm only going to get the police involved in this if I have to. All I care about is the accident."

"I don't know you for shit. How do I know I can trust you?"

"Because you have no choice." He didn't look too impressed. "You know, while the cops are interviewing you, I bet I could get them to check some of your parts numbers."

"You son of a bitch."

"Just who's being the son of a bitch here?"

He took the cigar out of his mouth and considered it. Then he threw it into a wastebasket. "Okay, okay. What do you want to know?"

"First off, anyone in your car with you?"

He shook his head indignantly. "I wasn't in a car. I had one of the rollbacks."

I sighed. "You got some system worked out where you do tows without turning in the money."

He looked indignant. "You said you didn't care."

"I don't. It's fine with me. Keep talking."

"Anyways, it was dark and I was in no hurry. I seen some cars way ahead of me when we both got to the top of a hill, you know? I wasn't paying much attention. They went out of sight and I didn't see them after that. Like I said, I didn't think anything of it. Then I came over the hill and saw the bridge, with the car in the middle, burning. And this other car parked right by."

"What was it doing when you first saw it?"

"Nothin', 'cept that it was on fire. It was dead in the middle of the bridge, facin' back at me. I know 'cause I saw the grill in my lights."

"Tell me about the other car, the one parked right by."

"Piece-of-shit Sunbird, or something like that."

"So what did you do?"

"Pulled right around and drove like hell for a phone booth. Found one about a mile up, dialed nine-one-one."

"Any other cars around, besides the parked one?"

"I seen some taillights way ahead when I got to the bridge, but they was a long way away. What does the boss have to know?"

"Nothing at all." I gave him one of my cards. He grunted and shoved it into his shirt pocket.

"One more thing," I said. "How many rollbacks you got?"

"Just the one. Why?"

"Where is it?"

"Out front, near the gas pumps. What about it?"

"Nothing," I said. "Thanks."

I went over every inch of his truck and couldn't find so much as a bug spatter.

I wasn't much looking forward to my next stop. I pulled up in front of Maria's apartment and rang the bell. After a few moments the landlady answered. Up close she was even heavier than she'd looked on the porch with Lisa. Her gray hair contrasted with her dark skin. "What can I do for you?" She was pleasant, but there was suspicion in her voice. White men usually meant trouble of one kind or another, and I was guilty till proven innocent.

"My name's Dave Garrett. I'm here about Mrs. Winter."

"I'm Florence Grace, the landlady."

"I guess you know—"

"I heard," she said quietly. Neither of us said anything for a moment. She looked around the tiny porch. "She was just here, last night. . . . We stood right here, talkin'." She shook her head. "Awful, ain't it?"

"Yes, it is."

"She was one of the nicest tenants I ever had and she's gone, just like that." Her voice sounded tired and old. It sounded like Maria was the latest addition to a long line of people she'd known that wouldn't be coming back.

"Did you get to know her very well?"

"She had supper with my daughter and I some nights. She was fixing to have a little party this Saturday night. We was invited, and some of the neighbors, too."

I showed her my ID. "I'd like to see the apartment, please." She squinted at it, but her eyes didn't move left to right. I wondered if she was illiterate. After what she thought must be a decent interval she handed it back. "Are the police investigating this?" she asked.

"Yes, ma'am. You'll probably be hearing from Trooper Carter, state police." If she wanted to assume I was a cop, too, that was her own business. "Could I see the apartment now?"

"I guess so, long as I comes in with you."

We entered a short hallway with a door to the left and a steep set of stairs going to the second floor. The floor was old green linoleum, but clean, and the stair treads were covered with new black rubber. As we headed up the stairs I smelled oil soap and furniture polish.

At the top was a cheap hollow-core door with a peephole and dead bolt. She unlocked it and we went inside.

It was a three-bedroom apartment, spacious and airy, with the kitchen in the front and the bathroom all the way in the back. It was spacious, in part, because it was so empty. The only furniture in the living room was a card table and chairs. A single bed, a nightstand, and a cheap dresser in one of the bedrooms. The second bedroom contained only a dresser with a row of books on top. The last bedroom was completely empty. Presumably that was the bedroom Maria had wanted to sublet to Lisa. No pictures on the walls and almost no food in the kitchen cabinets.

"Looks like she wasn't planning to stay long."

"She signed a one-year lease," Mrs. Grace said, "with a two-month security deposit." She made it sound like the crowning achievement of her career as a landlady.

"Could I see the lease, please?"

"I gots my copy downstairs." She shuffled to the door and disappeared down the stairs.

Now that I was rid of her I could take a good look. The bathroom medicine cabinet was empty except for aspirin. No bottles or cans in the wastebaskets. No evidence of drug use. The closet in the first bedroom was filled with suits and dresses, some for the office, and lots of others that were too dressy for everyday.

I'd taught Lisa what I could, and I'd learned from her, too. Like how to tell good clothes from junk. The labels were Nordstrom, I. Magnin, and Saks. Not junk. On the closet floor were thirty, forty pairs of shoes; some flats and some heels, all of them in good condition. I checked a couple pair and saw that they were Ferragamos. *Definitely* not junk. The top dresser drawer was filled with fancy lingerie decorated with lace and bows, the kind that women never buy for themselves. The next two drawers down were her everyday underthings. Again, good brands, and more spare pairs of panty hose than I could count. I thought about the neighborhood and about the clothes. For whatever reason, Maria was living on a lot tighter budget than she was used to.

I opened the closet doors all the way and looked in both ends. In one corner was a small cardboard box that once held a couple of thousand sheets of copy paper. But now it was overflowing with envelopes and thick documents.

I dragged the box out for a better look. A shipping label on the outside told me it was from New Directions Realty in Jenkintown. The papers were a jumble; letters, phone messages, draft agreements of sale, title searches, and sketch plans were jammed in together. Different pieces of land, different banks, different purchasers and sellers. The only common feature I saw, from a quick glance, was that New Directions represented the seller each time. Toward the bottom of the pile was a stack of reports from a company called Eco-Protect on environmental conditions on each property. I'd never heard of them, but their letterhead bore an address I recognized: the Meeting House Business Center in Plymouth Meeting. I glanced at a couple of the reports, but Maria's name didn't appear anywhere. For that matter, I didn't see her name on any of the other documents, either. I pushed the box back into the corner where I'd found it.

Maria's bed was made and the bedspread was on. It smelled faintly of perfume. The bedside table was covered with a collection of small framed photographs of family members. I checked the drawer but found just the usual jumble of pencils, loose buttons, paper clips, and rubber bands. I thought how this was the second time in two months I was searching the bed table of a dead woman. I finished my job and got out of there.

The dresser in the second bedroom was empty—I assumed it was for Tom's use when he moved in. The books on top, though, were clearly hers—all hardcovers, and judging by the dust jackets, well thumbed. Mainstream romances, a few best-sellers. On one end were several larger books, photo albums. Most of them were the large, inexpensive kind sold in discount stores, and they showed their age; but one, wedged in between the others, was thinner and bound in what looked like real leather.

I couldn't find an address book, but next to the phone in the kitchen was the next best thing, a corkboard covered with business cards from a variety of services—cable TV, dentist, photography studio, gynecologist, trash hauler, optometrist, and auto repair. And the card of Mark Louchs, a lawyer I knew who handled domestic cases.

Before I could search any further Mrs. Grace came up the stairs, breathless with the effort, and handed me the lease. It was a standard Realtor's form, signed six weeks ago. I nodded while I looked it over, as if I was learning something that made her trip downstairs worthwhile.

I handed it back. "Ever meet her husband?" I asked.

"No. She didn't mention no husband."

"She had one, and he'll probably be around. Name's Pat. "When did you see Maria last?"

"A little after nine last night. She was on her way out and she stopped off to ask me to tape a show for her. She said she wouldn't be back till after it started and she didn't know how to work her VCR to tape if she wasn't here."

"She seem okay to you?"

"Maybe a little steamed up, but she didn't say 'bout what."

"She seem high?"

"I never saw her take nothin', 'cept a glass of beer oncest."

"Did she say where she was going?"

"No, she said she had something to do. That's all. Is it important?"

"Whatever she was doing got her killed. For her sake I hope it was important."

"Ain't nothing worth dyin' about."

10

Wednesday, 11:00 A.M.

THE STATE POLICE garage where Maria's car was impounded wasn't exactly what I expected. A shiny black Porsche was on a lift right in front of me, having its underside torn off with air chisels while two men in badly fitting business suits looked up anxiously. My guess was that if the car wasn't carrying drugs there was going to be hell to pay. Next to the Porsche was a perfectly ordinary Plymouth sedan peppered with bullet holes. Further down was the front half of a new Jaguar sedan in British racing green with a New York license plate. The rear was nowhere to be seen and was presumably on the highway somewhere at this moment, attached to the front end of some other Jag. They didn't call them chop shops for nothing. In the far corner was the blackened hulk of a Mack truck tractor sitting on four flat tires. The room was filled with an unpleasant, sweet barbecue smell, and I had a bad feeling that it was coming from the truck.

In the context of all the automotive carnage, Maria's Colt fit right in. It was on a lift to one side of the Mack tractor with three men clustered underneath. One was wearing gray-green coveralls like most of the other men in the place. I assumed he was a state trooper. The second man was also in coveralls, but his were white. He was sporting a salt-and-pepper beard that I was sure wasn't standard state police issue. The third man, in a suit, was Preston. His hair was badly combed and he hadn't shaved. His tie was knotted loosely a full inch below his unbuttoned collar.

He looked over when I was a few feet away, and we nodded at each other. He looked up at the car. "We'll have to talk." He paused. "Nothing here so far . . . " He made a vague gesture at the underside.

"You okay?" I asked.

He passed a hand over his face. "I didn't sleep well after Pat's call."

"What did he expect you to do in the middle of the night?"

"He wanted it investigated. He can be very insistent, as you know. His own case has problems because we could never locate the witness who saw him go off the loading dock." He kept staring at the underside of the car, lost in his thoughts.

"Look, there's no point in hanging around here. Let your man do his work. Had any lunch yet?"

"Not even breakfast."

"There's a diner across the street. Buy me lunch while we talk."

He introduced me to the man in the white coveralls, who turned out to be Les Hecht, a mechanical engineer whose deposition I'd taken some years before; then we crossed the street.

We sat down at the counter and ordered without looking at the menu. I summarized what I'd learned from Arronomick and the landlady. It wasn't a lot.

"So how did Maria get off the road?"

"She could have been drinking," I admitted, "but the

autopsy will tell us that. She could have been tired. She had worked a full day and it was past eleven."

"I'd hate to have that autopsy come up positive for blood alcohol," he said. "A witness who could say that she was sober when she left the bar would be nice."

"Don't even bother to hire me to take statements. When you file suit, just include a count against the bar. The owners, the manager, and every employee would be happy to swear that when she left she was the very picture of sobriety. Even the ones who were over in Jersey that night will come forward." Preston nodded. The Dramshop Act has probably resulted in more perjury than all the other statutes of Pennsylvania combined, and any experienced civil trial lawyer knew it. "Besides," I said, "I searched her apartment top to bottom and didn't find any booze at all."

"What did you find?"

"Nothing that's got much to do with a wrongful death claim. Mainly that she had a business card from a divorce lawyer." I realized something. "You know, in the divorce, his personal-injury settlement would be a marital asset. She might have gotten half of it."

"I know what you're going to say, Dave: that it would be a lot of money out of Pat's pocket."

"Did Pat know that?"

"If he knew, it wasn't from me." He sipped his coffee. "There's something I didn't mention yesterday," I said. "Not that it matters anymore, but Pat's already paid for it. It's in my supplemental report, but you probably haven't been to your office yet. Maria's boyfriend was a guy named Tom Evans, from Broomall. Has a wife named Virginia. Sells Audis and BMWs. Maria was coming back from meeting with him last night when it happened."

He looked at me, startled. "Evans . . . is he young?"

"About forty, maybe a little less. No younger than thirty-five. Why?"

"Because—this sounds crazy, but I think I met him once, at an AIDS benefit a couple of years ago. Big blond fellow, very smooth. Is his wife sick or something?"

"She has a phobia about leaving the house."

"Then it has to be him. I remember. He was married, but he was there alone because his wife couldn't leave the house."

"This AIDS benefit—tell me about it."

"A classmate from high school was opening a card store on South Street. Ralph Torino. It's still there; I buy my Christmas cards through him. I think it's South Street Cards or something like that." He paused. "I wonder if he met Maria there."

"She was there?"

"She sure was. What a small world."

"How's Pat taking this?"

"He was pretty numb last night when he called. He rambled a bit and it was hard to tell what he was saying at times. I think he'd been drinking on top of his medication."

"He said some pretty strong stuff in your office yesterday."

"Whatever happened in my presence is privileged, and you know that," he said sharply.

"I just wonder if he has an alibi."

"For an accident?"

"Don't you think it's a hell of a coincidence that within a few hours of a jealous husband finding out where his estranged wife lives, she turns up dead?"

"David," he said slowly, "I'm going to have to ask whose side you're on."

"Maria's. If she died from her own stupid fault then she's got no business with anybody. If she died because some Penn-DOT engineer cut corners, her estate should recover. If she was murdered, somebody owes."

He pulled his trick with the deep breath before he answered. "You're sounding a little histrionic."

"I have a great affinity for the dead. They don't ignore your advice and they don't call you at home. And if they have solvent estates, they even pay your bills without complaining."

"You're afraid he may have had something to do with it, aren't you?"

I had my answer ready. "I wouldn't want to rush into a civil case if it would make . . .other difficulties for my client."

He looked down at the counter and thought about it.

I checked my watch. "Shall we take a look?"

Maria's car was off the lift, and the two men in coveralls were peering under the hood. The one in white, our engineer, saw us coming and came out to meet us in the parking lot.

"Mr. Preston, we're about done here." He wiped his hands on a rag. They were very dirty. I wondered how he kept his beard so clean.

"Find anything?"

He worked his jaw, and I noticed that he was chewing a wad of tobacco. He used it the same way a man can use a pipe —something to distract the questioner while he thinks over his answer. "So far, there's no evidence of a mechanical malfunction. Lights were on at the moment of impact, the brakes worked, the transmission *still* works, and as far as I can tell the steering was fine."

"You qualified what you said about the steering."

"Because the steering system comes in a hundred pieces from the factory, and this one is in about two hundred and fifty. Anybody who tells you he can eyeball a preimpact defect out of this mess is a liar or a fool. There's a lot more testing we can do, but it's going to get expensive. She hit a concrete wall, huh?"

"Bridge abutment."

He nodded. "She was probably doing at least fifty to cause this damage."

"What are the odds of it being a mechanical failure?"

"Five percent, tops. You can have mandatory inspections till the cows come home, get every junker off the road, and it's not going to save many lives. It's still the loose nut behind the wheel that causes most accidents." He looked at Preston. "No disrespect intended."

"The police finished?" he asked.

"They're only interested in whether there was a crime or not, and they didn't find anything. Any authorized agent of the record owner can have it towed away."

"Will they need his signature?"

I heard a car pull up behind us, turned, and saw it was a taxi. The rear door opened. "If they do," I said, "he can sign for himself."

The others turned. Getting out of the cab was Pat Winter, wearing a T-shirt and a red baseball cap. As he came toward us he seemed to be limping.

"Pat," Preston said. He took Winter's hand in both of his own. "I am truly sorry. She was a wonderful woman."

Winter looked at him from under the bill of his cap, without expression. I wasn't sure that he understood what Preston was saying. He looked in my direction.

"Mr. Winter," I said, "I'm very sorry about your wife."

"My wife," he repeated. Then he shook his head slowly.

No one said anything for a moment. Then Preston broke the silence. "Her car's over there, on the rack."

Pat looked at it briefly. "Can we get it out of here?"

"Yes, they're through. They didn't find any evidence there was a crime."

He limped over to the car to look for himself, and Preston trailed after, leaving me with the engineer.

"Les, got a minute?" I asked.

"Till they're done making up their minds, I've got all the time in the world."

We found ourselves a quiet corner. "The trooper spent a lot of time on her car before I got here and you watched him work. Could he have missed something?" I asked.

"Like what?"

"Like, I don't know. Anything that doesn't fit an accident."

"You sound like you're investigating a murder."

"You never can tell," I said.

The tobacco shifted again. "Nothing, but that doesn't mean nothing happened. There's ways."

"I'm all ears."

"Smack her with another car or some other large object just right. A car's nothing more than an object moving in a certain direction at a certain speed. A little force at the right angle changes the direction of travel. Not much and not for very long, but twenty thousand cars probably pass by that abutment safely every day, and they're only a couple of feet further away."

"Wouldn't there be paint from the killer's car on the left side of Maria's?"

"Sure. You'd have paint transfer, rust transfer, maybe even some transfer of metal at the molecular level. For about ten seconds, till it all burned off and oxidized, along with the car's own paint job."

"Is it possible it happened that way?"

"Possible." He snorted. "That's why engineers think lawyers are assholes. They're always asking that. Except for things that violate one of the laws of thermodynamics, nothing's impossible." He paused. "No disrespect intended." To emphasize that this was his final word, he shifted around the tobacco again.

At that point Pat came back, trailed closely by Preston. His face was flushed and tense, but I couldn't read anything more. "So it looks like an accident," Pat said.

"That's what the engineer and the police think."

He pursed his lips. "Garrett, what should I do? Spend more money on this or not?"

I couldn't tell if he was putting me on the spot or if he really wanted my opinion. "Sleep on it. You don't have to make any decision about it today. Give it some time."

He lowered his voice. "Nobody's gonna think I'm hiding something if I dog it for a couple days?"

"Talk to your lawyer."

"I keep sayin', I'm asking *you*."

"And I'm telling you, I'm not going to give legal advice. You've got a good lawyer—listen to him."

He nodded, not really satisfied, and turned back to the car. I was still trying to figure him out when Preston came up beside me. "I'd like you to check out this fellow Evans," he said quietly. "See what you can find out about his movements since Monday night."

We both knew the law. Intentional acts by third parties relieve persons of any responsibility for mere negligence. If PennDOT could convince a jury it was homicide, they walked— even if they were negligent in the design of the bridge approaches. "He couldn't have done it," I said.

"He could have set it up." Preston looked over at Pat and kept his voice low. "If there's something for PennDOT to work with, I want to know it now and not three years from now."

"I'm going to start with Torino, if that's okay with you. And I'd like your permission to use my assistant. Sometimes she gets more out of an interview than I do."

"You don't need my permission for that."

"If I use her any further, it means telling her what's happened thus far." He nodded glumly.

"Want me to keep an eye on Pat, too?"

"What's that got to do with the case?"

"Because the same rule about criminal acts applies to him, too. And he's got motive."

"He still wanted her back."

"And he got here in a taxi. I wonder where his car is?"

Preston compressed his lips into a thin line. "Check out both of them," he whispered. "But don't put anything in writing unless I tell you to."

11

Wednesday, 3:00 P.M.

"SOUTH STREET" MEANS different things to different Philadelphians. People up in the Northeast, whose sense of the city below Cottman Avenue tends to be a little fuzzy, confuse it with the old Italian neighborhoods of South Philadelphia, which are generally at least a mile further south. Older Center City residents remember it as a deteriorated black neighborhood that pressed in on Society Hill. But to Philadelphians under thirty, especially the singles and most of all the gays, it's the place to party. The blocks of South Street near the Delaware are shoulder-to-shoulder clothing stores, bars, restaurants, and gift stores catering to the tourist trade and the upscale residents, and almost every night in decent weather they're all jammed. Parking after five is actually more difficult than in Center City during business hours. The side streets in the area are uniformly gentrified brick town houses, immaculately kept and bristling with security. Architecturally and from the standpoint of historic preservation it's a pale echo of Society Hill, but no one seems to mind. After all, it cash flowed.

Lisa and I were there before the start of South Street's real business hours, and I was able to find a parking meter only a few doors from the address we wanted—a card shop with two male mannequins in the window locked in an embrace. One of them was holding a bouquet of roses that on closer inspection turned out to be a dozen ingeniously packaged red condoms. I put two dollars' worth of quarters in the meter and we went inside.

The card rack had a special-occasions section, and a bright red, white, and blue card caught my eye. It was a closeup of a penis, painted white, with one ball painted red and the other blue. The inside message was a hope that the recipient would enjoy fireworks on the Fourth of July. I showed it to Lisa.

"And you thought patriotism was dead," she said.

"Nice to know that someone still believes in the old values."

We worked our way to the back of the store, past displays of increasingly bizarre merchandise: restraints, candles shaped like dildos, rows of massage oils and lubricants, and things I couldn't even identify. We stepped by two men with their backs to us who were evidently considering a purchase. "Even if he doesn't, it'll make a *great* conversation piece," one of them said. I couldn't see what they were talking about, which suited me just fine. I wondered how gays felt when straight people talked about sex, if they felt as awkward as I did right then. And I wondered what Lisa was thinking.

The counter in the rear was occupied by a slim youth with short blond hair and flawless, creamy skin. He had large blue eyes that moved lazily up and down over my body and said that since I certainly wasn't pretty enough, I'd better be rich enough. He never looked at Lisa at all. He was wearing a bright plaid shirt, unbuttoned to the navel. Some gold chains and hairless skin peeked out. "What are you interested in today?" he asked.

"My name's Dave Garrett. I'd like to see Mr. Torino."

He opened a door leading to the rear of the store. "Ralph!" he yelled in a New Jersey accent. "Somebody to see you!"

A tall, handsome man appeared in cream-colored slacks and a loud print shirt. Hairy, muscular forearms, tanned a color that spoke of lots of time in sunny climates. His hair was full and still black, and he moved with the bouncy stride of someone who works out regularly. Aside from some wrinkles around the eyes he could have been forty instead of fifty. "I'm Ralph Torino."

"Dave Garrett." The strength of his handshake caught me by surprise. I thought I detected a little smile in his eyes just before he let go. *Thought we all had limp wrists, huh?*

"Well, hello. Can I call you Dave?" I had to fight the impression that he was trying to sell me something and I just couldn't figure out what.

"Please do," I said. "And this is my assistant, Lisa Wilson."

Something happened then, so quick that I nearly missed it. He offered his hand and gave a brief courtesy shake, but then, just for a moment, his eyes narrowed and he looked down at her hand. Then he looked back at her face before he let go. Lisa blushed and took a step backwards. She would have taken another except she ran into me.

He turned to me, but it was a moment before he said anything. "Nice to meet both of you. So what can I do for you?"

"You know a woman named Maria Winter?"

"Sure. She's the one got killed out on Germantown Pike."

"We'd like to ask you some questions, if you've got a minute."

He looked at Lisa and then back to me. "Is—this going to take very long?"

"If you know anything important, it will."

He nodded. "This way."

We followed him through the door into a storeroom, then through another door, up a flight of stairs, into the living room of a second-floor apartment. It faced to the west, and the afternoon sun poured in through a series of red, blue, and yellow stained-glass windows that took up most of the front wall. The light provided most of the color for the apartment. The furniture was high-tech black metal with a matte finish, and the floors were carpeted in a deep pearl shag. A couple of small area rugs, red and orange, were scattered around for contrast.

"Nice place," I said.

"Thank you. Want a drink?"

I asked for coffee and Lisa surprised me by ordering a beer. She surprised me even more when she drank half of it in one gulp.

Ralph apologized that he only had espresso, not regular coffee. While we waited for the machine to warm up we settled around a glass-topped coffee table. He took off his shoes and socks and worked his feet into the pile of the carpet. "Go ahead," he said. "You'll like it."

I did, and he was right. The carpet felt like mink against my stockinged feet. "Nice," I said. "Very nice."

"It wasn't cheap. But you only go around once." He smiled some more. "It's important to indulge yourself."

"Does that include the clerk?"

He shook his head without losing his grin. "Andrew's just one of the employees." He hung on the last word in a way that made me think either that Andrew was something more or that since he had sex with all the employees, Andrew was nothing special.

"Did you know Maria very well?" I asked.

He looked at the ceiling and pursed his lips. "Not my very best friend in school, but pretty close. We were together in elementary school before that, too."

"I don't want to start this off on the wrong foot, but you don't seem very upset about her death."

He put his arms back on the top of the sofa. The smile stayed the same but his voice dropped an octave. "Dave, I'm HIV positive and I've just gone into active AIDS. If Maria's pissed at me for not making more of a fuss, we can discuss it ourselves soon enough."

"I'm sorry."

"So anyway, go on."

There was nothing to do but plow ahead. "Have you lived in the area since high school?"

"I was in the army after college, but after that I was back here."

"Oh? Where did you serve?"

"Laos," he shrugged. "Special Forces."

"You—must have been one of the original Green Berets."

"Till I was dishonorably discharged I was. But I don't think you're here about that."

"Let's start with Tom Evans."

At that moment the espresso started to flow. Ralph excused himself and went into the kitchen.

I leaned over to Lisa. Her skin was already flushed with the alcohol. "You okay?" I asked. I let my eyes drop to the glass in her hand. "What did you do that for?"

She swallowed and leaned close enough to whisper. "He made me. It's—never happened before, never."

"You mean—oh. Are you sure?"

"The way he looked at my hands. That's one of the things that doesn't change." She held up one hand for a moment and regarded it glumly. "I can put on nails and all that, but they're still a lot bigger than—they ought to be. I feel—I can't tell you—it's like one of those dreams where you're naked in public."

"He hasn't said a word."

"He *knows*, that's the problem."

"Well, *I* know."

She looked at me out of the corner of her eye. "That's another problem."

"Well, neither one are problems you're ever going to be able to solve. You can't rewrite history." She stared at her glass and didn't say anything back.

Ralph returned with a silver tray. I noticed that even though Lisa hadn't asked, he'd brought a third cup for her. She needed it more than either of us. She took a quick sip and excused herself to the bathroom. As she walked past I watched him studying her ass.

He settled back in his chair and picked up his cup. "Did you know Maria was down here, a couple of years ago?"

"Yes," I said.

"Did you know she and Pat were having trouble back then?"

"No, I didn't."

I saw another of his smiles. He was enjoying himself more than I liked. "I didn't think so," he said. "They came down for my grand opening—except Virginia, that is. Even she made an effort. Took some Valium and everything. But she couldn't handle it and Tom had to leave her at home."

"Tom didn't go to high school with you. He's years too young."

"Tom was here because his boss is heavy into supporting AIDS relief. He came as their representative. I never met him before that night."

"So how did it go?"

Another sly smile. "Like I said, Tom was by himself."

"By any chance, did he spend most of his time with Maria?"

"For what difference it made."

"I'm listening," I said.

"It takes two. She wasn't paying any attention."

"Sure about that?"

"Sure I am. My opening, it was a big event. We sent out invitations by the hundreds, everyone I've ever known, spread it out over two nights. It was part of an AIDS benefit so we had lots of coverage, lots of people thinking it was a good idea to show up. Anyway, I hadn't seen some of these people in years. I was curious how they'd get along after all this time—old friendships and jealousies and all that."

"I didn't think you had X-ray vision."

"It's got nothing to do with that. It's just a question of seeing what's there to be seen. Being gay, you get used to paying attention to clues about what people are like. Things are a lot better than they were thirty years ago, but you still have to be able to size people up." He let his little bomb drop. "The two of you, for example."

"Us?"

"You and Lisa. You're a couple."

"How can you tell that?"

"The way you look at each other when you talk. How you sit, almost touching. Leaning toward each other. You're not afraid of body contact."

"That's one way of putting it," I admitted.

He leaned back on his sofa with his espresso, looking very pleased with himself. "So, am I right?"

"I'm sorry, but you *are* getting a little personal."

He smiled. He was used to winning at whatever he did, and he wasn't going to quit now. "You want the truth from me? My price is the truth from you."

"We had a thing. It's over."

He shook his head. "Not for her it isn't."

"Sleeping with the help isn't good for business, as I bet you already know."

He pursed his lips. It was a gesture intended to convey thoughtfulness, but it looked exaggerated and feminine. Or perhaps that was what he intended. "I don't want to be indelicate, but . . . I assume you know all about her?"

"That she's a transsexual? Sure."

"That bother you?"

"She's off-limits because she works for me. That's the only reason."

He nodded slowly. "You're a remarkable man, Dave."

I shrugged. "To me, she's just a woman with an interesting past."

"Does she see it that way?" he asked.

"You *are* good." I found myself smiling back at him.

"Lucky guess. What does she think? I'm interested."

"Who's being interviewed here?"

"Truth for truth, Dave."

"I think you're just pulling my chain."

"You want my confidences. I want to know what kind of person I'm dealing with."

I leaned back and sipped my coffee. "We dated for a few weeks after we met. We took a couple of weeks in Mexico together. It was going great. Then something happened. She turned moody and then we had a real screaming fight. She flew back the next morning, and that was it as far as anything personal between us. A couple of months ago I offered her a job and it's been strictly business ever since."

"So what was the fight about?"

It was the second very good question I'd been asked that day. I didn't have an answer for this one, either, but just then I heard Lisa coming back. "Ask her yourself."

Her face was freshly scrubbed, and she was a good deal more composed. She looked from one of us to the other and I'm sure she guessed what we'd been talking about. Ralph looked at her, rolling the question around in his mouth like a piece of candy. A half-smile played around the corners of his mouth. Then the smile went flat. He drank some more espresso and looked at me. "All right, Dave. You've paid the price of admission. What can I do for you?"

"Anything you can remember about Pat, Maria, or Tom. Anything at all, but at the opening in particular."

He picked up his coffee and looked at it. "Tom was making his move that night. Pat made it easy—he parked himself at the bar and didn't move once. He just looked at the wall. But Maria was safe with Tom. She was stiff as a board."

"Would you be surprised to know they carried on an affair for months?"

He considered his answer. "If it started back then, yeah."

"So what about Maria? Other than not being interested in Tom?"

"She was ready for some action. She kept looking around, even when Tom was talking to her."

"It could be she was just looking for old friends. Women friends."

"Not the way she was looking."

"So Pat just let it happen?"

"To a point. I heard that later he took her home before she was ready and they had a scene on the street outside."

"Did you talk to Pat?"

"Just to say hello. We were never close in school, and that night he was really blasted. He was pissed at just about everybody. For having jobs and being at least halfway healthy. He started a scene at the party; the once and future king had to cool him down."

He saw our puzzled looks. "Sorry. That's what we always called Charles Preston."

"Back in high school," I said slowly.

"You sure couldn't call him Chuck."

"So Preston was there?"

Torino laughed. "He favored us with his presence for at least twenty minutes."

"It sounds like you don't like him."

"Maybe I envy him, how easy his life's been."

"I don't know if he'd agree with you," I said carefully.

"Hey, even in high school everybody knew he was a man to watch. Most likely to succeed and all that." He paused to drink some espresso. "You know, we all had such a clear idea of what it meant to succeed when we were eighteen. It gets a little fuzzy over the years."

Lisa cleared her throat. "Tell us about Preston and Maria."

"Well, they dated in high school. She dated a lot of guys,

though—if you've seen her picture you'll know how pretty she was. Anyway, they broke up around graduation. He was going off to California for college."

"And what about at the opening?" she asked.

He thought about it. "He was here for just a few minutes. I don't recall seeing them together at all."

It was my turn. "Could Preston and Maria have been an item over the years?"

He shook his head. "I really doubt it. They traveled in different worlds. Maria was busy raising her boy and Charles was climbing the ladder."

I asked a few more questions, but it seemed I had exhausted his relevant recollections. He led us back downstairs and walked us through the store and back to the street, where we said our good-byes. I left him with one of my cards just in case he remembered anything else.

It was the middle of rush hour, but the traffic moved smoothly. Somewhere there was probably a hell of a tie-up, but not on our route. I wondered aloud about why Preston hadn't told us that he'd known Pat, Maria, and Ralph for thirty years, but Lisa didn't respond. Except to mention she had a date with John that night, Lisa sat wrapped in her own thoughts. I let her be, all the way back to her apartment in Overbrook.

When we were parked outside I asked her what she was thinking.

She took a moment before she answered. "Monday afternoon. Reading tombstones in the graveyard in King of Prussia and how mad I was at you."

"I wasn't too thrilled with you just then, either."

She didn't want to banter. "Graveyards are places of power," she said slowly. "They make you think about dying, even if you don't want to."

"Myself, I always liked the line about letting the dead bury the dead."

She moved uncomfortably in her seat. "These people we're investigating. They're all so damn full of *regrets*."

"Who isn't at fifty?" I asked.

"When this job is over I'm going to make John take me back to that graveyard at night."

"What for?"

"Maria dying, and those tombstones." She played with the end of her braid. "I want to fuck there."

"I never tried it in a graveyard," I said.

"Sure you did. With me, in Mexico."

"That was just some ruins."

"There were graves, too."

"We split a whole bottle of tequila that night. How can you remember?"

"I remember how the moon was only a sliver, how the sand felt under my back, how the animals were making noises in the jungle, all of it."

"The last half hour, you been thinking about the case at all?"

"Torino likes getting attention, but he's telling the truth," she said.

"What in the world made you ask about Preston and Maria? Where did that one come from?"

"There's ten thousand lawyers Pat could have used—why go back to somebody he hadn't seen in thirty years, who he wasn't all that close to in school? Maybe Maria steered him to Preston."

"But why, after all this time?"

"Could there have been something going on, now, between Maria and Preston?"

"You have any evidence for that?" I asked.

"Am I on trial?"

"I just mean, it doesn't sound like him."

She played with her braid idly while she thought about it. The tip fell down between her breasts. I looked out the window and tried not to think about Mexico. "No," she agreed. "You're right. From what you tell me, Preston's scared of his own shadow." She picked up her purse and put her hand on the door handle.

"That was a good hunch about Preston and Maria, anyway."

She opened the car door. "You make enough guesses, you get lucky. Isn't that what you've told me?"

I shook my head. "Women's intuition."

She started to speak. Then she stopped and just said "Thanks" in a low voice. She turned away and walked inside.

12

Wednesday, 5:00 P.M.

S W E D E S T O W N A U D I - B M W was on a busy four-lane
just west of town, with the usual floor-to-ceiling glass showroom
and the usual overpriced toys inside. Just walking through the
doors put me in a bad mood. It reminded me that I was annoyed
at Lisa for throwing so much of her money at an expensive car,
and seeing the Audis made me think of how my ex-wife had the
better deal in our divorce. Even if the car smelled funny in the
summertime.

The cars in the showroom were sleek, and the salesmen were
even sleeker—earnest, hungry men, relentlessly clean-cut, watching the doors with studied nonchalance. I was glad I made an honest
living out of threats, lying, and general sneaking around.

Tom Evans, wearing a blue suit and white shirt, greeted me
before I was ten feet inside the door. He had the muscular build
and rough, ruddy complexion that women call "ruggedly handsome." At a certain age it deteriorates into simply looking beat-
up, but he was still years away from that. Our fingers hadn't

even touched before his smile flickered. "Hello, I'm Tom. Haven't I seen you somewhere before?" His handshake was just the right mixture of firmness, warmth, and brevity. Even though the shake made my hand hurt, I found myself wondering if a BMW just might be a good investment after all.

"I'm Dave, Tom. Uh—I don't know. I live around here. This is my first time in—"

"I saw you very recently," he said slowly, still not placing me. "In the last few days. I never forget a face."

"You're doing better than me. I can't say I recall it."

"Well, what can I show—" he froze. "I remember now," he said. His voice was small and tight.

"Monday night at the shopping center," I said. "Small world, isn't it?"

"What's—going on here?"

"You have an office?"

He showed me to a small cubicle decorated with his sales awards. A large photograph of a boy and a girl on his desk, and a smaller copy of the wedding portrait I'd seen in their living room. He shut the door firmly behind me and sat down with his hands spread out flat on the desktop. The fingertips were white. "I think you'd better tell me what's going on."

"I think you should tell me," I said.

The hands left the desktop and played with each other. I could see sweat breaking out on his forehead and on the sides of his neck. "I don't know if I should be talking to you."

"I'm working for an attorney, investigating her death. There may be a civil suit against the Department of Transportation, or the county, or whoever built the bridge where she died."

"There's nothing I would know that would help you," he said. "What lawyer are you working for?"

"That's confidential. I can tell you that what you and Maria were doing doesn't matter. I'm only here because you were one of the last people to see her before the accident."

The hand dropped to his lap, and he looked around the room. Everywhere he looked his eyes landed on a picture of his family. After a moment he stared down at his hands. "I called her office this morning. She wasn't in. I tried her at home but no one answered. I thought she might be there, but not picking up. Then I saw the afternoon paper."

"Why wouldn't she answer?"

"She was pretty upset."

"She sure was. How about you?"

He was starting to get his courage back. He raised his eyes and even stuck out his pink chin a little. It was kind of cute. "That's none of your business."

I sighed. "She wanted you to leave your wife and you were giving her the stall. I was just hoping you'd tell me yourself."

"If you knew as much as you pretend you wouldn't need to talk to me in the first place."

"She was mad at the motel Monday night, so mad she stormed out of the room. When you got together Tuesday night she gave you an ultimatum, and you turned her down."

"I didn't really—" he hesitated. "You're plain guessing. You don't know."

Every good hand of poker has a bluff, and now it was time. "Monday night, you remember her saying she'd met a possible roommate?"

"So?"

"She say anything about her?"

He couldn't see any harm in answering the question. "That she was pretty, that she seemed nice."

"Anything else?"

"She made a joke that if this girl moved in she'd have her hands full keeping me away from her. That this woman had dark hair and was really pretty and how I have a thing for brunettes."

"The woman is my assistant, and she was right by you Tuesday night in Collegeville."

"So why didn't Maria recognize her?"

"Come on, between the bad lighting and how upset she was?"

He folded. It didn't happen all at once, but he leaned back in his chair and the air just slowly ran out of him. "Please—don't tell my wife."

"I don't intend to unless you make me."

He looked at the sales awards on the wall. "I'm not the kind of guy to do a thing like this."

"I've met your wife," I said carefully.

"You did?"

"I didn't tell her a thing."

"You're the investigator who was asking about insurance. She told me."

"I feel sorry for both of you."

By way of an answer he looked at the wedding picture.

"Tell me about last night."

"She called me first thing yesterday morning and said she had to see me that night. We set it up for ten, at the bar in Collegeville. We talked till around eleven."

"You see her car after that?"

"When I pulled out she was ahead of me, but I stopped to call home." His tone became more private. "You must think I'm a shit."

"I try to avoid judging people. Lately I've gotten pretty good at it."

"*I* think I'm a shit. I got two great kids and a wife who can't help herself."

"The Boy Scouts and the army are the only places that give medals for good conduct."

"I've never met anyone like Maria. You know, I loved her."

"I'm sure you did."

"But not enough. Not enough to do any good."

"Love doesn't always do anyone any good. No matter what

you talked about that night, she was still going to drive off and hit that bridge."

"Do you think he ran her off the road?"

It was time to be very careful. "Who?"

"Pat. He tried, you know, just a couple of months ago. That's why she finally left him."

"Back up and tell me from the beginning."

"The end of March she was going to Fort Washington on the turnpike. It was night. A car pulled up alongside, then dropped back, then pulled up again and smashed into her. It forced her off the road, but there was a shoulder and all she did was run up on the bank. She was scared but she wasn't hurt. She didn't see the driver but she told me she was sure it was Pat. She started looking for an apartment the very next day."

"Was this reported?"

"Sure, but they never arrested anybody."

"Did she confront Pat about it?"

"No. She said he'd just deny it and she didn't have any proof."

"What about the other car?"

"Wherever he got it, it wasn't his. She didn't recognize it."

"When you left last night, how was it between you?"

"I don't know exactly. But I'm afraid it might have been over. She didn't want to hear what I was saying."

"And what was that?"

"I told her I'd been thinking about it all day and I couldn't leave my wife, not the way she is. And what about my kids? They need me. I can't just walk away from them and pretend they never happened, can I?"

"People do it every day."

"Telling Maria no was the hardest thing I've ever done in my life. And I thought I'd made up my mind. . . ."

He could wallow on his own time. "Anyone know about the two of you besides me?"

"No."

"That's an advantage of marriage over adultery. Now you have to keep this all bottled up."

"I thought you didn't judge."

"I don't," I said. "It's just a fact. Can you think of anyone else but Pat who might have wished her harm?"

"With him on the list what more do you need?"

"Just answer the question."

"Nope. Working in a real estate office may not be the most exciting job in the world, but you don't make many enemies, either."

"Could your wife have known?"

He thought about it. "No. She's too focused on herself to pay any attention."

"I thought you felt sorry for her," I said.

"Hey, I do. Like you said a minute ago, it's a simple fact." He turned around her wedding picture for me to see. "Till our first child was born we had a great time. Did you know she was a computer programmer? Made fifty a year. We traveled every chance we got—the islands, Europe, wherever. She had hair to her waist and a black bikini the size of three Band-Aids." He looked at the far wall, and for a moment he was on a beach somewhere. The sun was hot and she was coming toward him, carrying a couple of beers. Her sunglasses were hiding more than her bathing suit was. She was going to lie down beside him and ask him to rub sunscreen on her back. Then he was back in Swedestown, Pennsylvania, with me. "Like I said, then everything went to hell."

I gave him one of my cards and left him alone with his memories and his life. My own didn't seem so bad by comparison.

I called the Limerick state police barracks and learned that Trooper Carter would be coming on duty at seven. Pausing only for a cheese steak and fries, I was there at twenty till.

It was like all the other barracks buildings I'd ever seen—hastily thrown up in the fifties out of cheap concrete block and second-string linoleum, and badly maintained ever since. At some point the interior of this particular barracks had received a slapdash coat of yellow paint, but otherwise it looked unchanged since the days of the Scranton administration. The banks of overhead fluorescent lights bathed everything in a sickly greenish light that emphasized the cracks in the walls and the defects in the paint job. The receptionist paged Carter, and she met me in the lobby.

"Mr. Garrett?" I hardly recognized her. She was in civvies—a simple white sleeveless dress that hugged a slim figure. A flurry of wiry black hair spread out around her face. Her skin was that creamed-coffee color that can mean black, Hispanic, or even a deeply tanned Caucasian. It occurred to me that she could have passed for white if she'd wanted to.

"There's something different," I said. "Let me guess—you're not wearing your hat."

"Or the body armor, either. It may save your ass, but it don't exactly lift and separate."

"Hope you got some sleep since I saw you last."

"That was a bad one." A shadow crossed her face. "I slept as well as I could."

"Trooper—"

"You can call me Roz."

"Only if you call me Dave. Is there a chance of a cup of coffee around here?"

She led me down linoleum corridors to a grimy break room with no windows. In the far corner a couple of mesomorphs with crew cuts were struggling with an incident report form, and losing. A vending machine robbed us of seventy-five cents apiece for five ounces of something dark and hot.

We sat down at a small Formica table. "Well, it smells like coffee, at least," I said.

Roz folded her arms and put her elbows on the table. "How well did you know her?" she asked.

"She was a tail job."

"How well?" she asked.

"Is this official?"

She pursed her lips, just a little. "No, it's not."

"I followed her the night before. I only met her once, the afternoon of the day she died. She was in real estate and I was posing as a customer."

"That's it? That's all you knew about her?"

"Except for the tail last night, yes."

She took a sip of coffee. "You're a man who feels things, aren't you?"

"She deserved better."

"I meant it as a compliment," she said.

"Last night you said I was getting mushy when I told you that you'd done a good job."

"When I'm on shift I'm all business. Being a black woman, you don't ever relax."

"Got a minute for a little business now?" I told her what Evans told me about the March incident on the turnpike.

"You think that the husband may have gotten it right last night and that he was practicing back in March?"

"Maybe."

"You probably know this already, but the official finding is accidental death. We're not pursuing it any further."

"I'm not surprised."

"Unless it's part of an active case I'm not supposed to spend time on it."

"Then let's say I need a favor."

She tried to look grumpy, but she was too young. "I have a feeling what this favor is going to be."

"Uh-huh. I need you to check out this March business for me. Unless there's more to it than my source told me, there's probably just an incident report with no follow-up."

"You wouldn't happen to have the incident number, would you? Or the investigating trooper's name?"

"If I did I'd give them to you. I don't want to make this any more difficult than it already is."

She checked her watch. "I'm going to be working traffic later today, but I've got a friend in Records." I gave her another card and wrote my home number on the back. "I'll give you a call as soon as I have something for you."

"Thanks. And take care."

She played with her empty cup. "That was my first fatal."

I was ready to go, but she wanted to talk, and Maria bound us together. "It's hard. I was in the war."

"They found the seat belt buckles jammed under her seat. If she'd just had her belt on she wouldn't have hit her head. She could have gotten out before the fire took hold."

"Maria was old enough that she never got used to wearing belts when she learned to drive. It never got to be a habit."

"But it's such a little thing. It could have made all the difference."

"Or maybe not. Know the story of the appointment in Samarra?"

"No."

"I don't know where it comes from, exactly. Somerset Maugham tells it. Anyway, a servant in Baghdad sees Death in the market. Death makes a gesture. The servant runs home, tells his master, and begs the master for the loan of a horse so he can flee to Samarra. The master gives him the horse, and then goes to the market for himself. He sees Death and demands to know why Death is trying to frighten his servant. Death replies, I wasn't—I was just surprised to see him here in Baghdad, because I have an appointment with him tomorrow in Samarra."

She shivered. "Dave, you think too damn much."

"I get by." I stood up. "And you have to get to work. Take care."

"You, too, Dave." She put her hand on mine and gave it a brief squeeze. I gave her a nod and went outside.

No, twenty-five was way too young.

13

Wednesday, 7:00 P.M.

PAT WINTER'S HOUSE was on a quiet suburban side
street midway between Norristown and Ambler. And, I noted,
not far from the Fort Washington turnpike exit. I parked around
the corner, just out of sight of the house, and walked toward the
front door.

A blown-down branch at least twenty feet long lay against
one side of the house, and it looked like it had been there for
some time. The lawn hadn't been cut in weeks and the trees
hadn't been trimmed in years. The house was a fairly new Cape
Cod, painted in a shade of pale gray-blue I'd never seen before.
I wondered if Maria had picked it out. If she had, it wasn't going
to be one of her more lasting memorials. The paint was gone
from large parts of the southern side and was peeling everywhere
else.

I rang the bell, armed with a cock-and-bull story about need-
ing some further information from him. The need was real
enough, but what I wanted to know wouldn't come from an in-

terview—at least not yet. The story wasn't necessary; no one answered. After checking around to see that no one was watching, I went around to the back of the house and found a burglar's dream—a sliding-glass door off the patio. I looked around; the houses on both sides were dark, and to the rear was nothing but a patch of woods. In a minute I was inside.

The first thing that hit me was the smell—a stale combination of mold, old food, and dirty clothes. The glass door opened into the dining room, and occupying most of the table was a pile of filthy laundry. The bare areas of the table were covered with a fine coating of dust. Beyond the dining room was the living room, equally dusty but obviously unused. I made a right into the kitchen. Every flat surface was covered with dirty dishes and glasses. The wastebasket was overflowing with beer cans and the remnants of meals, a lot more of the former than the latter. A check of the refrigerator revealed a case of beer and a number of covered dishes whose contents were in various states of decay. I shut the door as quickly as I could.

Next to the wall phone was a calendar. The entries for the previous months were mainly in a small, precise handwriting that I assumed was Maria's. The entries for May were in a larger, barely legible scrawl. I checked the entries for this week. Pat Winter was a busy man. Monday at nine to see a Dr. Rothstein; physical therapy ten till noon; three to four at the chronic pain clinic; and then an appointment at seven with a Dr. Rakosky. Tuesday started at eight with a work-hardening program over at Bryn Mawr Rehab, which involved a twenty-mile round-trip. His appointment with Preston and me didn't show, which wasn't surprising. Pat only had a couple hours' notice, so he didn't bother to write it down. After he'd kept our appointment, he'd met with the Office of Vocational Rehabilitation at four at the Valley Forge Corporate Center. About two miles from where she died, six hours before it happened. Nothing for the rest of the evening. Wednesday morning at nine he'd gone in for more physical therapy. I wondered if it was a regular appointment or if he'd done anything Tuesday night to throw out his back.

I found an address book by the phone, but it didn't help much. A few Winters, evidently relatives, in the Midwest and Texas; a number of doctors, and a lot of names I didn't recognize. Preston's name didn't appear. I found Tom Evans's work number, in Maria's handwriting, under "Evans' Dress Shop." Smart lady. I sighed. In the last few months I'd run into any number of clever, interesting people who just happened to be dead now. I copied down every unfamiliar name and phone number, just in case.

I gave the living room the once-over, but my imagination failed me as far as what I might possibly find there. The books on the shelves—popular novels, romances, and self-helps—all looked like hers. No gaps on the shelves, just like there were no empty places where furniture ought to go. Wherever the books on her dresser had come from, they hadn't been from the living room. Evidently Pat was right when he said she'd taken little more than her clothes when she left. I had come there only looking for information about him. But maybe there was something to learn about her, too.

The bathroom on the first floor was just a powder room, primarily for guests, and it looked like they hadn't had any in some time. No door to the basement, so I assumed the house was built on a slab. The only other room on the first floor was the laundry room, which was equally unused. I thought about the pile of clothes on the dining-room table. How could a man who could drive an eighty-thousand-pound machine a hundred thousand miles a year in all weather be stymied by a washer-dryer? Or a coffeepot?

I checked outside to make sure Pat wasn't walking up the block and then went upstairs. The first bedroom was being used as a den, which in modern America means a room for watching television. A twenty-six-inch colossus presided over one corner, facing a reclining chair surrounded by remote controls, bags of potato chips, and empty beer cans. A stack of half a dozen rented videotapes was next to the TV—action films, westerns, and comedies. I was a little surprised not to find even one X-rated tape. Then I remembered about his back. This was the room for his own reading materials, which consisted of books on hunting, fishing, archery, camping, and the outdoor life generally. I began to feel sorry for Pat. Everything in his life, his leisure as well as his work, depended on his back. Without it he was nothing. I wondered how much time he spent in this room thinking about just that.

Across the hall was Pat's bedroom, his king-size bed unmade and clothes strewn around the floor. I checked the drawer of the side table but found only some old insurance papers. Opposite the bed was a ten-foot-long dresser. Half of the drawers were empty. I wondered if she'd moved to her own room before she moved out completely. Pat's closets yielded a variety of hunting and camping equipment, all neatly stowed, but no real surprises. Neither did his dresser drawers. His medicine cabinet was jammed with every anti-inflammatory, analgesic, and antidepressant I'd ever heard of, and some I hadn't. The man had enough drugs to kill himself and half a dozen people besides. I thought about the girl I'd watched die of a self-inflicted drug overdose. I thought about dumping half of them down the toilet and decided it was none of my business.

The other bedroom, judging from the furnishings and a few clothes still hanging in the closets, had been used by Maria. The bed was covered with a bedspread, but underneath was a bare mattress. I sat on the bed and tried to put myself in her place. She's moving out and she's not planning to be back. But she has a half-hour round-trip to Cherry Street for each load, and she can only take what she can get in the car. She picks a day when Pat's away for as long as possible. Let's say she has four hours. Things have to be loaded here, driven to Norristown, and unloaded and carried up a flight of stairs by a woman who's closer to fifty than forty. With a little luck there should be something left behind.

The drawers in the bedside table were still full, for what difference it made—a telephone book, an unused appointment book, photos of a hunting cabin somewhere, a box of blank envelopes, and a flotsam of loose paper clips, pushpins, cheap pens, and erasers. Checking under the bed and dresser didn't help, but it gave me an idea. When I looked under the dresser I found myself looking at the underside of the bottom drawer instead of at a solid wood base. I realized that the dresser had no drawer liners and that things could get caught in the runners. I pulled out every one of the nine drawers and felt around inside. The third time my hand closed on a piece of paper, but it turned out to be part of a dress pattern. Nothing behind the rest—till I tried the very last drawer. A slip of paper was stuck in the back. I carefully drew it out. From its crumpled appearance the drawer had been pushed against it a number of times. It was triangular in shape and was torn from a heavy stock paper. The writing on it was print, not type, but that didn't help me much:

doir

graphy

pointment

Paoli, Pennsylvania

I decided it was an invitation. Either that or an announcement. Or maybe a receipt. Or an invoice or an ad or a coupon or who the hell knew. I stuck it in my wallet and hoped for better luck in the rest of the room. I didn't get any.

I was ready to leave when I realized something was missing. Pat had obviously been an outdoorsman in his better days, but I hadn't seen any guns in the house. If there was no garage and no basement, where were they? Another trip to his bedroom closet, where I found cleaning kits for .22-, .38-, and .45-caliber pistols, plus a kit for a 12-gauge shotgun, but no guns and no ammunition. I didn't like the idea of Pat in possession of the arsenal that the kits represented. I certainly wasn't going to take them, but I would have felt better at least knowing what he had and copying down the serial numbers. So where were they?

I checked Maria's closet again but found nothing but old clothes and empty boxes. Then I tried the den. A stack of papers, topped by a high school yearbook, covered a side table next to his recliner. I moved them, hoping at least one of the guns might be underneath. It wasn't, but a thick packet of twenties in the middle of the pile caught my eye. I pulled it out. The twenties were paper-clipped to a crumpled receipt from a Phoenixville gun shop dated three weeks before. It was a purchase order covering a .22 Ruger automatic, a .357 Colt Python, a .38 Military and Police, a Colt .45 automatic, plus a Savage 12-gauge shotgun, made out to Maria Winter. The total sales price, $820, matched the amount of cash. Like I said, a smart lady. And no wonder the receipt was crumpled. I tried to imagine Pat's rage when he came home from physical therapy to an empty house, growing madder as he stalked from one room to another, and then finding she'd sold his guns out from under him.

I locked the sliding-glass door from the inside and let myself out the side door, locking it behind me. Just then I saw a car coming up the road. I pulled back behind the corner of the house and waited. It slowed, signaled, and turned into the driveway. I counted to ten and stuck my head out. I saw Winter's back as he shuffled toward his front door. He stiffened, and for a moment I thought he'd sensed I was there. But it was just a muscle spasm; he grunted, paused, and rubbed the small of his back. Then he dragged himself the rest of the way to the house and went inside.

I made a quick run for the street, ducking down behind his car for cover, a five-year-old Chevy Beretta. He wasn't kidding when he said he bought American. I waited a few seconds and then peeked up over the hood. As I watched, he turned on the lights in the front room and slowly headed back toward the kitchen till he was out of sight.

I ducked down again and planned how best to get clear of the property. Staying low was my best chance of not being seen by Winter, but it would look suspicious to any neighbors who might be watching . . . but before I could move something stopped me.

A smell.

Not the faint, sweetish smell of the lawn, or the hot, oily smell radiating from the engine; this was a chemical smell, like turpentine or acetone. Fresh paint. From the fender of the car. The light was starting to fade, but a careful look at the body showed the usual dings and scratches on the right quarter panel and door. The only part that had been freshly painted was the right front fender.

I went back to my car, to wait.

14

Wednesday, 8:00 P.M.

I MOVED THE CAR until it was under a weeping willow close to the corner. Pat had never seen my car, and I could afford to wait for at least a few minutes to see what would happen. I couldn't afford to sit very long—the neighbors might start wondering about me. To really blend in I needed a woman in the car. I thought of trying Lisa, but that would mean leaving Pat unobserved. I could hear her already, "David, if you just had a car phone . . ."

I decided to give myself half an hour. And just what was I waiting for? Was I afraid to have him about without someone keeping an eye on him? Well, Maria had been afraid of him, afraid enough to take precautions, to dispose of his guns and to hide from him. And she'd been safe until I found her. The thought was an ugly dark lump in my belly that had been growing ever since last night. I'd killed people in my work, but always in self-defense and always as a last resort. I'd never made a mistake that killed anyone, or worked for a killer before. I hoped my record was still clean.

The shadows were lengthening when Pat came out and started his car. A few seconds later he drove by while I pretended to be looking for something in the backseat.

I started my engine but didn't move till he'd made the turn at the corner behind me. Then I made a U-turn and headed after him. I thought he might go west, toward Norristown, or east, toward Ambler, but he surprised me by going north. I followed him as far back as I dared through a suburban landscape that turned into farms and then into open land. As it grew darker he put on his lights. I waited as long as I could before I did the same. We were in the northern corner of Montgomery County, approaching the Green Lane Reservoir. What was he doing up here? Ever since January, I couldn't be near a reservoir without a bad feeling about what might be hidden underneath.

Being out alone with Pat Winter in the middle of the night didn't appeal to me, but fortunately it didn't work out that way. About a mile short of the tiny town of Green Lane he turned off onto a side road. The tail would have been impossible from there, except that one of the cars in between us took the same turnoff and screened me the next four miles. I looked around but all I could see were farmhouses and trees. Where the hell was he going?

The two cars ahead of me made a left onto Gun Club Road; I took a chance and dropped back another couple hundred yards. Not more than a quarter of a mile later I saw Pat and the other car pulling into a dirt lane marked with a wooden sign: TYLERSPORT RIFLE AND PISTOL CLUB. Underneath, in smaller letters was OPEN TO THE PUBLIC—SALES AND RENTALS. I stopped, counted to a hundred, and pulled in after them.

After a short drive between two stands of pines I found myself in a gravel parking lot with a long, rambling log building on the far side. The windows were larger than residential windows and the place was brightly lit, so I assumed it was the clubhouse. Pat's car was in a handicapped parking space right next to the door, and I didn't begrudge it to him one bit. I parked as far away from Pat and the lights as I could, taking care to leave the nose of the car facing toward the exit.

I assumed Pat was inside the clubhouse, so I bided my time. To the left was a knoll, obviously artificial, with a row of tables and seats for rifle shooting. I could see a hundred-yard range immediately next to the clubhouse, and a longer range beside it. To the right of the clubhouse was a long bench, roofed over, with seats for about twenty shooters, about half of which were occupied by men shooting pistols. The whole range was lit up with floodlights.

Pat came out of the clubhouse carrying an automatic, a set of earplugs, and a box of shells. He looked tired, and his limp was worse than ever. He found a spot near the far end of the pistol benches, which was fine with me. I waited till he was busy fiddling with his gear and went inside the clubhouse. It was one long, narrow room, decorated with deer and moose heads, with aisles of shooting accessories—holsters, ammunition, targets, and clothing. The floors were linoleum, with obviously artificial Navajo rugs scattered here and there. A bearded, beefy man in a long-sleeved checked shirt and jeans presided from behind a glass-topped counter. "Evening," he said.

"Evening."

"Can I help you with something? We close at nine, you know. You want to get any serious time on the range, you'd better get started now."

"I think a friend of mine just went over to the pistol side, Pat Winter."

"Yeah," he said casually. "Rented a Government Model forty-five."

"How much?"

"That was my last Government Model. If you want a big bore there's a Smith and Wesson forty-four magnum, fifteen dollars an hour."

"Okay to shoot my own gun?"

"Sure. Range fee's ten an hour, one hour minimum. We require ears. If you don't have 'em, that's two."

"Ears?"

"Hearing protectors." He handed me what looked like a set of headphones. "Gets pretty noisy under that roof."

"I've got a Browning Hi-Power. Better put me down for a box of shells, too."

"Need some targets? Two bits for three."

I put my money down, went back to my car and fished out the gun from under the seat, and headed for the range. I wanted to get a seat a good distance from Pat, but since he was at the far end, my seat had to be near the door. If he came back toward the clubhouse, as he was certain to do at some point, he'd come right past me. There was nothing to do but keep alert.

I was startled by a sound of a heavy gun going off nearby and hastened to get my protectors in place. Next to me a skinny, pale youth with greasy long hair and a hint of mustache was firing a .44 magnum revolver one-handed. Each time he fired the gun jumped almost straight up in the air, but he put all six shots into a six-inch circle at twenty-five yards.

I waited, keeping one eye on Pat. He was leaning against a post, waiting for the other shooters to finish so he could put up his targets. After a couple of minutes there was a lull in the firing. I heard him yell, "Man on the range! Man on the range!" A couple of other shooters echoed him, and we all put down our guns. Pat and several other shooters went out to post targets and I went with them, being careful to keep my face away from him and towards the clubhouse.

When the range was clear again I faced off at my target, holding my gun in both hands. I struggled to control my breathing as the sight danced merrily around the target. The marines train mainly in rifle marksmanship. A rifle is special to a marine—a pistol is simply one more piece of equipment. Except for some point-blank shooting associated with my job, I hadn't fired a pistol in years, and I'd never fired this particular weapon at all.

I tightened my grip, and the sights settled down a little. I tried to remember what I'd been taught—legs apart, only the tip of the finger touching the trigger, a firm but not crushing grip— and waited for the sights to line up. The front sight came up and gave me a perfect sight picture. I gave the trigger a little more pressure and the gun went off. I couldn't see where the round hit, but it felt good. I squeezed off two more, both of which felt like bull's-eyes.

"Say, buddy?" The skinny kid on my right was bent over his spotting scope.

"Yeah?"

"Which target you shooting at?"

"Uh—the bull's-eye on the extreme left."

"You just put three rounds into mine, the one next to it."

I bent over and looked through the scope for myself. "Oh, Christ. Sorry about that."

"Let me see your gun a minute." I took out the clip, ejected the round from the chamber, and handed it over. He turned it over slowly in the light, his eyes glinting as brightly as the gun. "Boy, stainless steel finish, black rubber grips, target sights, gold trigger . . . you take this away from a stickup artist in North Philly?"

"No," I said. "It was in Center City."

"No shit?"

"He never had a chance. I had a trash can."

He looked at the gun again and then at me. "Want me to help you sight this in?"

"Wouldn't mind a bit, thanks."

He handed me a tiny screwdriver. "Try eight clicks to the left, just to get started. Leave the elevation alone for right now."

I spent the next fifteen minutes fiddling with the sights,

walking the rounds closer to the center of my target. All the time I kept one eye on Pat. A number of shooters were in between us, but I could see that he was all business. He loaded, set his feet, held his gun in both hands, and fired off clip after clip as fast as he could. It was pure combat shooting, practicing hosing down a target with as much lead as he could in the shortest possible time. I couldn't see for myself how he was doing, but judging from the crowd that collected behind him, it was impressive. I wondered who he was imagining as a target.

I finished adjusting the sights. The rounds were falling in a circle nearly a foot across, but at least the center was the bull's-eye. I looked over and Pat was headed straight for me, the gun in one hand and his ear protectors in the other. I yelled, "Man on the range!" and stepped out. I got a couple of dirty looks from shooters who were set to fire, but there was no question of what to do. Everyone put down their weapons and waited while I collected my targets. By the time I sounded the all clear, Pat was inside the clubhouse.

Leaving my ear protectors on the table, I took my gun back to the car and waited behind the wheel. I expected that I would barely beat Pat to our cars—all he needed to do was hand in his rented gun and leave. But a minute stretched into two, then three, then five. Nine o'clock came, and the other shooters packed up and drifted away. A couple went into the clubhouse, but most of them had their own guns and just drove off. Each departing car made mine more conspicuous. I moved my car away from the entrance, sheltering it between two blue spruces. It was almost twenty minutes later when Pat emerged, carrying something in one hand. He got into his car without looking around and drove away.

The lights were still on in the clubhouse. The only other car was a rusted Jeep with an NRA sticker, which I assumed belonged to the clerk.

He was behind the counter, getting ready to lock up, when

he saw me come in. He didn't look pleased to see me. "We're closed now, friend."

"That's okay."

His first instinct was that I was planning a stickup. His right hand started for whatever he kept under the counter, then stopped when he saw I was standing still and that my hands were empty. "What's going on?"

"I want a little talk. About Pat Winter. How much did he pay you?"

His whole face tightened up, and his head sank down between his shoulders. "Whatever it is for the rental and the shells. What's it to you?"

"You never saw him before tonight, did you?"

He thought about his answer. "Maybe I did, maybe not. Maybe the boss knows him."

"Then let's call the boss and find out. Otherwise there's a problem here."

"There's a problem with your fuckin' attitude, that's what's the problem." He produced a sawed-off baseball bat from under the counter. "Beat it."

I dragged my eyes off the bat and looked into his face. "There's lots of problems here. One, you just sold a man a gun without the five-day waiting period. Two, I know about it. Three, your paperwork has got to be messed up—either your purchase receipt is backdated or your delivery slip shows a day five days from now. One way or the other, you've filled out bogus paperwork for the feds. We're talking loss of your boss's federal firearms license. Oh—number four—the guy you sold it to just may be a murderer."

"You're full of shit."

"A used, knocked-around Government Model, the kind you'd rent out, nothing special about it—you'd sell it for two or three hundred, four tops, right?"

He started to sweat. "Get the hell out of here."

"He came in here with eight hundred bucks in cash and I bet a good half of that never makes it into the cash drawer. It's in your pocket right now."

His mouth compressed into a thin line as he hefted the bat. He was even smiling a little. This was the kind of thing he understood. "Gonna come look for it?"

I shook my head and took a half step back. "I don't need to. The paperwork is what matters."

For a moment he didn't say anything. Then he put the bat down on the counter. "Okay. A hundred to forget it happened. Something in this for both of us." He pulled out a wad of bills from his hip pocket and peeled off five twenties.

"What did he say he wanted it for?"

"Money talks. He didn't."

"What did you put down in your records for the sale?"

"I bought it in my own name. Tomorrow I'll put through a criminal records search on myself. On paper the gun's still here."

"He paid twice what it was worth. Did he know that?"

"He knows his guns. Said he wanted a forty-five, nothing smaller. I had a Model Ninety-two Beretta, the one the military uses, and he wouldn't even look at it. He even got some frangible bullets. They're illegal in Philly, but we can sell them out here."

"You have them for my Hi-Power?"

"They're not going to hit as hard as they will in a forty-five, but yeah." He put a small box on the counter next to the twenties. I shoved it into my shirt pocket. Then I picked up the twenties and folded them into my shirt. What the hell.

"This guy really kill somebody?" he asked.

"I wish I knew for sure."

"You going up against him?"

"I wish I knew that, too."

15

Wednesday, 9:30 P.M.

I TRIED PRESTON'S house from the first phone booth I found and left a warning about Pat's gun on his answering machine. I tried his office, but, as I expected, no one answered. Then I was struck by one of the inspirations that have made me the leading detective of the northern corner of Radnor Township. I had Leah's last name from the nameplate on her desk; and under the listings for Bryn Mawr was an "L Starniski" and an address. It was worth a try.

Half an hour later I was walking down a narrow street behind the college. Old trees crowded the sidewalks and met overhead, shading out the streetlights. Judging from the parking stickers on the cars, it was a neighborhood of student rentals, with a few junior faculty and administrators. The events of the last few hours hadn't prepared me for Bryn Mawr; but then, nothing does, except a degree from Haverford, Swarthmore, or Penn. The evening classes must have just finished, and the sidewalks were busy with earnest young people, in couples and small groups, whispering among themselves. People in Bryn Mawr, at least the ones from the college, don't raise their voices. The loudest sound was the click of my own leather heels on the sidewalk.

The address I wanted was a brick bungalow that barely peeped out between two clusters of thick maple trees in the front yard. I went up the wooden porch, which echoed with every step. The doorbell was the old-fashioned pull type, with a large ivory knob. Around the knob was a man's tie, knotted.

The door was answered by a pretty blond girl in tight jeans and a Bryn Mawr T-shirt. She favored me with the cheerful smile of someone who's never been bruised by life. It was good to see a smile like that. "Excuse me," I said. "Does Leah Starniski live here? My name is Dave Garrett."

She had the same eyes as a girl I'd dated as a freshman: large, brilliant, and light blue, almost a pale gray. I didn't want to think about the possibility that this could be her daughter, or that I was old enough to be her father.

"She lives here," she said cautiously.

I handed her one of my cards. "Could you check if she could see me, please?"

She took the card without reading it and shut the door. She was back within the minute. "Come on in."

"Thanks."

"I'm Carla."

"Nice to meet you."

"Leah's upstairs. She'll be right down." She led me to the living room and headed toward a door in the rear of the house. I thought about the other girl with blue-gray eyes, twenty-five years ago, and made an effort not to stare at Carla's backside. It was like trying not to think about penguins.

"Right down" turned out to be ten minutes, which gave me lots of time to look around. The room was like student housing everywhere: bare wood floors, crates and scattered oversize pillows for furniture, and the smell of lemon furniture polish and incense. Posters and cheap prints taped to the walls. Bookcases made of painted rough boards and concrete block. I looked through the titles: *Love Story*, *The Web and the Rock*, a half dozen King Arthur stories, and lots of poetry anthologies, the bindings swelled with bookmarks . . .

Leah came downstairs in a long cotton dress with a high neck and long sleeves. A print of tiny pink flowers, rosebuds, maybe. The fabric was flimsy, and it molded itself to her body as she moved.

"David, I'm a little surprised to see you." She smiled hesitantly. Her hand went to her hair, brushing it away from her face.

"Sorry about the hour."

"That's fine. I'm a night owl, anyway."

"You have a nice place."

"Thank you." She looked around the room. "Carla and a friend of hers live here. It pays the mortgage." Without her makeup she looked younger, hardly any older than Carla.

I was thinking of what to say when Carla breezed through and nodded at both of us. "Don't want to be in the·way. I'll be at the library." As she opened the door she unknotted the tie. She waited until she was sure Leah had seen her, waved goodbye, and let the door slam shut behind her.

We stood together awkwardly. Leah's fingers played with the material of her dress. "David, would you like a glass of wine?"

"Anything you've got, as long as it's not a chilled red."

"There's some burgundy, a rosé, some Riesling, some white zinfandel, a—"

"Anything's fine. Really."

"I've got some leftover Chinese."

"No, thanks."

"It'll only take a minute in the microwave—"

"Just a drink would be fine."

She returned with two large glasses of something cold and yellowish that tasted like urine. "Ah, the Riesling," I said.

"Have a seat."

There were no chairs. We sat down on a pair of pillows; not touching, but close enough so I could smell her perfume. It was a heavy, sweet scent; not unpleasant, but somehow it made me think of Lisa, who never wore perfume at all. "That tie," I asked. "It's a Do Not Disturb sign?"

She looked down and blushed. "That's for Carla and Jenny; not for me."

I didn't know if she meant that she and her fiancé didn't need time alone or if he had a place of his own, so I gave an all-purpose shrug. "Did you go to Bryn Mawr?"

She nodded. "Three years of psychology."

"You didn't finish?"

"I ran low on money and decided to work for a while. I went to work for Charles and never went back."

"How long?"

"Ten years this October."

"How come?"

"Did you ever find a situation where you felt you really belonged? Not just fit in, but the place you were meant to be?"

"I used to think I did. I was wrong."

"What happened?"

"I trusted somebody."

She sipped her wine before she asked her next questions. "That you shouldn't have?"

"She was my wife. I had to trust her. It's just that I shouldn't have married her in the first place."

"You sound like you still care about her."

"It's been a long time."

"An ambiguous answer if I ever heard one." When I didn't respond, she went on. "You sound like you have unresolved feelings about her."

"I've got unresolved feelings about every woman I've ever known."

She played with the rim of her glass. "I imagine you've been with lots of women." She blushed. "You're an attractive man."

"Some of the most complicated relationships aren't about sex."

"I always thought sex complicated relationships."

"Sometimes it lets people know where they stand."

She thought about that one. "Some more wine?" She ignored the fact that her glass was empty and mine was barely touched.

"Please. I'll try the burgundy."

She got up and collected my glass. "I'd never have guessed."

She came back with a glass—a red, this time—and settled down on her pillow. Her feet were bare, with long toes and high arches. She saw me looking and looked away, but she didn't cover them with her skirt. Again I found myself thinking about Lisa. Why couldn't I remember what her feet looked like? I could remember every other part. . . .

"Leah, I'd like to ask you some questions about Preston."

"All right."

"How well do you know him?"

"Like I said, I've had ten years in a small office with him."

"He have a good practice?"

"Very good. He's very selective in who he represents."

"Didn't he just let some staff go? And an associate?"

She hesitated before she answered. "Yes."

"Aren't things kind of lean?"

"You'd need to ask him that."

"Leah, I'm working for him, you know."

She turned her head a little to the side. "Are you?"

"Sometimes the person who hides the most from you is the person you're closest to. Like your client."

"Pat Winter?"

"No, I mean my client. Your boss. You need to help me. He could be in danger."

"Pat isn't dangerous."

"Then who killed his wife?"

"Her own bad driving."

"Pat wants to kill somebody pretty bad and your boss is about the only target I can think of. He went to a lot of trouble to buy a gun tonight. And some special bullets. Frangible bullets. When they hit they don't make a neat little hole. They shatter into hundreds of fragments that tear you up like a shotgun. Somebody gets hit with one of those, you can't sew it shut or pull out the bullet; anywhere someone's hit is just hamburger."

She swallowed. "Shouldn't we warn Charles?"

"I left a message on his machine."

"How long ago?"

"Maybe an hour."

"Let me try again." She went to a low table in the corner with a phone, found his home number on a sheet of paper, and dialed. While she waited for an answer she stood with her arms folded across her chest, looking away from me.

She finally put down the phone. "Just the answering machine," she said. She came back to her pillow, but she sat lightly, full of tension.

"Where is he, do you think?" I asked.

"Probably his hunt club. They're meeting to set up the fall hunts. Foxhunts."

"Could Pat know where he lives?"

"I don't think so. Charles isn't in the book, and he's way over on the other side of the county. Shouldn't you call the police?"

"He hasn't done anything yet. He hasn't even made a threat."

"Didn't he break the law in buying the gun?"

"Technically. The seller is really in more trouble because he can lose his dealer's license. The guy who sold it to him could say that he just loaned it to him, or that he has the gun on approval, or something like that."

"Still, shouldn't we tell the police? Just to let them know?"

"I will." It seemed that all the women in my life were nagging me.

"No matter what Pat's thinking about, Charles is safe enough for now. I'll keep trying him till I get him."

"I don't really think Pat's a killer."

"I wish I was as sure as you."

"Just look at him," she said.

"Try me. I look like a killer?"

She looked into my eyes for what seemed like a long time. "Yes."

I looked away. "I guess you got your money's worth from those psych courses."

"The war?"

"And my work, too."

She didn't ask me if I wanted to talk about it; she must have known the answer. "Winter doesn't like him, does he?" I asked.

"They're different people."

"If Pat didn't like Charles, why bring him his work? He could have gone to the union lawyer."

"I don't know. But clients talk right in front of you, like you're not there. He thought Charles was stuck up, and that he didn't spend enough time on his case."

"I think their dislike was mutual."

"Charles never said anything to me."

"Has Charles talked about Maria's death?"

"Almost nothing else. He's a private person, but after ten years . . . It's affected him. He wonders why he's still alive, what he did to deserve more time than her."

"How much younger was she?"

"Pat and he were the same age, same year, and she was a couple of years younger. They all went to high school together. You'd hardly believe it now, but according to Charles, Pat was the school jock. Lettered in four sports, had all the girls he wanted, would cut class anytime he felt like it because he knew none of the teachers wanted to blow his eligibility."

"You don't care for Pat much, do you? Or Maria, for that matter?"

"She had a husband of her own. What did she need with someone else?"

"He wasn't much," I said.

"Still, he was hers."

"Everyone wants more, no matter how much we have."

"What's wrong with wanting things to just stay the same?"

"Nothing, except they don't."

"You have a lot of depressed thoughts, David."

"Sure you didn't have a whole four years of psychology?"

"I'm sorry." She hesitated. "I get personal too easily."

"It's a fair question. My ex-wife used to say I was depressed, too. You live alone, it's easy to get down."

"You live alone?"

"Ever since the divorce. I've got an apartment the other side of Villanova."

She put her hand lightly on my arm. "Have to be going anywhere now?"

I looked down at her left hand. "Is that an engagement ring?"

For a moment she seemed surprised it was there. "Ah—sort of."

"He's a lucky guy."

She turned her hand slightly so that the ring was hidden. "Psych majors can cure depression."

"I'm sure you can."

"David, the ring—he's—it's okay; really it is."

"I just ended an affair with someone who was involved with someone else. She said the same thing at the start."

She withdrew her hand. "So why did you come here?"

"To see you."

"For me, or to ask questions?"

"You're a very attractive woman, but I came here about the case."

She looked down, and her hair fell into her eyes. "I'm sorry."

"There's nothing to be sorry for."

"Sometimes I read too much into what people say."

"We all do. Or not enough." I stood up. "And now it's time for me to go."

"I'm embarrassed."

"It's not you; it's me."

"Then why am I the one who feels like an idiot?"

"Of all the people you meet in your life, there's only a few that anything happens with. For lots of reasons. The timing isn't right, that's all."

"Have you ever read Thomas Wolfe?"

"How that true love lies behind a door we never open, how we all die a little half hour from the one mated ecstasy that we were destined for? No, never have."

"Did you know you're a very interesting man?"

"My ex said that about me, too." I gave a small wave and took a step toward the door.

"David, on the way out, would you retie that tie?"

"Leave it untied awhile. It'll be good for her to wonder."

16

Thursday, 8:00 A.M.

I WAS IN the passenger's seat of Lisa's mother's Plymouth, wearing dark glasses, a sweatshirt, and a Philadelphia Phillies cap. Lisa was in the driver's seat. We sat in silence, as we'd done for most of the past hour. Lisa's moods were reflected in her clothes; the happier she was, the lighter the colors and the more skin she showed. Today she was wearing a black leotard top with a high scoop neck and a single gold chain. No makeup. Black jeans with a thick leather belt that had a thin band of gold running through it. And, as far as I'd been able to determine, no bra. I'm a detective; it's my job to notice details like that. Her hair was still braided over to one side, and she played with the braid absently as she stared glumly at Winter's car in the driveway up the block. I was willing to bet five bucks she was still thinking about Ralph Torino, and another ten that she'd never admit to it. It was drizzling, too.

The households on this street were up early. We'd been here

since quarter to seven, and it seemed that at least one car, if not two, had left each house—except for Winter's. None of the neighbors paid us any attention. The car was even more anonymous than my Honda Civic, and if Mrs. Wilson was ever ready to sell I was ready with my bid. In that car we could have pulled off a hit-and-run at Broad and Market at high noon and the only description would have been, "Well, not too light but not real dark; kinda boxy, I guess."

"Want to run down to the WaWa for some coffee?" I asked.

She answered without taking her eyes off Pat's car. "If he wants to get something done first thing in the morning he'll be leaving in the next few minutes."

"I just meant you looked a little beat."

"I'll live."

I sighed. Getting Lisa to open up was like shucking clams barehanded. "So what's your call on the gun business?"

She didn't look at me. "All last night proves is that he feels a need to own a gun. Maybe it's just reassurance."

"Then why does he have to have it right away? He paid through the nose, and committed a minor crime or two."

"He just knows he wants."

After that we sat in silence for another twenty minutes till we saw him come out and start his car. We followed him east, to a gas station near Ambler with a U-Haul rental lot.

"Want me to get in closer?" Lisa asked. "He's never seen me."

"Be careful." In response I got a sour look.

She parked around the corner from the garage and got out, leaving me alone with my thoughts. Last night, after my interview with Leah, I'd checked Pat's house again. His car was in the drive when I arrived and the engine was cool. I'd waited till eleven-thirty, half an hour after the house lights went out, but he stayed in. He'd been in a hell of a hurry to get a gun, get home, and do nothing with it. And now a truck rental. The more I thought about his movements in the last twelve hours, the less I liked it. Especially the part about the special ammunition for his .45.

Lisa slid into the driver's seat. I wasn't being much of a detective that morning; I didn't see her walking up. "Guess where Pat's going."

"You got that?"

"I was hanging around right next to him. The attendant must have thought I was with him, and Pat never noticed me. He was as nervous as they come."

"Limping?"

"Not that I noticed. But he could be on pain pills."

"Go on."

"He's renting their biggest truck for a one-way run to California. And he's getting the tow bar to take his car with him."

"Anything else?"

"He took down the name of a local short-haul moving-and-storage outfit to do the packing and loading. And he asked them how to go about finding somebody to drive it for him. He said he was going to fly out. He was hoping they could be out there to start packing this morning."

I worked my fingers, trying to keep the burned skin from stiffening. "This guy's in quite a hurry about everything."

"Is he from California?" she asked.

"No. Maybe he knows people out there."

"Maybe he doesn't, and that's why he's going."

"I was thinking the same thing myself. And I'm also thinking it's time to have a talk with Preston."

"No argument."

"That's a first."

She shrugged. "Hey, sometimes you're right."

I decided to tear a little at the scab Lisa kept over her feelings. "I'm surprised you're not more upset about Ralph recognizing you."

"Every once in a while you say something smart, you know that?"

"What did I say this time?"

"Back in his apartment. About rewriting history."

"Remember what the Greeks said?"

She sighed. "Am I going to be subjected to your classical education again?"

"I can't remember anymore who said it, Herodotus or Thucydides, or whoever. But he said that the secret of happiness was freedom, and the secret of freedom was a brave heart."

She turned it over in her mind. "I like that," she said.

"Yours to keep."

I had Lisa drop me off at my apartment and arranged to meet her back at my office later. Ten minutes later I was in Preston's office.

Leah was at her post, eating an orange and reading a paperback romance. The cover gave me a glimpse of a tanned, bare-chested mesomorph holding a disheveled blond in an awkward but interesting pose. His hair was a good deal longer than Leah's.

"Morning, Leah."

She looked up quickly and looked away when she recognized me. "Good morning, David." We shared one of the awkward silences for which I'm so famous. She was the one who finally broke it. "Here to see Mr. Preston?"

"I don't have an appointment, but it's pretty important."

"He's doing a will execution now, and he doesn't have anything more till after lunch, so just have a seat." She didn't have to look at his appointment book.

I stayed standing. "About last night . . ."

She swallowed. "Yes?"

"I'm sorry if I embarrassed you."

Her smile was tight, but it looked sincere. "I'm sorry, too."

"Friends?"

"Friends."

Before I could sit down the door to Preston's office opened and he ushered out a young couple carrying a small baby. I leaned close to Leah. "I hope his wills practice consists of something more than clients young enough to be his children."

"It's a good bet for an estate," she whispered. "They both smoke."

Preston saw me even before Leah could catch his eye. "David, come on back."

We shook hands and he offered me the seat in front of his desk. He looked more rested this morning, but he wasn't at ease. "Would you like some coffee?"

"No, thanks. I won't take up more of your time than I have to."

He nodded slowly. "Go ahead."

I told him what I'd learned about Pat, forgetting to mention the part about burglarizing Pat's house. I ended with a question. "Did you know about his plans to leave for California?"

"He's given his testimony in the comp case. We're just waiting on the referee's decision."

"That's not what I asked you."

A deep breath and a look out the window. "I don't know what to say."

"Exactly how well do you know this man?"

"You're talking about your own client."

"Maria Winter died the day after I told 'my client' where to find her. I want some answers."

He touched the fingertips of both hands together and looked at me over the top. "Or?"

"Or I'll go to the police."

"What he tells you is protected by the attorney-client privilege."

I was ready for that one. "He hasn't *told* me a damned thing. I saw it all for myself. There's nothing privileged about an illegal gun or a freshly painted fender."

Preston looked uncomfortable. "I keep forgetting you were a lawyer."

"Don't."

"How come you're getting so unpleasant with the person who's paying your bill?"

"The bill isn't as important as knowing whose side you're on. I want to find out if Maria's death had anything to do with me. Either you're with me or against me, and you'd better make it clear."

Another breath, but this time it didn't seem to be an affectation. "I tried to talk him out of leaving. If he goes the police will get interested all over again. He doesn't need that kind of aggravation."

"Doesn't need it, or can't take it?"

"He's tougher than you think, David."

"I know he's dumber, and I wasn't thinking about his emotional state. I was wondering what the police would turn up when they take a close look after he splits."

"As far as I know, nothing at all."

"Good." I wasn't sure whether I believed him, but the question was asked and answered. It was time to move on. "Any progress on the bridge case?"

He nodded. "I located an engineer who knows the bridge, and he gave me the name of a lawyer he worked with ten years ago. Two kids were seriously hurt at the same bridge, but coming the other way. Same thing as we're thinking—car gets off the road and can't get back on because of the slope of the shoulder. PennDOT paid out some serious settlement money but never fixed the shoulders afterwards."

"So far, so good."

"I'll need your written report, and photographs of the approach, as soon as they're ready. You can drop them off with Leah and she'll give you a check for your additional work."

I detected the signal that our meeting was over and ignored it. "Has he told you where he was Tuesday night?"

"He had a meeting with OVR in the late afternoon; I know because he'd asked me about whether I should go with him."

"What did you decide?"

"The meeting was supposed to go to at least five, maybe a bit longer. I had to be in Center City at six. So I told him to go alone and let me know if any problems came up."

"What were you doing?" I asked.

"The Philadelphia Bar Association had a seminar on the new amendments to the realty transfer tax."

"How long were you there?"

"A lot later than I wanted to be. The questions and answers weren't over till nearly eleven."

"Would there be any witnesses that you were there?"

He put his hands together so that the palms touched. "Are you investigating me or Pat?"

"If Pat comes up with an alibi that includes you, I'd like to know in advance," I said.

"I didn't see anyone I knew. And Pat never stopped in at the seminar," he said dryly.

"Did he tell you where he was that night?"

This time Preston gave me both a preliminary breath and a long pause. I could have counted to five before he started to speak. "Home alone. He had a pizza brought in, but that was at seven."

"Who thought to bring that up?"

"He did. He may be crude but he's not stupid."

"And the police?" I asked.

"A couple of state police detectives were here yesterday afternoon. They didn't like him very much and they liked his alibi even less. But they didn't say they were filing charges."

"You really should get him to stay," I said.

"I'll try to talk him out of going. I'll do my best; I know how it's going to look." He played with his pencil. "I've got a dead woman with the better part of a twenty-year work-life expectancy left, good liability, and I can prove the state knew there was a problem with that shoulder. This could be a hell of a big wrongful death case, Dave."

"Yeah."

"I've never had a million-dollar verdict. This could be the one."

"Well, good luck."

"You sound like you disagree."

"I agree with your analysis. Yes, there's a lot of money at stake. No, it doesn't change anything I'm going to do. After I left yesterday, did you tell Pat that the boyfriend was Tom Evans?"

"No. It wasn't in your preliminary report. His name, I mean."

"Does he know now?"

"I certainly haven't told him," he said, a little too quickly. I found myself smiling. "And why not?"

"I think you're dead wrong about him, Dave, but . . ."

"But what?" I persisted.

"Well, he doesn't *need* to know, does he?"

"If you can keep him from finding out, at least for the moment, do it. If nothing else, I'll sleep better."

"It stays in my file," he promised.

"Your nice clean accident case keeps trying to get dirty."

He caught something in my voice I'd been trying to hide. "You don't trust me, do you?"

I thought about bringing up how he'd forgotten to mention he'd known the Winters for thirty years, and then I decided to keep it to myself. Holding it in reserve? For what? I realized he was waiting for an answer. "I think you want to protect your client and his cases."

"You've got a fixation about Pat and I don't want to make it worse."

"Hiding the ball doesn't help me do my job."

"I'm going to tell you something that has to be kept confidential. With your attitude, I don't want you finding it out on your own and saying I was trying to hide something."

"Go on."

"The police don't know it yet, but Pat had more motive than they realize. He's still on his union list as a member. One of the benefits is a hundred-thousand-dollar term life policy on dependents, with double indemnity for accidental death."

"Jesus."

"The two of us were meeting with a union representative just a month or so ago, discussing his options, and we specifically talked about it. I was trying to find out if we could drop the benefit and lower his expenses. There's even correspondence about it. The police could prove he knew all about it."

"What's his financial picture?"

A thoughtful pause. "Well, Maria's income helped but they were pretty far in the hole. He's been pressing me to get his case resolved quickly, but I've been moving as fast as I can."

"Just a straight answer, all right?"

"He didn't say so in so many words, but I got the impression he's under a lot of pressure to repay some loans."

"Who isn't?"

"Well, you know the kind of people I mean."

"If you mean loan sharks, I do."

"He was introduced to them through some people in his union. He apparently borrowed a good deal of money."

"Any idea how much?"

"I know this much. He used to make sixty thousand a year, and Maria didn't work during the first year of his disability."

"Has he applied for the insurance benefit yet?"

"No. I can't decide if it looks worse to apply right away or wait awhile."

I thought about it. "That makes two of us."

17

Thursday, 11:00 A.M.

LISA WAS WAITING for me in the reception area at my office, reading one of my books on criminal investigation techniques. I nodded at her to follow me upstairs. Normally I sent her up first so I could watch her ass on the stairs, but my shoulder was acting up and I was in a bad mood.

I unlocked the door to my office and we sat down. I went over my meeting with Preston in as much detail as I could remember.

"Do you trust him?" she asked.

"He had nothing to do with Maria. I checked with the bar association about the seminar; he was registered, at least, and he showed up. They're checking to see if he could have left early."

"That's not what I asked."

"No, I don't trust him; and no, I don't think he did it. So what if I don't trust him?"

She rested her chin on her hand. "So what now, boss?"

I pulled out my notebook. "I've got a list of names from the Winter address book that need to be checked out—who they are, what they know about the Winters. Or we could go back and keep an eye on Pat—"

"Sit outside and watch him pack?"

"My point exactly. Instead of wasting time, we can give Maria's place a good toss."

"For what?"

"If there was a man other than Evans, we might get a lead on him."

"We might."

"I have a piece of paper." I took it out of my wallet. "This was torn off in one of Maria's drawers. Whatever it was, it was important enough to take the rest of it with her, and she didn't take much."

She looked at it a long time. "Could be anything."

"Don't get carried away by your enthusiasm."

"I'm sorry," she said. "I didn't sleep too well. And it seems like a long shot."

"In lieu of a better idea . . ."

Forty minutes later we were standing on Cherry Street in Norristown. To be precise, we were on Maria's front porch and Lisa was ringing the bell. Mrs. Grace answered, wearing a screaming orange kimono with purple dragons, in a size normally used by draft horses, and a matching scarf. It wasn't a pretty sight.

"Well, am I glad to see you." She registered just a moment's surprise at seeing Lisa with me. She might be illiterate, but she caught on fast.

"Why is that?"

She looked up and down the street. "Come on inside, honey."

We entered the foyer, and she shut the door behind us. "You still working for the lady's husband?"

"Yes, ma'am."

"He don't want that apartment, do he?"

"No."

"I can rent it, if he can let me clean it up right away. I can let him outta the lease, you knows." Her hands worked the cloth at the sides of her body.

"I'll mention it." I didn't feel like pointing out that the lease wasn't the husband's problem.

"You know, her husband's been here already."

"When?"

" 'Bout ten. But that was before the folks called 'bout the apartment. They—"

"Balding, about fifty, bent over?"

"That's right. I made him show me his photograph off his driver's license. He didn't have no key, but I let him in. He was up there a long time." She indicated a tiny color TV at her feet in a cardboard box, just inside the door, the size for a kitchen counter. "He took stuff to his car, said he'd be back for this later. I suppose it's all his now, anyways. He said he'd send somebody back to clean out the apartment."

"Did he ask you any questions?"

"Nothing at all. He seemed in a hurry, real nervous. The new people, they can move in day after tomorrow. That be all right?"

"Like I said, I'll ask."

"Can you call me todays yet? The new people be in a hurry. They got flooded—"

"Give me your number and I'll try to get back to you today. And I'll need you to let us in. We need to do an inventory."

Anything that might help her turn the place over was fine with her. Two minutes later we were alone in Maria's apartment. Already it was starting to feel neglected, abandoned. Like Maria, it was turning cold.

"So where do we start?" Lisa asked.

"We start by taking our time. Walk around, look at every damn thing. Don't rush."

"What are we looking for?"

"Anything that looks out of place. It's a Zen thing. Just study the rooms and let *them* tell *you* what's wrong."

"You studied Zen?" Lisa asked.

"I read half of *Zen and the Art of Motorcycle Maintenance*."

It didn't take a Zen master to find out what was wrong in the kitchen. It had a door with a window insert, going out onto a small back porch that doubled as a fire escape. There was glass on the floor, and a pane was broken out near the doorknob.

"Was this intact when you were here Tuesday morning?" Lisa asked.

"I think I would have noticed," I said mildly.

Lisa squatted down and studied the glass. "No tape or anything; the glass is smashed, not cut. So it's an amateur, right?" She seemed pleased with herself.

"Or a professional making it look like an amateur."

"Oh."

Lisa was better at detail than I was. She started in the living room and scoured every surface, moving every piece of furniture and looking everywhere anything could be hidden. I started in the kitchen and worked my own way around. Fortunately, the place was nearly bare. A careful search of a fully furnished apartment that size would have taken hours.

I checked the spare bedroom with the dresser. I opened each drawer, and each was empty. The books looked the same. Well, did they? One of the volumes of poetry stuck out farther than the others. Had someone touched it? I was sure I hadn't. Using a tissue from the bathroom, I picked up the book and saw that it was a little oversized; it was as far back as it would go already. It must have been that far out all along. So much for Zen. Maybe I should have read the whole book.

I went into the master bedroom and walked around. Nothing was obviously out of place. The clothing in the drawers hadn't been disturbed, as far as I could tell. I opened the closet. The clothes hung, just as before, and the shoes were scattered just about evenly around the closet floor, the way I'd left them. But when I reached into the corner for the box from the real estate office, my hand closed on air. I felt around carefully, on both sides, but it was gone.

The area around the bed looked much the same, and the bedclothes still held a whisper of her perfume. Maria's alarm clock was in the same spot on the bedside table, and the little huddle of framed photographs looked the same. Well, almost the same. A little more open. One was missing.

"Lisa! Come in here."

"What's up?"

"There's a box of stuff missing from the closet in the other room. And a little framed photograph. And there's a photo album missing."

"Tell me about the album first."

"There was a photo album, new, in between these two big ones. Now it's gone."

"You're sure?"

"Absolutely."

"What kinds of pictures?"

"I didn't look. I'm even guessing that it was photos. It was in between a couple of other photo books."

She studied the small gap between the other two albums. "Can you describe it any better than that?"

"It was as big as the others, nine by twelve or whatever, but it was thinner, maybe only an inch thick. The binding looked expensive, like leather."

"Any markings on the spine?"

"No."

"Could it have been their wedding photos?" she asked.

"Maybe. But it looked new."

"Maybe they took good care of it," she said. "Most people do."

I nodded. "If it was their wedding album, I could see where he might want that back."

"Okay, let's go to number two. What about this photograph?"

"It was on the nightstand. Sitting up in a frame, maybe a five-by-seven. They were all family photos, I think."

We sat on the bed and looked over the ones that were left. An old photo, hand tinted, that looked like her parents' wedding picture. The same couple, many years later, in front of a trailer in the desert. A young Maria in a perm and heavy eye makeup holding an infant. A shot from about the same time, showing Maria with her arm across the shoulder of a woman who was a taller, darker version of herself. A shot of her son at ten or twelve playing baseball.

"There's no picture of Pat," I said.

"Damn right," Lisa said. "Why should there be?"

"I guess the missing one was a more recent picture of their son."

"Pat wouldn't really want the others, would he?" she asked. "All the rest are her family."

"Unless he'd want them for their son, I don't see he'd be interested."

"Okay, so let's try number three," she said. "What about this box?"

"Records from the office where she used to work. A place called New Directions Realty." I told her what I could remember about the papers. "When I looked at them I didn't see how it could be important."

"Somebody does." She shivered. "Let's get out of here before our somebody comes back."

We split up again and searched the rest of the apartment in silence. Lisa came to rest opposite the wall with the business cards. She folded her arms across her chest and studied the cards a long time.

"Ready to go?" I asked.

"I'm thinking."

"Yes?"

She pointed at the bulletin board. "Every one of these cards, it's clear why they're here. You move, you need cable and a mechanic and a doctor and all these people. But why the photography studio?"

"If she and her husband were splitting up, she'd want to get family photos duplicated."

"This piece of paper you found. I bet it says 'boudoir photography,' and I bet it's a receipt. And I bet that the missing album was those kind of pictures."

"For Evans?" I asked.

"Most likely."

"But she didn't give it to him," I said.

"Maybe she was planning to. Or maybe he left it with her. He couldn't very well take it home or to the office."

"So, either way, why would Evans want them?" I asked.

"Maybe she'd written in the album, or he may have been in the pictures, too."

I took down the studio's card from the wall. "If you're right, I sure hope Tom has the book."

"Oh?"

"It would put Pat over the edge."

We stopped downstairs and told the landlady about the broken glass in the kitchen. She feigned shock that something like that could happen in her building. It wasn't very convincing.

"You hear any noises upstairs since she died? Like someone was up there?"

"No, sir. If I did I would have called the police right away. I ain't foolin' with nobody breakin' in."

"When her husband left this morning, what did he take with him?"

"I just saw him on the stairs the once. He didn't show me. He put it in a grocery bag."

"The bag seem heavy?"

"No. Least, he didn't have no trouble with it, and he didn't look like no weight lifter."

"Did he make any other trips to his car?"

"I wasn't payin' no attention. You know, she had a VCR up there. If he don't want it, is that mine?"

"You'd have to ask him that."

We stepped out onto the porch. It was getting warmer, and a brisk wind was taking care of the clouds. "So which lead first?" Lisa asked. "The photography or the real estate?"

"Time for some carefully considered strategic planning."

My quarter came up heads.

The photography studio was on a narrow street in an older section of Paoli, blocks from the slabs of glass-and-steel office buildings that had torn the heart out of the town. The trees on either side of the street were in full leaf, and the bushes out front were neatly trimmed—except for a single forsythia, which was still in its first bloom of golden yellow.

The studio was converted from an old house. We entered by a side door and found ourselves in a large, airy reception room. Except for the gold in the highly polished wood floors the room was entirely monochrome. Matte white walls, black baseboards, black modern light fixtures that hung down like flying saucers. Directly in front of us was a white receptionist's desk and chairs, all empty. The walls were covered with black-and-white framed prints, mostly portraits of couples or families, but a few landscapes, too.

When we shut the door a bell sounded. A moment later a bearded man in his fifties shuffled out from a room in the back, a pipe in one hand and a sheaf of papers in the other. His movements were deliberate, and his hands showed the ravages of arthritis. A copper bracelet protruded from one sleeve of his tweed jacket.

His blue eyes darted from one of us to the other, then settled on Lisa. "Bring your portfolio?"

"Portfolio?"

"You're here about the modeling job, aren't you?"

She laughed and stuck out her hand. "Sorry, no. I'm Lisa Wilson. I work for Mr. Garrett here."

He turned to me politely and told me his name was Bob Pegritz. I tried to shake his hand as gently as possible, but he winced anyway. "Could we sit down for a moment?" I asked.

He waved us to the chairs on our side of the desk and I handed him one of my business cards. He looked at it carefully and tucked it inside his jacket. "So what brings you to me?"

"We're investigating a death case. A woman who may have had her picture taken here. Maria Winter."

"Oh," he said slowly. "A very beautiful subject. She's dead?"

"I'm afraid so."

"I'm sorry to hear that. A very nice lady."

"We were hoping you could help us. We have some questions about her business here."

"You have some kind of release or something from her heirs?"

"No, I don't. I'd just like to know—"

He shook his head. "I can't tell you anything."

"I'm sorry? I don't understand. The—"

He knocked his pipe into the ashtray and set it down. "If you're here, you must know what kind of photography it was."

"You advertise it as 'boudoir,' I think."

"A silly word, but it means something to people. I suppose that's what counts. It means lingerie poses. Revealing clothes and situations. Nudes, sometimes."

"Do you remember what Maria Winter wanted?"

"That was between her and myself."

"She's dead."

"You have to understand, the women who have this done, it's a very private thing. They want an album for their husband, or maybe a fiancé. Once in a while someone wants a portrait for the bedroom wall, but that's about as public as it gets. These pictures aren't for general distribution."

"We don't want to see any pictures," I said. "The—"

He waved me off, gently but firmly. "My customers aren't professional models, Mr. Garrett. They're often shy people, and . . . not all of them have flawless figures. I sell privacy as much as I sell pictures. Can you think of a surer way of ruining my business than have it get out that I'm talking to strangers?"

Lisa spoke up. "We don't want to embarrass anyone. I can imagine how I'd feel. We don't want anything personal."

He picked up his pipe again and filled the bowl. Then he took his sweet time lighting it. "You see the pictures on the walls?"

"Yes."

"The landscapes, I mean. For thirty years I made my living that way. They called me the Ansel Adams of the East Coast. I climbed in Maine in midwinter, stood in swamps up to my ass . . . I can't do that anymore. Tell me, are you going to guarantee me a living if this blows up in my face?"

"We'll do everything we can to keep you out of this."

"Guarantee?" He pointed the stem of the pipe at me.

I sighed. It was time to recognize a blank wall when I hit one. "Sorry to take up your time, Mr. Pegritz."

"You have to understand . . ." He gestured vaguely around the room, his hands twisted almost into claws.

I nodded and stood up, but Lisa stayed where she was. "You said something about a job?" she asked.

He studied her face with interest. "Ever done glamour?"

"No."

"Come over here, if you don't mind." He got up and she followed him to the room in the back of the studio. She sat on a chair in front of a blank background. He turned off the overhead and flicked on a couple of small lights, which left most of the room in shadow. "Just look toward the window, please." He moved a large camera on a tripod and studied her through the viewfinder. "Turn your head to the left. Pull the hair away from your face, please. Now look to the right. Turn your shoulders the opposite way. Raise the chin a little."

He considered the result, then backed away. "Are you sure you never did glamour? Or anything else?"

"I'm sure."

"There's very much a market for your look, you know. You have strong features—nose, cheek, jaw—we could do some interesting shots."

"Go on."

"How old are you?"

"Thirty-seven."

He studied her face from a few inches away. "You'd be great. If we work without makeup, bounce the light a little, I can make you look forty, forty-five. But you've got the body of a twenty-five-year old."

"Low mileage."

"Your face is old enough for the clients to identify with, and your figure will convince them I can make them look good." Lisa and I both looked at him blankly. "For the kind of work we're talking about," he added.

She swallowed. "Boudoir?"

He made another expansive gesture, except this time there was a hint of a shrug, too. "People come in, they want to see a sample of what I can do. I don't want to show what I've done for other customers. Without samples, people have to take it on faith."

"You'd like me to pose for you?"

"I'll pay agency scale. And I'll need you to sign a release."

"I'm no model. And I told you how old I was."

"That's why you'd be good. The customers are older than that, most of the time." He thought about his words. "This isn't a honeymoon thing for kids out of college; it's women who are looking to . . . rekindle something."

She hesitated, but she wasn't blushing. "I don't know. I've never done anything like this."

"You'd be great. And I know somebody in Cherry Hill who's looking for someone just like you for his own studio."

She gave her head a small toss, so that her hair swung freely. "You make it sound tempting."

"I promise you, nothing is going to happen. My assistant will be here, and the prints are only to show to customers. No commercial circulation."

She bit on the end of a fingernail and looked worried. It was a gesture I'd never seen before. It took me a moment to realize she was acting. "I'm not a professional, either," she said. "Any more than the other women. I don't know if I trust you to take my photograph if you can't trust us."

"Me trusting you?"

"We'd like some basic information about Maria. It won't go anywhere. No one will know you gave it out. If you can do that, I'll do the shots for you."

"Trust, huh?"

"Trust," she said firmly.

He looked at her, and then over at me. A funny smile played around the edges of his mouth. He'd been had and he knew it, but when he looked at Lisa again and thought about the pictures, I knew we had a deal. "Come out front," he said, and led us back to his desk. He rummaged through a file cabinet and drew out a form, which he briefly scribbled on before handing it to Lisa. "Here's my standard contract, release, and so forth. Look it over and call me if you'e got any problems with it. Then call for a date for the shoot. Mondays generally good for you?"

"Mostly."

"Good. The beauty shops are closed and we can get a girl

in to do hair and makeup. We start at nine or ten. Should take till lunch, early afternoon. Call in and my assistant will set it up."

"All right," Lisa said.

He looked from one of us to the other. "I hope my trust is not misplaced." Then he turned to the file cabinet and withdrew a slender folder. "Now, Mr. Garrett, what do you want to know?"

"Anything at all you can tell us."

He consulted the file. "The photos were taken just three months ago, delivery of the finished prints was last week. Our standard package, one album of fifteen different poses in eight by ten. She paid cash and picked it up herself."

"What was her address?"

It was unfamiliar to me, but when I checked his suburban phone book, it matched New Directions Realty.

"She gave her work address," I said. "You said she paid cash. Was it her own check?"

"I mean greenbacks."

"Isn't that unusual?" I asked.

He took his pipe out of his mouth and considered it gravely. "Not everyone wants their purchases to be traceable. I don't require a proof of marriage."

"Did she say who they were for?" I asked.

"No, she didn't. Except that they were a birthday present."

"Was anyone with her? Or in the pictures?"

"No. I'd remember that."

"Did the album come with any writing?"

"It said 'Happy Birthday.'"

"No name?"

"No. There would have been an extra charge for the extra word."

"Can you think of anything else about her?"

He gave a sad smile. "She was a lovely lady. A pleasure to work with."

We thanked him for his time and headed back for the car. Lisa trailed behind me, studying the contract. Her eyes were wide.

"What's the matter?" I asked.

She came to a dead stop in the middle of the sidewalk. "David . . . Do you have any idea how much *agency scale* is?"

18

Thursday, 1:00 P.M.

WE STOPPED AT a fast-food joint, and I used their pay
phone to call my office. Lisa ate their biggest hamburger, with
fries, and talked about modeling while I forced my way through
a chicken sandwich.

"Are you all right?" she asked. "You look beat."

I could feel myself slipping away, even though it was still
early in the day. My shoulder was bothering me, too. I leaned
back in my seat and closed my eyes. "I didn't realize how much
last month took out of me. I'm still not over it."

"You're not twenty anymore, David. You have to learn to
pace yourself. Go home. I can do some interviews."

"Pat's going to be leaving soon."

"You're not responsible for Maria's death."

"If my information helped somebody, I'm responsible." I
took one more bite of my sandwich and threw the other half
down. "You did a good job just now."

"Thanks."

"How about a ride to see Trooper Carter? She left a message that she has some information for me."

"So I can't get you to go home and get some sleep?"

"Not till it's over," I said.

We pulled into the parking lot of the state police barracks, and Carter responded almost as soon as she was paged. She was in full uniform this time, which made her look thirty pounds heavier. I introduced her to Lisa, and the two of them eyed each other uneasily.

"Well, Trooper, what have you found out?" I asked.

"You owe me for this one. Took some digging."

"I appreciate it, believe me."

"We look at these phantom-vehicle cases pretty close. There's a lot of insurance fraud associated with this kind of thing. You lose control, spin out, get hurt, and wreck your car, you're stuck. But if you say it was a mystery car that ran you off the road and kept going, you have a civil claim for pain and suffering from your uninsured-motorist carrier. Because there was no contact between the vehicles, this one got looked at *real* close."

"So was it phony?"

"It really happened. She phoned in from a call booth right on the turnpike. We had a cruiser there within a couple of minutes. There was a witness in a following vehicle that saw the whole thing. According to him the other car came up alongside Ms. Winter and cut over hard. She was in the right-hand lane and went over on the shoulder. The other car kept coming and she left the road and went up on the embankment."

"Any chance it was an accident?"

"No. The other car didn't just change lanes to the right—it came over onto the shoulder after her."

"Can I talk to the witness?" I asked.

"He's a long-haul trucker out of Nevada. The investigating trooper needed some follow-up information and it took six weeks for him to complete his report."

"It hasn't been cleared, I assume."

"The trucker didn't get a plate, or even a description of the car except that it was an older American car, light in color. He was too busy watching Ms. Winter and trying to keep clear of the two of them. He was pulling two trailers and he was afraid of a jackknife."

"What kind of investigation was done?" I asked.

"Not a hell of a lot. The victim couldn't identify any enemies."

"What about her husband?"

She gave us a funny smile. "We check spouses anyway, regardless of what victims say. He said he was home alone. No verification. We took a picture of his car and sent it to the truck driver—that was what took so long. Typical bullshit ID. The driver said it didn't look like the car, exactly, but he couldn't be sure it wasn't, either."

Lisa spoke up. "Did Maria say where she was going or where she was coming from?"

Carter consulted the file. "Funny you should ask that. It's a routine question, but it's not here."

"Looks like she refused to answer," said Lisa.

"The trooper that investigated this? I know him. He's been around a long time and I'm sure he asked."

"If a married woman wasn't going to tell the police after a murder attempt," Lisa said, "she was probably meeting someone."

Carter thought it through. "So two people knew about the trip, besides her, I mean—the man she was meeting and the one who tried to run her off the road."

"Or maybe just the one," said Lisa. No one could think of anything to say after that.

We thanked Trooper Carter and decided to pay an unscheduled call on Tom Evans.

I should have picked it up right away when we entered the

showroom. The prosperous air of benign self-confidence was gone. The cars were as enticing as ever, but the people were on edge.

A salesman, very much like Tom but with dark hair instead of blond, introduced himself and asked if he could help.

"We'd like to speak to Mr. Evans, please."

His expression froze. "I'll get the sales manager for you, sir."

It must have been five minutes before he returned, introduced an older, stouter version of himself, and disappeared. I noticed that the older man was in the middle of a hair transplant. The rows of hair grew as precisely as Iowa corn. I wondered if you could see straight down the rows if the angle was just right.

"Uh—how can I be of service?"

"We wanted to speak to Mr. Evans for a moment. It won't take long."

"What do you need to see him about?"

"We're private investigators. I'd rather not say too much more, if you don't mind."

He dropped his voice. "Is this about the Winter business?"

"I'm afraid it is."

"Well, as you can see, we took action at the first opportunity." Despite his nervousness, he seemed at least a little bit pleased with himself.

"I can see that," I said, not seeing anything. "Who contacted you, exactly?"

"Mr. Winter himself. He said he'd been in touch with his attorney, but that he hoped we could deal with this without litigation."

"When was he here?"

"Early this afternoon. He was very—concerned, of course."

"We work for Mr. Winter," I said. "We know what kind of stress he's been under."

"If you're invest—you were the ones who traced him to that motel?"

"That's right."

"Well, then there's nothing I can tell you about this sorry situation." He paused to mop his forehead with a handkerchief and misunderstood my expression of alarm. "No, no, I want you to know how sorry we are about this. When an employee takes company time for an assignation—not once but dozens of times—with a married woman, it's simply intolerable." I wasn't sure if he was objecting to the sex or just the absenteeism.

"I thought this was on his own time."

"No, no. He volunteered to work evenings. We don't get as many customers then, so we pay an hourly rate to make sure we have full coverage. All those hours he said he was here . . ." Concern over the lost sales, or maybe that someone else was getting some when he wasn't, was written on his face.

"And nobody turned him in."

"They covered for him. And I wonder if he didn't cover for them, somehow, other times."

Lisa produced one of my cards and handed it to him. "If you decide you want an employment security investigation, it's one of our specialties. Now, what did Mr. Winter want you to do?"

"Exactly what we did—fire Evans. And I'll tell you what makes me the maddest. I only let him have the evenings because of his troubles at home. Look where it got me."

"Troubles with his wife?"

"Yes. It's a sad situation. She would come in here sometimes and make a scene complaining about this or that, make—"

"She comes in here?" I asked.

"Oh, not very often, of course. We asked him, very firmly, to make sure there were no incidents at work. It's probably been a year since she was in."

"But she still leaves her house?"

"Not frequently, of course, but yes, she did."

Lisa and I exchanged looks. "I'll say hello to Mrs. Evans tonight," I said. "Let's go see the Realtor now."

19

Thursday, 3:00 P.M.

NEW DIRECTIONS REALTY occupied a deteriorating clapboard bungalow on a main business thoroughfare in Jenkintown, sandwiched uncomfortably between a discount furniture store and a down-at-the-heels strip mall peppered with vacant storefronts.

We parked in the tiny front lot and got out. "Looks like Maria moved up in the world," I said, "getting away from this."

"Those clothes weren't from Goodwill," Lisa said. "She made money here."

We went in through a narrow alcove into the main office area, a grimy place with heaps of disordered papers and a couple of desks. One of them was occupied by a pale man with thinning black hair and an off-green suit. Even at fifteen feet I could tell it was polyester.

He stood up when we came in and headed toward us. He was bowlegged and stooped, and moved in a crabwise fashion. His tie was dirty and he needed a haircut.

"How can I help you folks?"

"My name's Dave Garrett. This is Lisa Wilson, my associate."

"John Speicher."

His arms were so short he had to move in close for a hand-shake, but as soon as the formalities were over he stepped well back. He didn't look like the kind of person who trusted strangers within arm's reach.

He looked from me to Lisa and back again. "Yeah?"

"We're here about Maria Winter."

His jaw clenched. "So?"

"We'd like to talk."

"Who are you?"

I gave him one of my business cards.

"What's your angle, Garrett?"

"I'm looking into her death."

"I think maybe you'd better leave." There was nothing tentative about the way he said it.

"We ought to talk," I repeated flatly.

He considered me, then stood back behind his desk. His right hand dropped below the desktop and began to ease open the top drawer.

"Take it easy, Mr. Speicher. We're just here to talk."

His hand stayed where it was. "I don't think we got anything to talk about."

I spread out my arms away from my sides and showed him my open palms. "No trouble. A couple of questions and we're gone."

"Who you working for?"

"Maria's husband."

"What's he want?"

"He wants to know if it was an accident."

His forehead furrowed with puzzlement. "Sure it was, wasn't it? I saw the paper. Ran slam-bang into a wall, right?"

"That's what I'm here to talk about."

He took his hand out of the drawer and sat down. He didn't invite us, but we took the two chairs across the desk from him. "I met her," I said. "The day she died. Nice lady."

"Yeah."

"How long did she work here?"

"About a year, I guess, maybe a little more."

"What did she do?"

"What's that got to do with the accident?"

"In a civil case, when the survivors sue for lost income, the earning capacity of the deceased is a big issue."

He was satisfied enough with my explanation to give me an answer but not enough to be specific. "This and that. You know, general office stuff."

"Did she have a license?"

"Associate's sales license, sure."

"She sell many properties?"

"We don't do much sales."

"What do you do?"

He looked at me. I think he was weighing what Maria might have told me already. "Is it important?" he asked at last.

"The lawyer's going to need proof of how she made her living."

He rubbed the side of his forefinger against his chin. "Lawyers."

"Her husband's lawyer is preparing a case. We're supposed to be helping him."

"So who's this lawyer?"

"Charles Preston, from Wayne." I saw his surprise. "You know him?"

"How do *you* know him?" he asked.

"Me? I just met him this week. How about you?"

He looked at me for a long time before he answered. "We had some business once. Long time ago."

"Condemnation cases, when the Blue Route came through?"

"Yeah, that's right." He leaned back in his chair and he

relaxed a little. "Hey, if you're working for Preston . . . what do
you want to know?"

"What you do here."

"Property management." He said it the same way Maria had,
with an unspoken "sort of" at the end.

"Rentals?"

"Mainly small commercial. Shops, offices, gas stations, stuff
like that."

"I wouldn't think those kinds of places would need management."

"If they close, they do. Business closes up, like say a gas
station, we go in, secure the site, help market it, deal with the
bank that holds the paper, that kind of thing."

"She told me she made a good living here." Well, her closet
told me that.

"Business is good."

"So why did she leave?"

"You've got me."

"Come on, John. It was just the two of you." When he didn't
answer I pressed on. "You make a pass?"

"She's outta my league." He gave a thin smile. "Yours, too."

"So why, then?"

He shrugged. "Better opportunities."

"Why?"

His manner turned frosty again. "I gotta make some calls."
But his hand didn't move toward the phone.

"I can wait awhile."

His hand slid off the desk and back into the drawer. "We're
through talking, you and me. You can leave now."

"Maria's dead and you're playing games with me."

"So she's dead. Her husband—what's his name? Pat?"

"That's right."

"When you see him, tell him I'm worried about his
health."

We stood up. When we reached the door I turned back. He was dialing a number and staring in my direction.

About a mile down the road was a diner I remembered from years ago. An old Greek couple ran it then, and the food was great. Feta cheese omelettes, any time of the day. Real gyros, seasoned nothing like the way convenience stores made them, and so big that one was a full meal. I prevailed upon Lisa to stop for a strategy session.

The old couple was long gone but I decided to give it a try anyway. Well, I never said I never made mistakes.

We took a corner booth, with a view of a scrapyard and the traffic roaring up 611. A waitress in a dirty pink uniform grudgingly brought us coffee.

"He's lying, you know," Lisa said.

"That's the easy part. About what, exactly?"

"At the very least, about why Maria left."

"It wasn't the money, so it was something about the work. We'll have to figure that out for ourselves."

"How, boss?"

"When she left her job she took some paperwork from the office and those environmental reports from Eco-Protect."

"What's the environment got to do with New Directions?"

"When you buy a property, or when a bank forecloses, they want to make sure they're not getting a Superfund site. The reports are routine enough."

"So?" she asked.

"I'm suspicious of companies with cute names."

"You want me to check them out?"

"I'll drop you off there. They may know something about her and they may not care so much about talking to us."

"Anything else?"

"Yeah. Try the Philadelphia Bar Association; see if they have anybody that remembers Preston being at the seminar late Tuesday night."

"What does Preston have to do with Maria's death?"

"Nothing, I hope."

"No problem." She picked up her coffee, took a sip, and made a face. "David, this stuff is really ghastly."

"Maybe it grows on you."

"It grows on something, I'm sure." She paused. "You have any other work for me?"

"Not for right now. Once you check out those leads, I'm fresh out."

"Want me to be on call?"

"I got you out of bed today and kept you out late the night before that. Take a day off."

"Okay, then. John and I will be going away tonight when he gets off work, if you're sure you don't need me. We were thinking about going to Cape May for a long weekend."

"One of the Victorian bed-and-breakfasts?"

She nodded. "He showed me a picture. And I bought this nightdress, all cotton, with lots of lace, a big flouncy hem, long sleeves, and little pearl buttons up the front."

I took a sip of coffee. She was right—it *was* ghastly. "Sounds nice."

"And I won't be wearing anything underneath."

I put the cup down, a little harder than I intended. "John's a lucky guy."

We asked for our check for the coffees. Two dollars and fifteen cents.

"What are you going to do now?" she asked.

"I don't know," I admitted. "I've got bad feelings about nearly everybody in this case. Like they're all holding out on me."

"We know Pat is."

"I think I'll pay him a visit."

I dropped Lisa off at the business center where Eco-Protect had its offices and ran into a WaWa for a cup of coffee to clean out my mouth. As I was getting back into my car I saw a glasses case on the floor on Lisa's side. It must have fallen out of her purse when she picked it up. Inside was a pair of reading glasses I'd never seen before. I thought about her upcoming weekend at the shore and wondered if she'd be doing much reading. I stuffed it inside my jacket pocket and made a mental note to drop it off. One more thing that wasn't going right.

It was raining: a soft, warm rain, hardly more than a mist, under low clouds. Whoever thought of the little gadget that allows wipers to work intermittently ought to get a medal. Come to think of it, I'd read in the paper where he'd sued Ford and won ten million dollars, and that his claims against GM and Chrysler were still pending. I guess he didn't need a medal after all.

When I pulled into Pat's drive his car was gone. It was as good a time as any to try the neighbors, and the hell with Preston's instructions. I put up my umbrella and looked around.

The house right across the street was obviously vacant—the lawn hadn't been cut in several weeks and a big For Sale By Owner sign dominated the front yard. The number to call had a 609 prefix—south Jersey. I wrote it down anyway—just in case all the other leads were bad.

On one side of the Winter house was a small two-bedroom rancher with a plaster deer out front. The lawn was edged with a tiny wooden fence, no more than six inches high, painted white. One car, a Chevy Nova.

I rang the bell and got exactly what I expected. A woman, about sixty, in a faded pink housecoat and fuzzy slippers. She was wearing some kind of face cream, and her hair was in curlers. "Yes?"

"Hi. My name is Dave Garrett. I'm a private investigator and we're doing some checking on one of your neighbors. Would you have a moment to talk?"

"Is this about Maria and Pat?"

I didn't know if she meant the divorce or her death, or both. "Yes, it is."

Her eyes narrowed. "Who are you investigating? Him or her?"

"Right now, him." The fact that he was also my client didn't seem all that important. As a matter of fact, the more I learned the less important it seemed.

"Then get on in."

I followed her down a cramped hallway into a small breakfast room off the kitchen, jammed with a big TV, cheap furniture, and souvenirs of long-ago trips to the Jersey shore and the Poconos. I cleared away enough pillows to make a place for myself on an armchair and she sat across from me with her hands folded daintily in her lap. "You'll have to forgive me," she said. "The place is such a mess."

"It's very clean," I said truthfully. And wondered why women always apologize about the house. Just once I'd like someone to say, "I busted my ass all day cleaning this place. Looks pretty good, huh?"

"Now what can I do for you, Mr.—"

"Garrett." I handed her one of my cards. "I'm doing a background check concerning Mr. Winter. You know that he has an insurance claim pending?"

"Isn't it awful about his wife? She was such a nice person."

I decided to play it close. "What about her?"

"Well, that she's gone. You must know about her accident."

"Why do you say that?"

"Because I saw you parked down the street this morning. I figured you were keeping an eye on him." She gave me a conspiratorial smile that turned sad. "Maria used to come by all the time, after my Ed left. She was a good friend to me."

"How recently did you see her?"

"Just before she moved was the last time. She hid his guns here. The last time I saw her was when she came by to get them."

"Tell me about that part."

"Well, she'd been planning to leave him for a while, and then she came to do it. She was afraid of him, so the day before she left she took his guns and left them with me. The next day, when she moved out, she took them and sold them."

"Why was she afraid? Any particular reason?"

"She'd tried to tell him twice before she wanted a divorce and he refused to let her leave. He'd start terrible arguments. The only way she thought she could get out was to sneak out." She paused for a moment. "It didn't have any dignity to it. When Ed left me at least he packed his bags and went out the front door. Not this sneaking around."

"Did he threaten her?"

"He'd hit her, a few times, over the years. But after the accident he couldn't anymore."

"Did you know where she went?"

"I asked her not to tell me. I didn't want to give him the satisfaction of forcing me to be a liar. But he never came over. He was just like my Ed. A man's man, as they say. Football and hunting and fishing. Trying so hard to prove he was a man and just showing how much of a little boy he really was." Her mouth curled in a bitter little smile. "Two of a kind."

"Did Pat and Ed see a lot of each other?"

"Ed died four years ago. His heart." There was a certain satisfaction in her voice, and I wondered if just possibly he'd died in the saddle with another woman. Even if she didn't know, I was sure that it gave her comfort to think he had.

I followed her eyes and saw that her kitchen window overlooked the Winters' front yard. I wondered what she might have seen out that window, and how to get her to tell me.

"I think that Maria may have been murdered," I said.

"I've wondered about that myself."

"You don't seem too surprised at the possibility."

"I honestly think he could have done it, I really do."

"I suppose we're all capable of murder. Or anything else, for that matter."

"No, I mean he went out Tuesday night, the night she died."

"He told the police he was home."

"His car wasn't. When I looked out the window after the lottery drawing at seven it was gone."

"When did it come back?"

"I went to bed around midnight. I heard him pull in and his headlights hit my bedroom. I got up at eight, but it was gone again. The next time I saw it was when I got back from bingo Wednesday evening. I always try to be home for the lottery, at seven."

I was glad for the Wednesday-night bingo—I'd left Pat's house only a couple of minutes before she got home. "Nosy Neighbor Costs PI His License—Burglary Charges Pending," said the headline. "Did he have another car?"

"Maria and he each had their own. There was no third car," she said definitely, "except for the one that was there Tuesday night."

I swallowed. "Tell me everything you can remember. And take your time."

She settled back into her chair, pleased to have my attention. I hoped she wasn't so pleased that she'd embellish what she really remembered. "I go for a walk about six, before I have my supper. I do the same walk every night except Wednesdays when I have bingo. I saw a strange car around the corner, up at the Perrones. I thought it might be one of their kids'."

"So what about it?"

"Well, Pat came home just about then. I waved at him coming up the street but he didn't wave back. He went right in the house and didn't look back. He seemed pretty upset. I went back in the house, like I said, and had supper. When I saw his car was gone I looked, and the car up at the Perrones was still there. In the morning the car was gone and I haven't seen it since."

She leaned closer. "And I checked with the neighbors on both sides, and none of them know whose car that was. I figure that Pat and the person in the car went off together Tuesday night for something."

It didn't hang together completely—why use your own car for the job? But it was the closest thing I had to a lead.

"Anyone in it?" I asked.

"Not that I seen."

"Can you describe it?"

She nodded. "It was a Chevrolet Impala. I think it was a 1966, because Ed and I had one and I remember those six little taillights."

"Color?"

"Light brown." That could mean anything from tan to copper to a real dirty white. It might even describe Lisa's mother's car. I wrote it down anyway.

"If you see it again, get the license plate. Call me if that happens or if you think of anything new."

She promised that she would, and I let myself out. My next stop was Tom Evans. It seemed like the next logical step—the problem was that I couldn't decide if I was arriving as an interrogator or a bodyguard.

20

Thursday, 5:00 P.M.

I PULLED INTO the Evanses' driveway and sat in the dark. Mine was the only car in the driveway. If I were him, would I be at home? More likely, out drowning my sorrows, and the more publicly the better. Then again, on ten thousand other nights things had been just as grim inside and he'd always come home. I thought about my days in Intro Psychology, when I learned that even earthworms could be taught to avoid unpleasant situations. And we think we're so smart.

The rain had stopped, and I left my umbrella in the car. As I went up the walk I saw that the kids' toys were still out in the lawn, a few feet from the door. I could understand being intimidated by Manhattan or Center City, or maybe even the regional shopping centers—but being too afraid to go out on your own front lawn?

I rang the bell and heard its chime through the door. While I waited I worked on a plan. The time for working under a cover to get general background was over. It was time to disclose exactly what I was doing—hopefully without disclosing exactly why I was interested in Tom. No matter how mad she was at him, I was sure that a wife would cover for her husband if the stakes were as high as a murder charge. Perhaps I could sell her on the story that he was a witness to the accident. Well, in a way he was. A lot depended on how much she knew about Maria.

As the possibilities floated through my mind, I became aware it was taking her a long time to answer the door, even longer than the other day. I rang the bell again and followed up with a knock. Still no response. Now I was getting annoyed. If ever I'd known that an interviewee was home, it was now, and it was too late at night for games. I paced the porch a couple of times, each time getting a little farther from the door, trying to get a peek under the curtains at the front window without being too obvious. I stumbled and looked down at the tricycle at the edge of the grass. A damned shame to let it get rusty, I thought. I bent down to pick it up.

At that moment I heard her yell through the door. "Tom? Is that you?" Her voice was high and shrill.

It happened so fast I didn't have time to straighten up. "It's—"

I never finished. A loud, muffled boom came through the door, and I felt my face being peppered with splinters of wood. I sensed something whizzing past my head. I threw myself flat on my stomach and pressed myself into the lawn, hugging the ground so hard that my fingers clawed up big handfuls of dirt. A moment later there was another boom, louder this time, and more wood splinters hailed down all around me. Again I heard something pass overhead. It sounded like a swarm of bees, all headed in one direction, and all of them going like hell. I heard a metallic rattling sound as the shotgun pellets bounced off the mailbox behind me.

I turned my head to look at the door. Even with just moonlight, I could see two ragged holes, one about belt-high and one at chest level. I didn't know which was the first shot and which was the second, but if the third one was going to be even lower I was right in line for it. I rolled hard to the right, landing on my bad right shoulder on the concrete walk. It hurt like hell, but I was clear. She could blow holes in her door all night for all I cared.

I waited for the third shot, or for the door to open, but nothing happened. I lay there on my back for at least a full minute, trying to get my breath and calm my racing heart. I figured that at least three of the neighbors, if not half a dozen, were calling 911 right now. Figure five minutes to respond and another five or ten to locate the source of the firing . . . I couldn't have cared less what they did with her, but whatever it was going to be, it was going to keep me from talking to her for Lord knew how long.

I sat up painfully, trying not to use my right arm. Pins and needles ran down from my shoulder as far as the elbow, and the base of my neck on the right side was stiff. I opened my mouth, but nothing came out at first. I swallowed and tried again. "Mrs. Evans. It's Dave Garrett. Not Tom. Put down the gun and open the door."

There was a pause, and then I heard the clatter of the shotgun falling to the floor. A moment later came the sound of the lock being worked. I stood up and walked unsteadily to the door. It opened before I could touch the knob.

She was wearing a dark, shapeless thing that I might have called a dress except that it had no shape at all—it simply fell down around her like a tent. Her color was splotchy, and she wasn't focusing her eyes on me. She was out of breath, and beads of sweat stood out on her forehead. With each breath her chest rose and fell a good six inches. "Oh."

"You know how close you came to killing me, you dumb shit?" I picked up the shotgun, a 12-gauge pump-action. A round was in the chamber. I set the safety; I was trembling so badly I was afraid to try my luck at unloading the weapon.

"I—I—"

"You thought I was Tom, didn't you?" She didn't answer. "The hell with it—we're not going to talk about you anymore. You tell me the truth right now, I'll leave before the police get here and you can give them a song and dance about scaring away a prowler. You give me even a little bullshit, I'll hang around and give them all the details."

"I have to sit down—this is so—"

"Stay right where you are and just answer my questions. What do you know about Tom?"

"He came home late in the afternoon, after he was fired. He told me about her. He'd been drinking." In another context she would have put some indignation in her voice, but she told it as a bald statement of fact.

"Did he say anything about the woman's husband?"

"No, he didn't." She licked her lips nervously. "You're working for him—the husband—aren't you?"

"Did you know about Maria before he told you?"

"I'm not going to discuss that with you."

I raised the shotgun and pointed it into her face. The barrel was warm in my hand, and it smelled of gunpowder and hot oil. I leaned close and spoke as softly as I could. "If I did you right now I could make it look like self-defense. Give!"

She looked into the muzzle. "There's usually been somebody or other, since I got sick. He never said anything, didn't flaunt it, but I knew."

"Did you know about Maria?" I repeated.

"No, I swear I didn't. Not till he phoned."

"Tom?"

"Her husband. He called here this afternoon, before Tom got home, and told me about Tom and his wife."

"Had you ever spoken to him before?"

"I didn't know him at all."

"What did he want?"

"He said he just wanted to make sure I knew."

"What's your alibi for Tuesday night?"

"I was home with the children."

"You go out at all?"

"No. And you can ask them. Anyway, we only have the one car," she whined. She could have borrowed one easily enough, but I wasn't going to argue with her. "Is her husband after him?" she asked. She couldn't keep a hopeful note out of her voice.

"Possibly. Where is he?"

"He's not here."

"No shit."

She smoothed down her dress, showing off a belly big enough to contain triplets. "He came home, packed a few things, and left. He didn't say where he was going or when he'd be back."

"What sort of mood was he in?"

"Frightened. And guilty." She stuck out her chin in a sick display of pride.

"Was he upset about being fired?"

"Tom's a good salesman. He can always get another job. I think he felt he deserved what happened." She stopped and considered what she'd said. When she began to speak again her voice was higher, like a child's, and I think she'd forgotten I was even there. "Well, *I* didn't. *I* wasn't chasing around. *I* wasn't—"

"Oh, shut up."

She burst into tears and covered her hands with her face.

I put down the shotgun. "If you don't mind, I'll take a little look around for myself." There was no indication she'd heard me, and I didn't care, anyway.

I moved down the corridor leading to the master bedroom. As I passed one of the doors a couple of young faces looked up at me, a dark-haired boy of about six and a blond girl who looked about four. They stood in the doorway without moving and without expression. If they were upset about their father being absent, the shots, their mother bawling hysterically, or the strange man prowling around the house, they kept a pretty good lid on it. With a mother like theirs, they'd needed to grow up fast. I smiled at them. The little boy gave me a solemn nod as I went by.

The master bedroom featured a fussy, feminine decor and twin beds. I wasn't surprised. I looked in the closet and saw a set of matched luggage. One was missing. I checked his dresser; handfuls of underwear socks, and sports shirts were missing. His business suits were still on their hangers. Wherever he was going, it looked like he expected to be away for at least a few days, and if he was looking for work, it wouldn't be a white-collar job.

I ran my hand quickly through the drawer on his side of the bed and found a box of .38 Special cartridges. One-hundred-twenty-five-grain high-velocity cartridges, to be precise. The box held fifty rounds and it was less than half full. I quickly patted around the rest of the drawer, but the gun wasn't there.

Virginia was on the sofa. She'd stopped sobbing, but the tears were still running down her face. She was breathing heavily again, and she had one hand on her chest. She glanced up when I came into the room.

"Tom has a gun, doesn't he?"

"A gun?"

"Don't bullshit me."

"A little one, yes."

"If it's the gun he has bullets for, it's not so little. Where does he keep it?"

"On his side of the bed, in his drawer. I—"

"Did he take it with him?"

"You can't—"

"Did he, goddammit?"

"I don't know. The—"

"You're lying. You were in the bedroom arguing with him and you watched everything." An ugly possibility crossed my mind. "Did he go after Pat?"

"He didn't say."

"Did you tell him to do it?"

"He does what he wants. You know that as well as I do."

"But you egged him on, didn't you?"

"He never pays any attention to me."

"Why didn't you call the police?"

"He cost Tom his job. And it was his wife that ruined my life. He's only getting what he deserves, too."

She started crying again, but I was already on my way out. I just hoped I wasn't too late.

21

Thursday, 7:00 P.M.

IT WAS RAINING again when I reached Pat's development, a heavy, driving rain with gusty winds that drove water through the shoddy waterproofing around the windows of my rental car. As I turned onto his street I had to slow to a crawl to pick my way around a couple of potholes that were almost invisible in the dark. The moon was hidden by the clouds, and the old-fashioned streetlights didn't help much.

Up ahead, at the very limit of my headlights, I saw a hint of movement. Larger than a person, and shiny. A car, pulling out of a driveway without lights. I saw the grill, and then, just as I was close enough for a good look, the headlights came on. The driver was using his high beams, and that was the end of my night vision. I tried to look past the lights, but it was a waste of time. The next thing I saw clearly were his taillights in my rearview mirror. Six small lights, three on each side. Like the old Impalas.

Another fifty yards and I reached the point where the car had pulled out. Pat's driveway.

I snapped the wheel all the way to the left, gave it the gas, and did a 180-degree turn, partly on the shoulder and mostly on Pat's lawn. Whatever was in the house could wait.

The other car must have speeded up when he saw me start to spin around, because by the time I was turned around he was already at the corner, making a fast right. I was only twenty seconds behind him, but by the time I reached the corner he was gone. I roared down the street as fast as I dared on the wet pavement. A four-way stop came up and I had to make a fast decision. It was a pure guess which way he'd turned, if he'd turned at all. And if I slowed down to make the turn and the Impala had gone straight, I'd never catch up. I gritted my teeth and I blew through the stop sign at forty. Fortunately, no one was coming. But when the road straightened out after a few hundred yards, no one was ahead of me, either.

Cursing, I turned the car around and checked the intersecting road, both ways, just in case the Impala was lying low in a driveway or along a curb. No luck. I gave up and headed back to the house.

I pulled into the drive behind Pat's Beretta and studied the house. Every light was on, both inside and out. It reminded me of Evans's house. Was Pat afraid of Evans? It didn't make a lot of sense—it ought to be the other way around. Unless, of course, he was convinced Evans had killed Maria. But Pat would have gone to the police. . . . Or maybe his thinking was more complicated than that. Extortion? Of what? Like most of my cases, the more I learned the more confused I became.

I reached under the seat and slid out my Hi-Power. I made sure the chamber was empty and got out, the gun in the pocket of my raincoat. It was bigger than my .357 and it bulged awkwardly, but without a holster it was the best I could do. I certainly didn't want Pat to see a big man in the middle of the night with a gun in his hand.

I knocked loudly on the front door and rang the bell, hoping that Pat hadn't taken so much medication and booze that he'd do something stupid. As I stood there I realized what a feeble hope that was. I knocked again and called for him, but there was no response.

I waited a good thirty seconds, then looked around to see if he might be observing me from somewhere. The door had a peephole, but the foyer was lit and I could see that no one was looking through it. The side windows on either side of the door were covered with light curtains, sheer enough for a look. I saw just the foyer and a section of the living room beyond it. Whatever he was doing, he wasn't watching me.

I rattled the doorknob. Looking back, I don't know if I had a plan or not. My skill at picking locks was mediocre at best, and if I were going to break in, the obvious choice was the tried-and-true sliding door in the rear. I think I just wanted to do something out of sheer frustration.

The knob turned freely, and the door swung wide open.

For just a second I stood there, thinking over the implications of Pat leaving his door unlocked; then I realized I was perfectly silhouetted against the light. I slipped inside, easing the door shut behind me, and flattened myself against the wall. I held my breath as long as I could, listening, but the only sound was the faint drumming of the rain on the windows. No music. No TV. No voices. I drew my Hi-Power and worked the slide, pumping a round into the chamber. The sharp metallic click echoed around the house.

I inched my way along the wall till I came to the door leading into the kitchen. I pressed my ear against the wall but only heard the hum of the mechanicals. Then I extended the gun at eye level in a two-handed grip and swung around into the doorway.

My eyes flashed around the room, the front blade of my sight dead in the middle of my field of vision. Nothing at eye level. The counters were covered with cardboard boxes of various sizes, but no one seemed to be sheltering behind them. No one crouched behind the kitchen table. The room was clear.

Keeping the gun pointed dead ahead, I inched into the kitchen. Packing boxes were everywhere, full of small appliances, dishes, glassware, and silverware. The bigger stuff—the larger skillets, the microwave, the bread-making machine, were still in place. Either someone else was going to be packing them, or he was leaving them behind.

I moved further into the kitchen and reached the corner where the breakfast nook began. The table was covered with moving paraphernalia—blankets, ropes, strapping tape. And on top of it all was the .45 automatic Pat had purchased the night before.

I looked around the room carefully. Partly I was doing my job; but just as much because I was scared to go further. Whoever was in that Impala had done something here they didn't want to be connected with. I could only hope that their business here was over.

Just as I was ready to open the door to the laundry room, my foot moved a little on the linoleum. I looked down, but all I could see was the floor. Kneeling down, I felt something wet. I smelled my hand and caught the smell of some kind of detergent or bleach. Someone had cleaned part of the floor recently, maybe just within the last few minutes. I stood up and moved around till the overhead light reflected off the wet area. It was big—almost the size of the breakfast nook—but whoever had cleaned up had done a careful job.

I checked the kitchen wastebasket but didn't find any bloody towels. I found a mop and bucket, both still wet, in the laundry room, but they'd both been rinsed clean. I wondered if with a little luck a good crime lab might isolate some blood traces from the mop. If so, I was going to be very interested to see whose blood it might turn out to be. Did it belong to Pat, or Evans? Or somebody else?

I checked the rest of the downstairs and saw the same indications about the move as the kitchen—some small things were in boxes or ready to be boxed, but a lot more was being left behind than taken. A few books had been taken down in the living room, but the vast majority were still shelved. As I stood by the fireplace I smelled something like paint, and I wondered what kind of fixup Pat was doing. I smelled again; it was a chemical smell, warm and sharp, but not paint. The smell of something burned.

In the fireplace was a mass of blackened ash, still square, and still warm to the touch. It smelled of paper and plastic, and on one side, unmistakably, was the blackened metal spine of a photo album. The length and width of the spine matched the one I'd seen in Maria's bedroom. I stirred the ashes with a poker and came across a bit of unburned cardboard, white with blue lettering. The box from New Directions Realty. All the things I'd seen and ignored. And now they were gone for good.

I sat there on my haunches looking at the fire, trying to figure it out. Who burned it, Pat or the visitor? And why? What was in the pictures? Someone was willing to go to a lot of trouble to keep anyone else from knowing. I shut my eyes and rubbed my temples and tried not to feel defeated.

Upstairs, Maria's remaining clothes were untouched, but his were mostly packed now. A number of his winter coats were still on hangers—either he planned to be back by fall, or he was moving to California for good.

Nothing was disturbed in the master bedroom or bathroom. I stuck my head in Maria's room, but it hadn't been touched. I stuck my head in the hall bathroom. I looked around and immediately detected . . . well, something. I looked from one side to the other. What the hell was different? The room had been empty when I saw it yesterday, it was empty now, and yet something wasn't the same. Still no towels on the racks, still no soap on the sink, the medicine cabinet still shut. Even the blind was still all the way down, the way I remembered it.

When it came to me I drew in my breath. I knew what was

missing and I knew that it meant trouble. Someone had taken down the shower curtain.

I went to the master bedroom phone, which I figured was the least likely one to bear any fingerprints of interest, and used a pillowcase to pick up the receiver. Preston didn't answer either at his home or his office.

I hung up and dialed 911. While I waited for the police to arrive I went back to my car, lifted the hood, and stuck my Browning behind the battery. When I'd taken the gun away from the person who'd been trying to use it on me, I'd neglected to get a proof of purchase. I didn't know who the police computers would show as the legal owner, except that it wasn't me. For once I was grateful I didn't have a holster. One less thing to get rid of.

I was standing in the driveway, the door wide open behind me, when the first Whitpain Township cruiser rolled up. They did a very professional job, which meant I spent a lot of time standing around with a police "escort" while they tried to figure out whether to arrest me for either trespassing, burglary, or murder.

In the course of the next two hours I told my story to a patrolman, a sergeant, and, finally, to a detective in a rumpled suit with eyes like a hound dog's. I don't recall that he bothered introducing himself. Like the rest of us, he couldn't make up his mind if he was part of the most interesting homicide of the year or a wild-goose chase.

When at last they were through with me, the detective escorted me out to my car. I gestured at his portable radio. "Learned anything so far?"

He thought over his words. "Nothing at any of the emergency rooms. Or anywhere else."

"Does a missing persons report go out now?"

"Gone out already," he said. "We don't wait twenty-four hours when it's this suspicious."

"Anything else I can do?" I asked.

He thought that was funny. "Yeah. Assuming it's a homicide, tell me who did it."

"Detective, even if I knew who was dead I wouldn't know who did it. And even if I knew who did it, I don't think I'd know why."

He looked back at the house. "One of those, huh?"

I nodded. "One of those."

22

Thursday, 9:00 P.M.

I FOUND A phone booth and called Lisa. It was a few rings before she answered, and until I heard her voice I was ready to believe I'd waited too long. "It's Dave. Hope this isn't too late."

"Late? It's only nine."

"I mean, you must be almost out the door. For your weekend with John."

"Oh. He's here. I was just waiting around for your call. No problem."

I didn't want to burden her with the events of the last four hours, especially when she'd delayed the start of her vacation for me. "Thanks for waiting. I'm sorry I couldn't call earlier. What did you find out?"

"Eco-Protect doesn't exist."

"Out of business?"

"Never in business, as far as I can tell. They've never had an office in Plymouth Meeting Towers, and the Plymouth Meeting Post Office has never heard of them. Nothing in the suburban or Philadelphia phone books. I called Harrisburg, and they're not a Pennsylvania corporation or a registered fictitious name. I even called the Department of Environmental Resources and a couple of environmental engineering companies. No one's heard of them."

"Any idea what any of this means?" I asked.

"Not a clue."

"Makes two of us. You have time to check out Preston's alibi for Tuesday night?"

"It stinks. The Philadelphia Bar Association confirms he bought a ticket for the seminar that night and that it was used. There were four hundred lawyers there. No one knows what time he registered or if it was even him using his ticket. And he could have left right after signing in, and no one would know."

"Hmm." For a man with home and office phones, he was pretty hard to locate at critical times. "Lisa, thanks. And now you need to get to Cape May."

"It can wait. John won't complain. I'll make sure of it."

"Thanks, but you don't need to bother."

"Sure?"

"I'm sure. I've imposed enough already. Have a great time."

"Then I'll call when we get back. Sunday night."

"Lisa, I just thought of something. I've got your glasses. Do you need them?"

"No, no problem. I can get them Monday."

"I can drop them off."

"No, thanks. We're leaving now."

"All right, then. Bye."

I put down the phone and got back in my car. I'd been striking out all over. Things were happening all around me, too fast for me to understand. I was looking at two murders, or maybe one murder, or maybe no murders at all, and I wasn't getting anywhere. I couldn't even manage to return Lisa's damn glasses.

Sometimes investigations are a straight line; but more often they circle, spiraling into themselves. It was time to circle around some more.

Even though it was a weeknight, South Street was jumping. Music poured out of every doorway and kids with boom boxes stood on every corner. Streetlights, illuminated signs, headlights, security lights, and the red pulse of the bar lights from police cars as they vainly tried to keep traffic moving. The sidewalks and streets were jammed with people of every age and style of dress. Society Hill matrons in basic black cocktail dresses rubbed elbows with panhandlers and high school kids with their baseball caps on backwards. Tired Center City businessmen stood in patient lines, waiting for their chance to spend thirty dollars for a couple of watered drinks and a chance to see a bored college girl in a bikini dance on a plastic runway. I looked at the publicity photo as I edged my way past the door, and then at the men. Most of them probably had wives at home with the same basic equipment who'd be happy to do a hell of a lot more than just dance, and would do it for free. But then, nobody asked my opinion.

If I expected it to be any less noisy inside Ralph's store I was wrong. His own PA system was blaring out a tune of its own, an upbeat disco number heavy on the drums. The store was crowded, mostly with gay couples, but a few straights, too.

Andrew was ringing at the register. When I first caught sight of him he was already watching me. For no reason I felt uneasy.

"Is Ralph in?"

He allowed himself a coy smile. "Back so soon?"

"We've got business."

He looked me up and down. "I'll say."

"Just get him, please."

The smile turned into a smirk. He picked up the phone and hit one button. "Ralph? That guy's back to see you." He listened for a moment. "Yeah, got it." He hung up. Before he spoke again, he brushed the hair clear of his eyes. "Go through the door to the back and wait for him. He'll be right out."

I went through the door and found myself in the same small alcove as before. I barely had time to shut the door behind me when Ralph came through the other door. Before it shut I had a glimpse of a large room with tables, bright lights, and some people. He had changed into a plaid jacket and a bright blue shirt with an open collar. Tan slacks and matching shoes. He stuck out his hand. "Didn't think I'd have the pleasure so soon, Dave."

"Neither did I." As we shook I noticed he was wearing English Leather. "You get this dressed up to sell greeting cards every night?"

He looked down at his clothes, ran his thumb along one of the lapels of his jacket, and smiled. "Looks good, am I right?"

"No question."

He shrugged. "Like I told you, I've learned to indulge myself a little. So what brings you down here?"

"We need to talk."

His smile started to thin. He moved closer. "What's the problem?"

"It's trouble. And it's private."

He led the way upstairs and unlocked the door to his apartment. The building was well insulated; all I could hear of the shop was a distant thumping noise from the drums in the music.

"You got a couple minutes, Dave?"

"Sure."

"Then let me show you something."

He turned out the lights and drew open the drapes to reveal a floor-to-ceiling window that ran all the way across the front of the living room. A thick oak rail ran about four feet off the floor, from one wall to the other. Outside, South Street was at our feet. The lights, the movement, the dazzle, the back-and-forth of the cars and the people—completely silent. It reminded me of watching TV without the sound. The people looked small and foolish. "Care for a drink?" he asked. "I've got some good single-malt Scotch."

"Don't know that I've ever had any," I said.

He poured a couple of generous ones. "Most Scotch," he explained, "is a blend—a little from one distillery and a little from another, maybe twenty or thirty in all. But a single malt is from just one. There's no two that taste alike."

He poured a splash of water into each glass. "I'd like mine with some ice," I said.

He shook his head. "No, either straight up or a little water to release the flavor. Ice cuts the nose off."

He handed me a glass and we stood together at the window. I had the feeling he stood there often, watching. It smelled like a good brandy, but smoky. I took a sip and let it roll around in my mouth. "What have I been missing all these years?" If heaven was a drink, it couldn't taste any better.

He leaned against the railing and looked out at the crowd in the street. "I warn you," he said quietly. "It's an expensive taste."

I leaned against the rail next to him. "And you don't care anymore."

"No reason to." He took a sip. "I spent my life putting off the good things, and now . . . It seems you either have time or money. One or the other, but never both." He looked at his glass, and walked slowly back to the bar. "It's funny, thinking that you might be doing something for the last time. Even something little. Makes you think of how you take things for granted."

"I'm sorry to be bothering you at a time like this."

He came back to the window and rested his elbows on the rail. "Hell, trust me—having you here doesn't make it any worse." He went to work on his second drink. "I'll tell you something, I'm glad you're here."

"You hardly know me."

"You're old enough to talk about dying." He pointed out the window. "Look at them down there, how young they are. They think they're going to live forever. Am I supposed to talk to

Andrew?" He snorted. "He's known a dozen guys who've died of AIDS and it's still not real to him. *I'm* not real to him."

"You're wasting your time. Make your peace with yourself and the hell with him."

"You sound like you've given this some thought."

I took another sip and let it go down slow. "Ralph, I dated a girl a couple of months back; she's dead now. She said something that's stayed with me. 'We all die alone.' "

He gestured with his glass at the people on the street below us. "It's like watching fish, you know?"

"I've just come from Pat's house. He's disappeared, and so has Tom Evans."

"So?"

"Can you give me some information?"

He sighed. "What do you want to know?"

"I'll start with where you were this evening."

"Why?"

"It was a neat job, no signs of a struggle, all cleaned up. Pat was on his guard. But you were Special Forces, you could have done it."

"Yeah, I could have. But I didn't."

"Got anyone to back you up for tonight between five and nine?"

"I was up here most of the time, downstairs a couple of times. I would tell you that the staff could back me up, but it's not true. Depending what time he got it, I might have had time for it. Besides, you wouldn't believe them anyway."

"How did you happen to invite Pat and Maria to your opening? You didn't invite your whole high school, did you?"

"Maria was an old friend, and I'd seen Pat off and on over the years."

"You're getting vague on me."

He sipped at his drink again, and I saw that it was almost gone. "Can I get you another one?" he asked.

"Not just yet, thanks."

He looked uncomfortable. "I can't tell you anything about Tom."

"So tell me about Pat."

"I hear things on the street."

"I bet you hear things in that back room, too, Ralph. What is it back there? Numbers? A bookie?"

"Just a friendly little social club."

The words "social club" have a certain meaning in south Philadelphia when spoken a certain way, and Torino was talking that way now. "So what was Pat's connection? How did he get to come to the opening? You didn't invite everybody you knew from thirty years ago. You had business with him, didn't you?"

"With the people in the back, he did."

"Was he a gambler?" I asked.

"Not with his credit." He turned to me and swished around the Scotch in his glass. "If I tell you anything, it's got to stop right here, between the two of us. Or you're going to be in trouble."

"All right."

"He was on the books with them. He came to me after his accident, said he heard I could put him in touch with people who could make a loan with no paperwork. So I did."

"How much did he owe?"

"It was well into five figures."

"And a point a week?"

"I don't get into details."

"He hadn't been paying, had he?"

He shook his head sadly. "No. And that's all I can say."

"Okay."

For a while he just looked out the window. "I'm sorry you didn't bring your friend along," he said. "She was interesting."

"I only have her along when I need her."

He looked over at me, and his old smile came back. "And how do you know that?"

"When I leave her out and it's too late," I admitted.

"She looks like she knows her stuff."

"I wish I had the work to keep her busy full-time."

He looked out the window for a while without speaking. "Dave, be honest with me about something. You say she's off limits 'cause she works for you?"

"That's right."

"Ever sorry about that?"

I sipped some more, letting it roll around on my tongue. The smoky smell penetrated my nostrils. I looked down at the people in the street. "I don't know. Why do you care about my personal life so much?"

"You want me to trust you. I need to know how you feel about people that are different."

"Do I pass?"

He nodded. "Dave, it's good you came to see me. And I got a message to pass along."

"From anyone I know?"

"When Maria left her job with Speicher she took something with her. There's people I know who want it back."

"What is it?"

"If you don't know, there's no point in telling you." But he said it mildly, and he even gave me a little smile.

"No games, Ralph. You want the Eco-Protect reports, don't you?"

"These people do."

"I don't have them."

"You know about them."

"Your people don't have them?" I asked. Then I caught myself—too little sleep and too much single-malt Scotch. "Of course they don't. We wouldn't be having this conversation if they did."

"That's right."

"I saw them in her apartment on Wednesday. When I went back today they were gone."

"Break-in?"

"Uh-huh." I took another sip. "I just assumed you had them."

"Any idea where they are?"

"It might help if you would tell me why they're so important."

"There's a ten-thousand-dollar finder's fee."

"That's not what I mean." I turned and looked him in the eye. "Trust for trust, Ralph."

"You're tough," he said.

"I'm just trying to keep up with my assistant."

He sighed. "Let's have another round first." He poured us each one more, a little shorter than the first two. "This goes outside this room, I can't be responsible for what happens to you."

"I understand."

"Do you? Sometimes it's better not knowing things."

"I understand."

"Let's say a guy's got a gas station or some little business. He owns the ground. It's worth three hundred, four hundred, but it's got a big mortgage. He can't make a go of it, he misses payments. Bank forecloses."

"So he's down the drain."

He looked at the Scotch in his glass. "Let's say . . . somebody gives the bank a report that the property is so polluted that if you put a match to the ground it would burn. You think a bank wants to spend its money cleaning up if they foreclose? Hell, no—they write it off, give the guy the property free and clear."

"Sounds like the guy got himself a deal."

"Well, he's got to pay income tax on the amount of the mortgage that's been forgiven, and he owes a percentage to the people who provide the report, but, yeah, it's a good deal. Bank wins, too—they get to take the bad debt write-off as a deduction."

"But the banks have the originals of these phony reports. What's so important about getting the file copies back?"

"Somebody could make trouble with just a list of the deals. But unless Maria made a list, you need the copies to see how big the scam is. The banks having them doesn't matter, 'cause the banks don't *know* they're phony."

I decided to tell a little of the truth, indirectly. "Anybody contact your people about the reports?"

"No, why?"

"They may not exist anymore. Maybe Maria took them with her for some reason when she went to Collegeville Tuesday night, and they burned up in the car with her."

"They didn't," he said flatly.

"How can you be sure?"

"They had a man following her. He jimmied her car when she was in Collegeville. They weren't there."

"Was his name Mike Arronomick?"

The name didn't mean anything to him, but it all added up. "I don't get into details. Why are you smiling?"

"Because a guy with a bad toupee and a smelly cigar sold me a bill of goods. Did he check her apartment after she died?"

"Maybe. If he could find it. Is that a question?"

"Just sort of thinking out loud." I looked down at the street. "I'll keep my eyes open for the reports, but I wouldn't be optimistic, if I were you."

He continued facing the window, but I saw him looking at me out of the corner of his eye. "When you can tell me something, let me know." I nodded.

After that we just watched the street together till my glass was empty. "I'll be back to you if I find out anything," I said when I was ready to leave.

We shook hands. "Come back anyway, Dave."

"I will," I said. "Anyway."

23

Thursday, 11:00 P.M.

I DROVE AWAY from South Street without paying much attention to my driving. I thought about Ralph, and about all of the people I'd known who were dead now. The list got longer every day, and most of the best people I'd known were on it.

I headed west on Kennedy, toward 30th Street Station and the entrance to the Schuylkill Expressway. I was ready to take the turn for the ramp when I remembered Lisa's glasses. She was probably long gone, but I didn't want the responsibility of remembering to return them later. I decided I'd stop in and put them through her mail slot.

Lisa lived with her mother in Overbrook, a residential section on the western edge of the city not far from Saint Joseph's University. The neighborhood was a little down at the heels these days—crime was up and the rows of late-Victorian mansions were showing their age—but no worse than the rest of the city. The blight that had engulfed west Philadelphia had taken the liquor store, which was surrounded with concertina wire and defaced with graffiti, but it stopped short of the the block with the church and the train station that formed the heart of the neighborhood.

The apartment was brick, with a short walkway, and next door was an Italian funeral home. I was a little surprised to see Lisa's Legend out front, but then perhaps they'd taken John's car.

As I came up the walk I saw light through a gap in the living-room curtains. Not the bluish light of a TV, and not the dim light of a lamp being left on for security. No one was supposed to be home.

The events of the evening had put me on edge, so instead of ringing the bell, I moved to the end of the porch and peeked in. Lisa was sitting on the sofa in a robe, reading a book and munching popcorn. No suitcase, and John was nowhere in sight.

My first thought was that their plans had fallen through somehow. I was just about to knock when I thought of another, simpler explanation.

Testing it was simple enough. I drove the few blocks to Lankenau Hospital and called her house from a phone in the emergency room. I called on the number we used only for business calls, so I'd be sure she knew it was me.

No answer.

Two possible explanations. One, she'd somehow had a falling out with John in the last hour, one so bad that the trip had been canceled.

Two, John didn't exist.

I thought about number two. John and Lisa supposedly had been going together since February and saw each other nearly every day. But he'd never called for her, never left a message. He never sent gifts. She'd never shown me a picture or even claimed to have one. On the few occasions I'd talked to Lisa's mother, Mrs. Wilson never mentioned him.

I walked back to my car and headed west on Lancaster

Avenue toward my apartment. Why would she want to go to the trouble? Was she out to fool just me, or herself, too? It was her own business if she dated one guy, ten, or nobody at all. . . . I didn't know what to think, except that, whatever was going on with Lisa, it wasn't my business; and anyway, it could wait until the case was over.

As I drove, my bad shoulder started going numb. One of these days, I was going to have to get that looked at. Whatever it was, I hoped they could fix it for something in the neighborhood of a hundred dollars and that it wouldn't cost me any time off work.

I checked my answering machine when I got home. The only message was from Preston, and it said to call his office whenever I got in.

He answered on the third ring. "Preston here."

"It's Dave. I just got back from an interview and I got your message."

A breath and a measured pause. "I'd like to have the benefit of your thoughts."

I repressed an urge to sigh thoughtfully right back at him. After all, he was paying the bills.

"Sure, but be patient. I'm still recovering from Ralph's hospitality."

"Ralph Torino? You saw him again?"

"I thought he might know something about Pat and Tom. He confirmed a few things. Nothing new."

I went over everything that had happened since our last meeting. It took longer than I would have thought. He didn't have the good grace to sound surprised or impressed even once.

"Let's start with the most obvious suspect," I said. "Pat. He could have killed Maria. If she'd lived she would have taken half his property, including half of his personal injury award."

"He loved her. He wanted her back."

"At times. And there were times he wanted her dead. I

wouldn't be too sure you knew him as well as you think."

"That business with his car—it's too pat. Whoever used his car was trying to put the blame on him."

Preston was right. I wasn't thinking things completely through. I stifled a yawn. Lisa had a point; I was getting too old to keep these kinds of hours. "If somebody loved Maria and thought Pat was responsible, they could have killed him in retaliation," I said. "Or maybe Pat had help, and the helper turned on him."

"What makes you think Pat had help?" he asked.

"Whoever was in the . . ." I fumbled for the make. "The Impala."

"That could be," he admitted; then he was quiet for a moment. "The wife of the boyfriend . . . What about her? She's shown she doesn't care much about human life."

"It's possible she had something to do with Maria's death, but she's in the clear about Pat. Even if she was out driving tonight, she couldn't have beaten me to Pat's."

"Could she have killed Maria?"

"Even if she knew about Maria, how would she have known where to find her Tuesday night?"

"Perhaps," he said, "by following her own husband." He might be pompous, I reminded myself, but he was quick.

"They only have the one car. And even if she'd borrowed a car, it leaves too much to luck. It doesn't seem to fit her." I stifled another yawn. "It's the oddest thing about this case. None of the people match up. They all want what they don't have, and they don't want what they do have. And it's even spilling over into my life. I found out tonight that Leah has an imaginary boyfriend—"

He was so surprised he forgot to breathe in. "Leah?"

"I'm sorry. I'm tired. I meant Lisa, my assistant. For months she told me she was dating this 'John,' but now I find he doesn't exist at all. At least I don't think he does."

"How interesting. Why would she do that?"

I didn't feel like violating her privacy a third time in two days. "I'm not sure. I think she doesn't want me to feel sorry for her, being alone. She's a very proud person."

"I just can't believe that Tom would be foolish enough to show up at Pat's house."

"Who says he went there as the victim? He had a gun and his wife was egging him on. Maybe he was at Pat's to get even for being fired, but Pat got in the first shot."

"So if Pat shot him in self-defense, why hide the body?" he asked.

"Pat likes to take care of his problems himself. With a good DA Pat would be pretty vulnerable, even if he was really innocent. The DA could make it look like an ambush," I said.

"You know," he said. "It's a difficult self-defense case for either one of them."

"Who loved Maria enough to commit murder to avenge her death?" I asked.

"Well, no one I can think of."

"That's the trouble here. There's lots of motive and yet no motive at all." We talked a little more and said our good-nights.

I still hadn't made up the enormous sleep deficit I'd run up in April, and Ralph's Scotch wasn't doing me any good, either. But I wasn't ready for sleep. The possibilities of the case were bouncing around too hard inside my head. Dead clients can be just as demanding as living ones.

I poured myself a short bourbon and put on a record. It was blues piano, no vocals, smooth and mellow. I sat down on the sofa, in the half-dark after the record was over, listening to the little sounds my apartment made in the night, the refrigerator and the soft rumble of passing cars. My head was full of middle-aged thoughts, the perpetual amazement of how we could have ended up, for good or bad, like *this*. All the decisions, the paths not taken.

I thought about the case. What was it that someone said about the Balkans? That they had too much history? This case had too *many* facts. Enough facts so that you could support just about any theory . . .

I don't know how long I sat like that, probably at least half an hour. I thought about what Lisa had said about none of the people fitting with each other. And about Torino and his account of the opening. And about how Pat could have found out about Tom Evans.

It was coming together.

24

Friday, 8:00 A.M.

MY FIRST STOP that morning was the Winter house. The entire lot was cordoned off with yellow tape, and Pat's Beretta was secured with a tape of its own. Two cruisers were out front, along with an unmarked car.

No one was in sight. I stepped over the tape and started toward the house. I was halfway up the drive when the front door opened and an unfriendly township cop yelled at me to get back behind the tape.

"Can I talk to whoever's in charge, please?"

"Get back over the tape, sir." The words were slow and distinct. When he wrote me up for Defiant Trespass he wanted to be sure he could say he'd given me fair warning. I moved.

From behind the tape, it was twenty or thirty yards to the house. I cupped my hands and yelled. "Now can I talk to someone?"

He waited, long enough to let me know who was boss, and then went inside. After a couple of minutes a big man in a cheap blue polyester suit came out and walked down the driveway to meet me. He wasn't in any hurry. Unless he'd put on fifty pounds since he bought it, or had a growth spurt, whoever sold him that suit should have been shot. When we shook hands his sleeve rode up almost to the elbow.

"Detective Morgan." He had a flat, square face with tiny dark eyes that looked me over slowly.

"Dave Garrett. I'm the one who called it in."

He looked at me blandly. "What's your business here?"

"Pat Winter was my client."

He looked puzzled for a moment, and then his face lost expression again. "Uh-huh." I noticed that his feet were spaced wide apart, and that his eyes were narrowing. I wondered if I was about to be arrested.

"I was checking to see if there were any developments."

He took out a notepad and wrote down the time. "Could I see some ID, sir?"

I produced my identification card. His expression told me that somehow, it didn't measure up; and for that matter, neither did I. "When did you see him last?"

"I think I covered all that last night, with the other detective."

"Cover it with me."

"At the state police garage, over in Limerick. I guess it was close to two in the afternoon."

"Not since?"

"That's what I said. Has he turned up?"

He put away his notebook and put his hands on his hips. His jacket fell open, showing me an automatic in a shoulder holster. His suit didn't look so funny anymore. "What exactly are you doing here?"

"Trying to find my client." Which was true, as far as it went.

"Well, you found him."

"Doesn't sound good," I said.

"It's not."

"Where was he?"

"Woods behind the house."

"Was he there last night?" I asked.

I didn't think he'd answer me, and I was right. "We're checking into that."

"It was a gunshot, though, right?"

He shook his head. "I don't want to be talking about a case under investigation." He didn't add "with you," but it was there anyway.

"Come on, Detective. At least tell me what I'm going to be able to read in the afternoon paper."

"I'll lend you a quarter so you can read it for yourself," he said.

"I might have something for you."

He didn't bite. "If you do, it's obstruction of justice not to turn it over."

"We both know that's bullshit. Let's get serious. I called this in, gave you guys every cooperation. You know damned well I didn't do it."

"Maybe a friend did."

"I'm not going to argue about it. But let me tell you this: I think I'm close to solving both of the Winter killings. All I need from you is cause of death and the time. Come on, if I had anything to do with it, I'd know that for myself already."

He sighed. "A single gunshot to the chest. No other injuries."

"Time of death?"

"You got to be kidding."

"At least tell me if he was dead last night."

"Yeah, he was. But that's all I'm going to say, Garrett."

"It's all I need. I wasn't kidding."

"I hope it helps you."

"To tell the truth, Detective, I hope it doesn't."

"You private guys like burning up the time, huh?"

"It's nothing like that. Mind if I take a look at the back of the house?"

"And mess up a crime scene? Forget it."

I shrugged, went back to my car for my binoculars, and went around to the back by staying on the neighboring property. Morgan and a uniform watched me with sour expressions, but without a complaint from the neighbor there was nothing they could do.

The neighbor's property was a little higher than Pat's, and I had a pretty fair view of the backyard. To my left was a small grove of trees and bushes, with the back of the house to my right. What I was interested in was dead ahead, in the lawn. They weren't easy to see, even in daylight, but once you knew where to look there was no doubt. Drag marks, running from the sliding-glass door all the way to the grove.

I stood there a long time, trying to get some other meaning from the evidence. I wanted to solve the case, but not the way it was going. I put down my binoculars and headed back to my car.

My destination was in the western part of Montgomery County, in Limerick Township, with an assist from a county road map and a crisscross phone directory. Open, rolling country, dotted with golf courses, farms, and parks. Spring was unfolding, and the new leaves sparkled even though the sky was cloudy. In the distance I got an occasional glimpse of the cooling towers of the Limerick nuclear plant, white against all the green.

Following my map, I turned onto a country road and slowed down. I was in farm country, but no one was working the fields. I supposed that it was still too wet from the rain the night before. I drove for several miles without seeing another person. The few cars I encountered were going the other way.

The mailbox wasn't marked, but after seeing the photo in his office, I couldn't have missed it. I drove through the open gate and over a bridge spanning a small creek. A gravel lane took me through a pasture at least ten acres in size. The lane expanded into a small graveled parking area right in front of the house, but I kept going around to the rear till I could park out of sight.

I got out and took a good look at Preston's domain. The house was surprisingly small, just one and a half stories, but big enough for a man who lived alone and spent most of his time at the office. Every chink of stone was perfectly mortared and every inch of wood neatly painted. No weeds in the garden and no moss on the flagstone. No horse manure around the barn. Even the watering hoses were neatly coiled. It was a place where nothing went wrong. Well, almost nothing.

I expected a security system, and I was right. Warning stickers on both the front and rear doors, and when I looked through the glass in the top half of the front door I could see the panel on the hallway wall. I'd seen similar systems a number of times, and I could guess at what the system could do. A keypad for entering the security code. A row of tiny lights, one for each downstairs door and window. An array of option keys—disable audible alarm, select siren instead of buzzer, volume control, automatic phone report, multiple user options, and so forth. But the only thing that interested me was the status light, which blinked red.

Unarmed.

Like so many people who lived in low crime areas, he'd grown tired of false alarms and just left the damned thing off unless he was out of town.

The doors to the main part of the house had no-nonsense locks, far beyond my ability to manipulate. But to one side was a wooden addition, a mud kitchen, with an agreeably flimsy door. A twelve-dollar lock set, and worth every penny. I went to work with a pick and was inside in less than two minutes.

I went through the mud kitchen and entered the main part

of the house. I was in a sitting room with polished broad-planked floors and intricately patterned Oriental rugs in reds and blues. One whole wall was a gray stone fireplace. From somewhere I heard the slow ticking of a clock. There was no other sound inside except for my own breathing.

Even a small house has hundreds of hiding places. Whole books have been written about the art of hiding and finding objects inside a home. I didn't have the time for a careful search, and if I came up dry I couldn't afford to leave any traces behind. All I could do was look in the most likely places and hope for some luck. I worked the first floor as best I could. I checked the kitchen drawers, the bookshelves, the closets. Unfortunately for me Preston was a pack rat. Everything—drawers, shelves, tabletops—was full to bursting. Books were piled on top of books. Videos about foxhunting were stacked on top of canned goods. I found jars of veterinary liniment in the kitchen cabinets and legal files jammed into drawers in a tiny table in the sitting room.

I found a narrow open staircase and headed upstairs. The kind of thing I was looking for would be in his bedroom, or maybe in his personal desk. I found the bedroom first.

It was in the front of the house, looking out toward the road. At this hour of the day it was shadowed. Even though the curtains were open, I still needed to turn on the wrought-iron chandelier for a good look. The room was dominated by a king-size four-poster with a canopy. On one side was a nightstand with a pile of books and legal papers. On the other was a dresser.

No one, at least no man, thinks about socks much. We put them on, take them off, throw them in the wash; and when they're clean again, maybe we fold them and maybe we don't. But when we want a place to put something very personal, something we want to keep close at hand but still out of the way, the sock drawer is the first thing we think of.

I opened the top drawer of the dresser and there they were, at least two dozen pair of black socks, neatly folded, all arranged in the same direction like cordwood. I slipped my hand underneath, being careful not to disturb anything.

I was so intent on what I was doing that my first hint he was there was a gun in the small of my back and a strong hand gripping my collar.

"Don't turn around. What are you doing here?"

25

Friday, 10:00 A.M.

MY FIRST THOUGHT was to swing around hard and try
to catch him in the face with my elbow. My second was to stamp
his instep and butt his face with the back of my head.

My third was to do nothing and not risk getting myself
shot.

I took a deep, easy breath and forced my shoulders to relax.
I kept my hands exactly where they'd been, inside the drawer.

"What does it look like I'm doing?"

"Find anything?"

The voice was too young and too excitable to be Preston's.
"Tom?"

My answer was a jab from the muzzle. "What do you want
here?"

"I don't have a gun and I'm not going to hurt you. Let me
turn around."

"Like I should trust you," he snorted.

"I was doing a job. I didn't tell your wife a thing."

He wasn't impressed. "So you told his lawyer and his lawyer told her. Thanks for the big fucking break."

"You've got better things to do than take up my time. Now let me turn around."

"What else should I be doing?" It came out snotty, but we both knew it wasn't.

"You're driving your own car?" I asked.

"Why shouldn't I?"

"Because every cop in the state is probably looking for it." The pressure of the gun in my back eased. "What for?"

"Back off and let me turn around."

I heard a creak on the floorboards behind me. "Okay, but keep your hands up."

I turned around and let my hands drop to my side. He was wearing a blue dress shirt, without a tie, and a pair of jeans. He didn't look like he'd slept very well. His hair was uncombed and a blond stubble of beard glinted in the light. In his right hand was a .38 with a snub-nosed barrel. "I'm too old for this 'hands-up' crap," I said. "Either shoot me or put that damned thing away before you shoot somebody by accident."

He looked down at the gun in his hand and then shoved it into a pocket. "It's not loaded, anyway."

"That's the first bright thing you've done."

He took it the wrong way. "I don't want anything off of you, Garrett. Just tell me what's going on."

"You mean you don't know?"

He looked at me with puzzlement. "We already talked about Maria."

"I mean Pat. That's why the police are looking for you. At least I think they are."

"Pat?"

"He's dead."

Tom sat down in a chair at Preston's writing desk. "Oh, shit."

"You'd better tell me what you did after you left home last night."

He looked at me sharply. "So you can tell his lawyer?"

"Do you know whose house this is? His lawyer's."

"So—what are you doing here?"

"Trying to find who killed Maria."

"Here?" he asked.

"Forget that one for a minute. I'll try and help you if you're straight with me."

"Why would you do that?"

"Because it doesn't happen to me very often and I could use a change of pace. But the first lie you tell me, I call the police."

"The last time I trusted you, my wife and my boss found out."

"You didn't trust me with a thing. I knew all about you and Maria before I said word one to you. I just want to find out who killed Maria."

He rubbed his hand across his face slowly. Then he nodded. "All right. When I got home, she already knew. We had a big fight. I drove around for a while, had some drinks at a couple of bars, spent the night in a motel. This morning I decided to see Pat. I slept in till after seven. When I got there I saw the police cars. I didn't know what they meant, if they were inside talking to him, or what. Then you came out and I decided to follow you."

"Try again."

"Dave, you've got to believe me."

"No, I don't."

"Please."

"Give it to me straight, Tom."

He swallowed. "Okay. It was almost like I said. I had the drinks and went to bed at the motel but I couldn't sleep. I went to Pat's—oh, it was around dawn. I saw the crime-scene tape and knocked on the door anyway. The whole place was locked up tight, no lights or anything. I went around the backyard and saw marks in the grass and I followed them to the body. He was dead. I drove around and thought about things for a while. I was on my way back to turn myself in when I saw you."

"Pretty good, except for the last part."

"What do you mean?"

"Last chance, Tom. I'm not kidding."

"I don't know what to tell you."

"How about, 'I wasn't going to turn myself in. I could have done that from anywhere. I went back because I was afraid I'd left some evidence.' Makes a hell of a lot more sense, doesn't it?"

"Can you leave fingerprints on clothing?" he asked.

"Under certain circumstances, I think so. You touched the body, huh?"

"Just to see if he was alive."

"You've given me an entire answer that's the truth. I like that in a man."

He looked away. "I've been under a lot of pressure."

"Who isn't? But not all of us do such stupid things."

"I didn't kill Pat," he insisted.

"Why did you go there?"

"This is going to sound dumb."

"If it's the truth I won't mind."

"I wanted to tell him how sorry I was about Maria's death."

"And?"

"He had a right to be mad. And even to get me fired. It was a risk and I took it. I didn't blame him. But we both loved her . . . I wanted to share—I don't know how to say it."

"You talk a lot smarter when you're not afraid of sounding dumb. And by the way, I know you didn't kill Pat."

"Who did?"

"That's what I'm here about."

"You think his lawyer did it?" he asked.

"Why did you follow me out here?"

"I didn't know where you were going. All I knew was, I didn't want to talk to the police and I thought you might be looking into Pat's death."

"That was a big assumption."

"I didn't have anywhere else to go. Anyway, I saw you come in. I thought maybe you knew where the murder weapon was. If I could get it I could clear myself."

I shook my head. "Tom, don't give up your day job. You think Preston would leave clear evidence of a homicide in his dresser drawer? The gun that killed Pat is at the bottom of the Schuylkill. At least you'd better hope it's there; that it doesn't wind up planted on you."

"What should I do?"

"Get out of here. The police have your plate and a description of your car and they're probably looking for you right now."

"I didn't do it," he repeated. "He was cold. He'd been dead for hours."

I sighed. "That doesn't prove you weren't there the night before, Tom."

"Oh, yeah." He paused. "So, if I killed him, why would I go back?"

"Exactly the reason you *did* go back—to check if you'd left evidence behind."

"Oh. That's right."

"So get out of here before a cruiser sees your car and gets us both in trouble."

"Where should I go?" he asked.

"You could always try going home."

"Don't be funny, Garrett."

"Either stay with her or leave. One or the other."

"What are you going to do?"

"I have to see a lawyer. Now go."

I listened to his feet going down the stairs and watched from the window while he drove away.

I opened the dresser drawer again. I'd been less than completely truthful with Evans. No, I hadn't found the Eco-Protect reports, but my fingers had touched something flat and hard. I drew it out.

It was a 5-by-7 color street scene, with palm trees in the background, of a tall young man in a graduation cap and gown. Maria, her hair up, had her arm awkwardly around him. Both of them were smiling broadly at the camera. Her hairstyle was a little dated, but even without paying too much attention to the cars I could tell it wasn't a recent picture. The better part of ten years old, I guessed. Pat wasn't in the picture. Perhaps he was working the camera, but somehow I doubted it.

I slid the picture into my pocket and let myself out.

26

Friday, 2:00 P.M.

PRESTON CAME OUT of his office and motioned to me with a brisk, foreshortened gesture that communicated that he was damned busy but that he could give me a couple of minutes if it was important. As we sat down he gave me his professional half-smile, but he didn't offer his hand. That was okay; my right hand was taken up with a paper bag. And I didn't want to shake hands with him anyway.

"I'm sorry to break in like this without an appointment," I began, "but I wanted to catch you before you threw any more money at Maria's wrongful death case."

"Who's that policewoman in the reception area?"

"That's Trooper Carter. I'm sorry, I should have introduced you."

Puzzlement crossed his face. He looked at me patiently, his hands crossed on his desktop. "I've got a busy day," he said.

"First of all, I'd like you to write me a check for all my time and expenses." I handed him an invoice. He glanced over it quickly.

"Certainly, but what's the hurry?"

"When we have our talk I'm not sure how much of a check-writing mood you'll be in."

"Bad news?"

"I'm afraid so."

He opened a drawer, pulled out a checkbook, and filled out my check. "All right, now what do you have to tell me?"

"All the times you've lied to me, I want to know if you were just playing for time or if you really thought I was dumb enough not to figure it out eventually."

His lips were white. "I think I'm going to have to ask you to leave."

"When I'm ready. I've been shot at and run around and I'm tired, so you'll have to pardon me if I don't put on my party manners. But if you'd been straight with me I could have gotten to the bottom of this two days ago, almost without leaving this chair."

"I haven't told you anything that wasn't true," he said primly.

I considered it. "Well, I suppose that's right. In a way that's the story of your life. You don't do anything bad, you just don't do the right thing."

"Say what you mean."

"You might have mentioned that you've been having an affair with Maria Winter."

"I most certainly have not!"

I took the graduation photo out of my pocket and laid it on his desk. There was no question that the features of the young man's were the same as Preston's.

"You son of a bitch!"

"Just doing my job. I can't help it if you made it harder."

He started to come out of his chair. "By breaking into my home? Your own client? I'm going to have your license pulled, I swear it!"

I didn't move. "Sit down. You're going to tell the truth for a change."

His face was flushed with anger, but he sat.

"That's better," I said. "First of all, you're not going to do a thing about my license. This little business here puts your whole career in the tidy bowl. I'd think twice before I made any calls."

"I can't believe how disloyal you are. I trusted you and you betrayed me."

For a moment I just looked at him, struggling to find an appropriate response. "What a crock of shit."

"Get out of my office!"

"You never trusted me an inch. This whole case was a fool's errand, right from the word go. You knew exactly where Maria was the whole time. You went there with your own key after she died and got the picture." I pointed at it. "It's funny, in a way. The only time in your whole life you got sentimental, too late to do anybody any good. Tell me, did you want the picture because of her or because he's your son?"

"I don't think I should be talking to you."

"Oh, but I do. Or should I call in Trooper Carter?"

"Don't threaten me."

"If you've got nothing to hide I'm wasting my time. If you do, you're wasting mine."

"You keep forgetting who you work for."

"No, you do. I'm working for Maria."

He looked away, out the window, and drummed his fingers on the desk. "I trust that what we say is confidential?" he said sharply.

"You're a funny one to talk about trust. But if you want to know if I want anything out of this from you, no, I don't."

"I'm not in a very confessional mood, Garrett. Why don't you just tell me what you want?"

"Clarity."

"I beg your pardon?"

"That's what I do. Punishment is for the cops and justice is for the judges—I guess. I just get things clear. The rest is up to somebody else."

"If it's all so clear then you explain it to me," he said.

"Let's begin at the beginning. High school. Maria was dating Pat, and some other guys, but she believed in you. She wasn't just good-looking, she was smart. A lot of people thought you were going to go places, but she was unique—she loved you, too. She would have left Pat in a minute for you—"

"Just what makes you think *that?*"

"The world gives you a test," I told him. "And what you do determines if you're going to shape your life or if it's going to shape you. It's not a test of good and bad—maybe it's even the opposite. It's about determination and taking risks, and even about being a bit of a selfish son of a bitch."

"And what was my test?"

"Tests. You had four of them and you blew them all. The first three were about Maria. You went off to Stanford instead of going somewhere local, and you left her behind."

"She was still in high school, for God's sake. And she married someone else right after we broke up, anyway," he pointed out.

"That was the second test. Of course she got married. To whoever would have her on short notice. To give your baby a name."

"I had my life in front of me. Marriage—I couldn't have gone to Stanford—I—"

"Save it. Did Pat know it wasn't his?"

"No." He looked around the room again. "When I told her I couldn't marry her, she told me to stay away. I did. I stayed away, all those years."

"Anyway, it's what happened two years ago that's important."

"Two years ago?"

"Or thereabouts. Whenever it was that Ralph had his open house on South Street. You saw each other. She was forty-six and married to a loser and you were still attractive. Did it start right away, or did a few months go by?"

"Why should I answer that?"

"Because I'd like to know if Pat brought you his personal-injury case before or after you started sleeping with his wife."

He swallowed. "I was reluctant, but she said she was sure I could do a good job for him."

"So everything went along swimmingly for a while. Maria got to sleep with the man she loved, you got a beautiful woman. Hell, Pat's case got lots of attention in your pillow talk, didn't it?"

"That's none of your business."

"You know, life was really kind. You blew two of your opportunities, a woman who loved you and fatherhood, when you were eighteen, and you got another one at fifty. But you blew that one, too. She didn't want half a loaf anymore."

"I never promised her anything."

"No kidding. If she was smart at seventeen she was smarter at forty-eight. She saw you weren't going to commit, so she gave you every chance and then started looking around."

"Evidently." There was a world of shame and rage in the word.

"She kept seeing you but she took up with Tom Evans. And she made sure you knew about it. Not to be nasty, but just to try to get you off the dime. Am I right?"

"I had no right to be jealous of what kind of a personal life she wanted."

"So that ploy didn't work. I want to hear you tell me why not."

He looked slowly around his office, as if trying to impress someone with its importance. Whether he was thinking of me or himself, I couldn't tell. "You met Pat. You know how vindictive he is. You saw how he got Tom fired. Can you imagine what he'd do to me?"

"On the one hand you've got a beautiful woman, the mother of your only child, offering you a second chance at happiness when you'd thought it was too late. Exactly what's on the other side of the scales?"

He looked down at his hands. His eyes closed and his chin began to tremble. Then he opened his eyes and forced himself to stare straight ahead. His hands made fists. Then, very slowly, they unclenched. He was back in control. "Damn it, the day after she moved out he was in here, demanding I do his domestic case. Against the woman I loved. I tried to tell him I wasn't interested, that I didn't do that kind of work anymore. There was no talking to him. That's when it really got out of control. I didn't want it, but what if he went to somebody else? What if the truth came out that way? I used to lie awake, thinking about what would happen. At best I'd be sanctioned by the disciplinary board. Suspended, even disbarred. In any event I'd be ridiculed. My whole life down the drain. It wasn't worth it."

"That's your problem—you've never thought anything but work was worth it."

"You're on quite the high horse, aren't you?"

"No. You see, I failed my test, too. I should have told my wife that failing the bar was her problem, not mine. But I was afraid she didn't love me enough, and I wanted the Mister Nice Guy Award more than I valued my own integrity."

"I would think you'd be more sympathetic, knowing how much there is to lose."

"I'm plenty sympathetic. But I'm after clarity, remember?"

He looked around the room, taking in the rows of books and papers. "I've spent my whole life learning. Cases, facts, law, procedures. And look how my life repeated itself. It starts and ends with Maria. I didn't learn a damn thing."

"Maybe you worked at learning the wrong things."

"You said life had given me four tests and that three of them involved Maria."

"Charles, I want to congratulate you on making legal history. Or history, anyway."

"What did I do?"

"It's what you *didn't* do. Half the lawyers I've ever known, sooner or later, got themselves into an office romance. Most of the time it blows up in their face, sometimes it doesn't. But you—if you'd fooled around with Leah maybe none of this would have happened. Either it would have worked out and you and Maria would't have gotten involved again, or it would have run its course."

"Now you've lost me."

I studied his face. "You know, I think I have. Did you know she was in love with you?"

I might as well have mentioned the queen of England. "Leah?"

"Yeah. The woman who's been falling all over you for years. The one who'd do absolutely anything, and I mean anything, for you."

"Garrett, you've been working too hard."

"She killed Maria Winter."

"You're expecting me to pay for wild accusations like this?"

"Pure fact. I don't know precisely how she did it, but I expect she was stopped in a driveway or somewhere around the foot of the bridge. She trailed me, or maybe Tom, to Collegeville, and stopped when she found the spot she wanted. Hell, it's the only spot there is. Anyway, she pulled out and forced Maria off into the abutment."

"Leah's not stupid. She couldn't have counted on the car catching fire. If that hadn't happened, it would have been obvious a second car was involved."

"The fire was God's gift to *you* and your dream of a personal-injury case, because it made a simple one-car-accident theory plausible. But Leah didn't care. Even if someone had gone looking at her car, they wouldn't have found any damage."

"Then how can you say she forced Maria off the road?"

"In Pat's car. She didn't care how much trouble *he* was in."

"Are you telling me she knows how to hot-wire ignitions?"

"She doesn't need to. Your little system here of leaving clients' keys with the receptionist? All she'd have to do is walk across the street to the Chevy dealer and get a duplicate. While I was waiting for you, I checked. She had a key copied on Tuesday. I'll bet you that check in front of you that the key was for Winter's car. He must have crapped in his pants when he went out Wednesday morning and saw his smashed-up fender, right in front of all the neighbors."

"Why, if she was trying to frame him, would Pat cover up for her by rushing out to fix his car?"

"He didn't know he was covering for her. He was covering himself. Did he ever suspect about you and Maria?"

"I wouldn't be sitting here if he had. The man had an unbelievable temper."

"He was Leah's second victim."

"What makes you think he's dead, let alone that she killed him?"

"He's dead, all right; it's going to be on the afternoon news. Leah killed him to protect you from the Eco-Protect mess."

"You know about that, too?"

"Maria made a mistake. Did she tell you that she'd taken the phony reports when she left New Directions?"

"Yes, she did."

"How?"

"When we were together, at her apartment."

For a minute I was stumped. "Then Speicher must have called you."

"He left a phone message. Nothing incriminating—just 'She

took the environmental information we discussed,' something like that. I called him back and said as long as he didn't do something stupid, he was safe as houses."

"He left the message with Leah."

"Most likely."

"And even if Leah didn't take the message, she could have seen it."

"But it wouldn't have meant anything to her."

"You've been working quietly, without litigation, with New Directions for years, haven't you?"

"Since the condemnations in the late sixties."

"She reads the files, types things. She knows your appointments. She sees these Eco-Protect reports come in, but you never meet with them, they never call, they're not in the phone book? Don't ever, ever, sell your staff short. She's too smart *not* to know. She wanted to protect you from exposure. She had it in her mind that Maria would try to blackmail you."

"That's silly."

"It's what she thought. She wanted to think it, because it gave her a part to play. She decided to get the records, but she couldn't get them without being able to find Maria. That's where I did my bit."

"Where are the records now?"

"You know, Charles, you really are a jerk. You want to know about the papers more than you do about Leah. But you don't have to worry. They're cinders, just like the album."

"What album?"

"Your birthday's coming up soon, isn't it?"

"The twenty-first."

"Maria had a birthday surprise for you. It doesn't matter now, anyway. Leah was damn careful. Pat didn't make the connection, but as long as the book existed, maybe somebody else would. It's just that it took me till this morning to see how complicated this all was."

"Go on."

"Half the reason for getting rid of Maria was so Leah could have access to the apartment. She probably went directly there, Tuesday night. She was in a hurry, it was dark, and she didn't dare turn on any lights. And she was probably shaking like a leaf. With one thing and another, she didn't find the papers. She didn't have a key and didn't know how to pick locks, so she had to bust a window. I thought that Arronomick broke the window, but a man who can do car locks can do a house lock with one hand behind—"

"Arronomick?"

"A small-time hood. The boys behind the New Directions operation hired him to get the Eco-Protect reports back. He got a lead somehow on Maria and checked out her car in the parking lot in Collegeville. He didn't find anything because the reports weren't there. He was tailing her, trying to get a lead on where she lived, when she was killed. He wanted to get to her apartment in the worst way, but he was stuck. I know he got there sometime, somehow, but by then Pat already had them. He took the papers and the album. Somewhere in there you showed up with your own key, but all you wanted was your son's picture. Were you sweating the records, or did you figure that no one would realize what they were?"

Preston ignored my question. "What makes you so sure Leah killed Pat?"

"Because he was so paranoid practically no one could get close to him without his gun. I can see it now. A knock at the door. Winter gets his gun. He finds out it's just Leah. Maybe she even has an appointment. He lets her in, puts away his gun. Bam."

"There's a flaw here. Pat didn't know she'd killed his wife. Leah didn't need to kill him."

"She did it for your sake, not hers. He had the phony reports."

"How would Leah know that?"

"He didn't know what to do with them, but he figured they were important. Anyway, what does a client do when he needs advice? He calls up your office. And he gets the receptionist."

"Why would Pat trust Leah showing up in the middle of the night?"

"Because he thought she was on his side. She'd done him a favor already—or what he thought was a favor. She told him that Tom was Maria's boyfriend."

"You're guessing."

"Only four people knew—you, Leah, me, and my assistant. Lord knows you had no reason to tell. For all you knew, Tom knew about *you*. If he did, and Pat confronted him, Tom might spill the beans."

"That's thin."

"No, she had two good reasons—one, she wanted to protect you; and two, she was hoping that Pat might go after Tom and that Tom would kill him. That would get Pat out of the way. But Tom was too smart, or too scared, so she had to do it herself. She told Pat she had some new information, maybe about the Eco-Protect reports, and went out to his house. She got the drop on him and made him give her the reports. Then she shot him, point-blank, in the kitchen, dragged him outside, and cleaned up the floor."

"Why clean up? Or hide the body?"

"The more mystery the more time she has to cover up both of the Winter killings. It's pretty hard for the police to solve a murder when they don't even know that someone is dead. And establishing time of death on a two-day-old corpse is a guessing game—makes it harder to break an alibi. You know, it was the drag marks that made me think it was a woman who killed him. If you're trying to hide a body the last thing you want to do is leave a trail leading right up to where you put it. You want to carry the body if you can. But if you're not strong enough, you have to drag it."

He rubbed his chin. "I don't know whether to believe any of this."

"Want to know the funniest part of all? I had it all figured out, last night, when I was talking to you."

"Then why didn't you say so?"

"Because I didn't *know* I knew. Remember when I said Leah had an imaginary boyfriend?"

"You said you meant Lisa."

"Yeah, but I really meant Leah all along. Her engagement ring is as phony as 'John' is. I checked your parking lot. She drives an old Impala."

"I had no idea Leah was attracted to me." He sounded like a politician talking for the record.

"Doesn't mean it's not so."

It was several seconds before he spoke again. "You're thinking in terms of criminal charges, aren't you?"

"That's why Trooper Carter is here."

"Thinking this through . . . there isn't a lot of evidence against her, is there?"

"I don't know if the police can prove paint transfer between the cars or not. And even if they can, I don't know if they can put Leah in Pat's car. As for Pat's murder, who knows? The police can do a lot if they know what to look for."

"Doesn't seem like enough for a criminal case."

"Well, they'll have ample evidence of motive."

"From you?" he asked.

"From you. You're going to roll over on a woman who loved you so much she'd do anything for you. You give the police your full cooperation, right now, and I'll do everything I can to keep the grimy details buried. Anything less and my next appointment is with the chief investigative reporter of the *Inquirer*."

I picked the check off the desk and put it in my jacket pocket. He watched the movement and moistened his lips. "I suppose there's no way to just send the trooper away?"

"I'd be more impressed if I thought you were trying to bribe me for Leah's sake instead of your own."

"What would it take to get the police out of here?"

"Bringing Maria back to life. If she'd given me the slip she'd still be alive."

"You're enjoying this."

"I hate it. I wish I'd never heard of you. Shall I send her in?"

His "Yes" was barely audible.

"One more thing," I said. He looked up blankly. "There's a man coming up from Florida for a funeral. A couple of funerals. You ought to take some time to get to know him."

I don't know if he heard me.

27

Friday, 3:00 P.M.

I NODDED AT Carter. "Mr. Preston would like to see you now." I'll give her credit—she marched in exactly like she knew what the hell she was doing. I took the chair nearest Leah's desk and sat down to wait.

"Would you like some coffee?" she asked.

"No, thank you."

"Was that the trooper from the Winter case? The auto accident, I mean?" She was trying painfully hard to sound chipper.

"Yes, it was."

"I thought so. We talked a little bit. She seemed nice." I didn't say anything back.

"I didn't have her in Mr. Preston's book," Leah said.

"It was my idea for him to see her. It came up rather suddenly."

"Oh."

She made a show of looking at her desk book, which I'm sure she had memorized. "He has a three-thirty. Do you think they'll be long?"

"I'm afraid so. He has a lot to talk about."

"Maybe I should take my break now, so I'll be here when they're finished."

"It might be better for you to wait. The trooper might want to talk to you, too."

"About Mrs. Winter? What could I tell her?"

"I guess that's going to be up to you."

I thought about what I was going to do when Carter came out. I'd told her not to attempt to question Leah herself, to get a couple of investigators in on this. It would still be her collar, but she wouldn't run the risk, as a rookie, of screwing up the interrogation of the defendant.

She looked at the closed door and back to me. "She's here for me, isn't she?"

"I'm afraid so."

I listened to the traffic noises through the window. I saw the pain in her eyes, and for a moment I felt sorry for her. Even thinking about what she'd done to Maria and Pat didn't help. No matter what she'd done, she was a victim, too.

Her mouth opened and she found her voice. "Then it's all been for nothing, hasn't it?" When I didn't answer, she went on. "She would have used them against him, sooner or later." She looked at me but I just stared back. She went on. "I'm not crazy. He's never looked at me all these years and I didn't have any illusions about *that*—but at least I could protect him."

"And if you did, just maybe he'd . . ."

Tears ran down her face but she made no move to stop them. "I guess I had more illusions than I thought."

I watched her cry. "You're right," I said after a moment. "She was planning to blackmail him."

Something hopeful crossed her face through the tears."Really?"

"If he didn't marry her when her divorce was final."

"Then—at least . . ."

I kept quiet. Maybe the truth would come out, maybe not. I'd had my fill of truth for one day.

We sat together without exchanging another word till Trooper Carter came out. Preston stayed in his office with the door shut. I nodded at Carter, and Leah, and turned away.

I found my way out to the street and thought about what I was going to do. I was going to dump Preston's damned check in the bank, that was certain, and get myself a bottle of Wild Turkey. No, for Ralph's sake I would buy a single-malt Scotch, no matter what it cost. It was a night to drink to Maria Winter. And who was I going to drink with? Lisa was pretending to be in Cape May; Ianucci and Carter were too busy; Kate was gone; and Susan was dead.

I looked at my watch. By the time I ran my errands and got down to South Street, it would almost be a civilized hour for a drink.

I got into my car and I realized I still had Lisa's glasses.

What the hell, I thought. It'll do her good to get out of the house.